The Tsar of Love and Techno

BY THE SAME AUTHOR

A Constellation of Vital Phenomena

The Tsar of Love and Techno

ANTHONY MARRA

HOGARTH
LONDON • NEW YORK

1 3 5 7 9 10 8 6 4 2

Hogarth, an imprint of Vintage,
20 Vauxhall Bridge Road,
London SW1V 2SA

Hogarth is part of the Penguin Random House group of companies
whose addresses can be found at global.penguinrandomhouse.com

First published by Hogarth in 2016

First published in the US by Hogarth in 2015

penguin.co.uk/vintage

A CIP catalogue record for this book is available from the British Library

HB ISBN 9781781090275
TPB ISBN 9781781090480

Penguin Random House is committed to a sustainable future for our
business, our readers and our planet. This book is made from
Forest Stewardship Council®-certified paper

Typeset in Walbaum MT by Palimpsest Book Production Limited,
Falkirk, Stirlingshire
Printed and bound in Great Britain by
Clays Ltd, St Ives plc

For Janet, Lindsay, and Rachel

It's a minor work.

—Pyotr Zakharov-Chechenets,
regarding his 1843 painting,
Empty Pasture in Afternoon

Contents

Side A

The Leopard

Leningrad, 1937

I AM AN ARTIST FIRST, A CENSOR SECOND.

I had to remind myself of this two years ago, when I trudged to the third-floor flat of a communal apartment block, where my widowed sister-in-law and her four-year-old son lived. She answered the door with a thin frown of surprise. She wasn't expecting me. We had never met.

"My name is Roman Osipovich Markin," I said. "The brother of your husband."

She nodded and ran her hand along the worn pleat of a gray skirt as she stood aside to allow me in. If the mention of Vaska startled her, she hid it well. She wore a blond blouse with auburn buttons. The comb lines grooving her damp dark hair looked drawn on by charcoal pencil.

A boy was slumped into the divan's mid-cushion sag. My nephew, I supposed. For his sake, I hoped he took after his mother.

"I don't know what my brother has told you," I began, "but I work in the Department of Party Propaganda and Agitation. Are you familiar with the job?"

"No," the boy said. The poor child had inherited his father's forehead. His future lay under a hat.

To his mother: "Your husband really didn't talk about me?"

"He did mention a brother who was something of the village idiot in Pavlovsk," she said, a bit more cheer to her tone. "He didn't mention you were balding."

"It's not as bad as it looks," I said.

"Perhaps you could get to the purpose of your visit?"

"Every day I see photographs of traitors, wreckers, saboteurs, counterrevolutionaries, enemies of the people. Over the last ten years, only so many per day. Over the last few months, the usual numbers have grown. I used to receive a slim file each month. Now I receive one every morning. Soon it will be a box. Then boxes."

"Surely you haven't come only to describe the state of your office?"

"I am here to do my brother a final service," I said.

"And that is?" she asked.

My vertebrae cinched together. My hands felt much too large for my pockets. It's a terrible thing, really, when said aloud. "To ensure that his misfortune doesn't become a family trait."

She gathered every photograph she had of Vaska, as I asked. Nine in total. A marriage portrait. A day in the country. One taken the day they moved to the city, their first act as Leningraders. One of Vaska as a boy. She sat down on the divan and showed each to her boy for a final time before bringing them to the bedroom.

She arrayed them on the desk. Her bedroom was mainly bare floor. The bed still wide enough for three, the blanket neatly pulled over a flabby mass of pillows. She must have only shared it with her son now.

I slid a one-ruble coin across the desk, hammer-and-sickle side up.

"What am I to do with this?"

I nodded at the photos. "You know what to do."

She shook her head, and with a sweep of her forearm that sent a small galaxy of dust motes into orbit, she winged the coin to the floor.

Could she have still loved my brother? Hard to believe. He'd been proven guilty of religious radicalism by an impartial and just tribunal. He'd received the only sentence suitable for a madman who poisoned others with the delusion that heaven awaits us. Paradise is possible only here on earth, possible only if we engineer it. One shouldn't envy this woman's blind devotion to a man who has proven himself unworthy of love. One mustn't.

She pressed her palms over the photographs, threw her elbows out to shield the images with her broad back, an instinct that suggested a starving creature protecting her last morsels, and this may be true: The stomach is not the only vital organ that hungers.

"Leave," she said, a ragged edge to her voice. She stared at the back of her hands. "Leave us be."

I could have turned, walked out of the room, closed the door on the whole affair. I'd done more than was required already. But something kept my heels pinned to the floorboards. Even though the concept of family was slipping into history as swiftly as the horse and carriage, I didn't have a wife or child of my own, and I wanted someone who shared my blood to live to see that paradise we've given ourselves to achieve. I wanted that little fellow out there on the divan to grow up, to become an active builder of communism, to look back on his life when he is a fat and happy old man, to know that the faultless society surrounding him justifies his father's death, and then, to be grateful for the lesson taught by the uncle he briefly met on a cold winter morning a lifetime ago.

It's silly. I know.

I grabbed her wrist and pinched the coin between her fingers.

"I'm not here to hurt you," I told her. "I'm here to make sure you don't get hurt. Your husband was an enemy of the people. What do you think will happen if NKVD men search the flat and find all these photographs? Must I go into greater detail?"

Whatever naked sentiment splayed itself across the table recoiled within her. She kept hold of the coin when I let go. That coin could have bought a meat pie, a sketch pad, a confectionary, a bar of soap; pressed into someone else's palm it could have become the bright spot in a dull day, but coins cannot choose their fate.

"Why can't you do it? You're the artist. This is your job."

I checked my watch. "I don't begin work for another hour."

When I heard the slow scratch of the coin on photo paper, I turned away. In the living room, the boy sat quietly peering at the thin lines etched upon his palms.

It was uncanny how much he resembled his father. A nose he hadn't yet grown into; a messy thatch of black hair, each follicle aimed in a different direction; lips pursed as small as a button. I would have been eight when Vaska was his age. Summer days we roamed the forests and fields, and at night we tapped coded messages to each other through the wall between our rooms; we each had our own. I made him sit for me in every shade and season of light so that I could sketch his likeness, could preserve his expression in charcoal on the page. If not for Vaska, I would have never become an artist. His face was my apprenticeship.

"Do you speak?" I asked.

He nodded.

"With understatement, I see. Tell me your name."

"Vladimir."

I clasped his shoulder and he flinched, surprised by the sudden gesture of affection. He shared his first name with Lenin—an auspicious sign.

"I want to see if you can do something for me," I asked. "Are you willing to try?"

He nodded.

"Stare straight at me," I instructed, then I flashed my fingers by his ear. "How many am I holding up?"

He held up four fingers.

"Very good. You've got keen eyes. Someday you might be a sharpshooter or a watchman. I'm going to tell you the story of the tsar and the painting. Have you heard it?"

The coin scratching in the bedroom might have been wind rustling leaves; we might have been far from there, near a dacha, in a field, the sun burning just over our heads.

"No, I didn't think you would have," I said. "It begins with a young man who overthrows an evil tsar. The young man becomes the new tsar. He promises his subjects that their troubles will disappear if they obey him. 'What will this new kingdom look like?' his subjects ask. The tsar considers it and then commissions his court painters to paint a picture of what the new kingdom will look like.

"First the painting is only a few paces wide, then a few dozen paces, then hundreds of paces. Soon the painting is miles and miles wide. Now, this is a big painting, no? Raw materials are essential to its success. The flax that would have clothed the tsar's subjects is requisitioned for the canvas. The wood that would have built houses is requisitioned for the frame.

"When the subjects are cold, the tsar tells them to look at the painting and see the beautiful coats and furs they will soon wear. When they sleep outside, he tells them to look at the painting and see the beautiful homes they will soon live in.

"The subjects obey the tsar. They know that if they turn their eyes from the painting and see what is around them, if they see the world as it is, the tsar will make them disappear in a big poof of smoke. Soon, all his subjects are frozen in place, unable to move, just like their reflections in the painting."

The boy stared with a bored frown. He must have been accustomed to excellent storytelling. Literature for children receives less attention from the censors than literature for adults, so naturally our best writers flock to the genre.

"How many fingers am I holding up?" I asked.

He put up three.

I slid my hand farther into his periphery. "How many now?"

He put up one.

"And now?"

He began turning his head, but I snapped. "Eyes ahead. Just like people in a painting can't turn their heads to see who's behind them, neither can you."

"I can't see how many fingers," he said. "Your hand is too far back."

"That's right," I said. "That's where your father is.

He's there, painted in the background, back behind your head, where you can't see. He's there, but you can never turn to look."

The coin scratching had silenced some time ago. When I looked up, the boy's mother was standing in the bedroom doorway. I followed her in. The photographs were lined neatly on the desk. In each one, a single face had been so violently scratched out that the desk's wood grain was visible through the hole. My eyes ached to see it. I closed them.

"Get photographs of your son every year," I advised. "If you're arrested, he'll be placed in a state orphanage who knows where. With a recent photograph, you'll have a better chance of finding him."

I was already at the door when she grabbed my wrist and turned me around.

"You're not finished," she said. "You owe my husband more."

"This is the best I can do."

Her hand was on my neck. The boy just sat there, across the room, watching with dark, dumb eyes. What did he see when he saw me? You remain the hero of your own story even when you become the villain of someone else's. His mother's chest indented on my forearm.

"You're in the party," she insisted. "Do something. Move us somewhere."

"I correct images. That's it."

"Then what more can we do? Tell me. When they go into an orphanage you never find them."

Her eyes were webbed with pink and her hands cupped my cheeks, her middle fingers tucked under my earlobes. There was something foreign in the hard, dense heat of her breath on my face. I couldn't recall the last time someone had breathed on me, nor the last time I had felt needed.

"You prove your loyalty," I said quietly. "That can work. In my own experience it has worked."

She looked to the boy, then took my hand. She led me past him, toward the bedroom, toward the bed still wide enough for two. All I wanted was to get out, to be rid of these people. Even so it was a relief to see that she would take her dead husband's brother to the bedroom, a relief to know that the boy might live to become that fat and happy old man because his mother understood, as his father never had, that it is not God or gravity but grace of the state that holds us upon the earth.

I shook my hand from her grip. She turned, uncertain. I leaned toward her, so the boy wouldn't overhear.

"You prove loyalty through betrayal." The words traveled no farther than the length of a little finger, from my lips to her ear. "You inform on someone close to you. This is what I know works."

Two years have passed since that morning. A month ago the department requisitioned my small office. A mean sense of humor, if little else, has filled the vacancy between my superior's ears: He has assigned me to continue our necessary work underground. Several hundred feet underground.

I bid the sky farewell and climb down. Amid dim electric bulbs, I imagine myself contracting within shadow, becoming Caravaggian. No matter how early I arrive, the workmen are already here: laying rail track, reinforcing tunnel cement, never raising their wary eyes to mine. I enter a sawdust swarm and on the other side emerge at the door of what will be the stationmaster's office.

Maxim, my assistant, has beaten me here. The worktable is already prepared with nozzles, cylinders of pressurized air, paint, sealed directives, and stacked files of uncorrected photographs.

Our Younger Stalins cabinet stands in the corner. It holds photographs of our *vozhd* taken ten to twenty years ago. When possible, we substitute a Younger Stalin for current ones. It's essential we convey to the people the youthful vigor of their elder statesman. The longer we do it, the further back in time we must go to find new material. Readers of certain periodicals may worry that he is growing younger with each passing year; by his seventieth birthday he will be a slender-faced adolescent.

"You're late, Comrade," Maxim says, speaking of slender-faced adolescents. The day we met, when the Department of Party Propaganda and Agitation first assigned him as my assistant, was the last day he saluted me. He sends letters praising the party leadership with the hope that the police will intercept, read, and record his expressions of loyalty. He makes no secret of wanting my post.

"I'm old, Comrade," I say.

Maxim, the little brute, nods in agreement.

By lunch we have corrected by airbrush three faces from a 1930 Foreign Trade Committee portrait that has been retouched so many times it's more painting than photograph. Or I should say, I have; Maxim contributes only cigarette smoke and a sour smirk. While concentrating on the face beneath my airbrush, I glance up to find Maxim concentrating on mine. The little brute couldn't erase pencil lead.

We lunch alone. Maxim stays in the mercury-vapor brightness of the office, while I wander through the tunnels. I have walked for hours through these tunnels and have found no end to them. Someday trains will carry the grateful citizens of a socialist paradise through this netherworld. All the work we have done here in their name will then be justified.

In the afternoon, we turn to an Isaak Brodsky canvas depicting Lenin's arrival at Finland Station in the city then known as Petrograd.

"Do you notice the perspective, Maxim?" I ask. "Do you see how the vanishing lines all center upon Comrade Lenin's open mouth, to give the sense that the entire scene is delivered through his speech? The technique goes back to the Renaissance masters. Think of Leonardo's *Last Supper*."

It's so rare to find good work.

Maxim frowns and gestures to Enemy Trotsky, lurking beside Lenin, whom we must erase, because he was never there.

"Come on," he says, disdainful, as always, of formalism. "It will take long enough to correct the painting without the entire history of Western Art. Painting should've stopped with Leonardo anyway. End on a high note."

Pity. I fear I'm among the last of the Leningrad correction artists who attended the Imperial Academy of Arts before the Revolution. The new breed, philistines like Maxim, have grown up in schools where children finger-paint watery ash over the faces of political enemies. They learn to censor before they learn to write. They were never taught to create what they now destroy, and have no appreciation of what, precisely, they sacrifice.

Last July I had the opportunity to correct one of my own paintings, a scene of the October Revolution oiled a decade ago, in 1927. Amid an ardent proletariat uprising, I had mistakenly included the figures of Grigory Zinoviev and Lev Kamenev, who couldn't have been there, not after having been proven perfidious in a recent public trial. I replaced our villains with our hero; Stalin was there, is there, is everywhere. In addition, I noticed other errors—slight skews in perspective, a poorly rendered poplar, a flat and sterile night sky—which, unasked, I took upon myself to correct. I spent two weeks on what should have taken an afternoon. One is so rarely given second chances.

Maxim places a new photograph on the desk.

In it a ballerina floats above the Mariinsky stage. Her left arm ascends into the brilliant wedge of an unseen spotlight. A corona of feathers laurels her black hair. The thick fingers of a silhouetted man corset her waist. He lifts her, throws her, carries or receives her. Photographed from backstage, the first five rows of spectators are visible.

"Who is this?"

Maxim shrugs. The woman is no one. That we have been given her photograph is proof enough that she no longer dances.

But in this photograph, she still has a tutu, tights, a full house, roses in water and champagne on ice in her dressing room. Still has a career. A home. A diploma. A birth certificate.

I know I should be priming the airbrush, bringing it to her pancaked cheek, but she looks so much like my brother's wife—ridiculous, I know—and to deface her seems a cruelty inflicted on her, on this piece of paper, on the ink in the airbrush, on any hand that will ever hold it, on any eye that will ever see it.

Nothing like this has ever happened to me before, I swear. I wait for the sensation to subside. Maxim must have noticed my expression and he asks if I am unwell.

"Dizzy," I tell him. "Light-headed."

"You should eat your lunch, rather than wandering through the tunnels," he says, and suggests we save the dancer for the next day.

By the time I climb the wooden steps to street level, the sunset is a coppery coin on the horizon. It is late October and the winter closes in. Soon night will wrap around the earth and all Leningrad will become a tunnel I walk through.

Pastel palaces line the Neva, designed by Francesco Bartolomeo Rastrelli or his later imitators; I have forgotten which are authentic and which are counterfeit. Rastrelli died here in 1771, and one can see the later additions of expanded drives, garages, antennas, barred windows, iron doors. Do these architectural changes undermine Rastrelli's original vision, or would he, as a fellow court artisan, understand that like one's politics, morality, and convictions, one's art is subordinate to the mandates of power?

A poster exclaims, WOMEN, DO NOT BE FOOLS, PARTAKE IN SPORT! Another displays a blindfolded man walking off a cliff: ILLITERATES ARE BLIND MEN WHO BELIEVE THEY SEE!

My spectacles fog as I enter my flat. I search for the vestige of furnace heat. A Polish émigré invented the radiator on this very street some eighty years ago; I'm still waiting for one. When I was promoted five years ago, a team of underlings, enough to field a soccer squad, swept through my flat and confiscated every image bearing my face. A precaution, they had explained.

My walls are empty but for a hanging portrait of our *vozhd*, Stalin. The portrait has been vignetted so Stalin's face seems to float freely in downy light, like a saint or savior in an old icon. If heaven can only exist on earth, then God can only be a human.

I flip it over. On the back, I have painted one of Henri Rousseau's jungle cats, a spotted golden glimmer peering through verdant leaves. A sense of belonging seeps from me in a sigh. Now I am at home.

In my generation the position of correction artist is a consolation prize for failed painters. I attended the Imperial Academy of Arts for a year, where I made small still lifes of fruit bowls and flower vases, each miniature as realistic as a photograph, before moving on to portraiture, my calling, the most perfect art. The portrait artist must acknowledge human complexity with each brushstroke. The eyes, nose, and mouth that compose a sitter's face, just like the suffering and joy that compose his soul, are similar to those of ten million others yet still singular to him. This acknowledgment is where art begins. It may also be where mercy begins. If criminals drew the faces of their victims before perpetrating their crimes and judges drew the faces of the guilty before sentencing them, then there would be no faces for executioners to draw.

"We have art in order not to die of the truth," wrote Nietzsche in a quote I kept pinned to my workbench. Even as a student I knew we die of art as easily as of any instrument of coercion. Of course a handful of true visionaries treated Nietzsche's words as edict rather than irony, but now they are dead or jailed, and their works are even less likely than mine to grace the walls of the Hermitage. After the Revolution, churches were looted, relics destroyed, priceless works sold abroad for industrial machinery; I joined in, unwillingly at first, destroying icons while I dreamed of creating portraits, even then both a maker and eraser of human faces.

Soon I was approached by the security organs and given a position. Those who can't succeed, teach. Those who can't teach, censor the successes of others. Still I could have turned out worse; I'm told the German chancellor is also a failed artist.

Most censoring, of course, is done by publishers. A little cropping, editing, adjusting of margins can rule out many undesirable elements. This has obvious limitations. Stalin's pitted cheeks, for instance. To fix them you'd have to crop his entire head, a crime for which your own head would soon follow. For such sensitive work, I am brought in. During one bleak four-month stretch, I did nothing but airbrush his cheeks.

During my early days in the department, I wasn't entrusted with such delicate assignments. For my first year, I combed the shelves of libraries with the most recently expanded edition of *Summary List of Books Excluded from Libraries and the Book Trade Network*, searching for images of newly disgraced officials. This should be a librarian's job, of course, but you can't trust people who read that much.

I found offending images in books, old newspapers, pamphlets, in paintings or as loose photographs, sitting in portrait or standing in crowds. Most could be ripped out, but some censored images needed to remain as a cautionary tale. For these, obliteration by India ink was the answer. A gentle tip of the jar, a few squeezes of the eyedropper, and the disgraced face drowned beneath a glinting black pool.

Only once did I witness the true power of my work. In the reading room of the Leningrad State University library, which I often visited to pore over folios of pre-Revolutionary prints, I saw a young man in a pea jacket search a volume of bound magazines. He flipped halfway through the August 1926 issue to a group portrait of military cadets. The cadets stood in three stern rows, ninety-three faces in total, sixty-two of which I had, one by one, over two years, obliterated.

I still don't know which among the sixty-two he had been searching for, or if his was among those thirty-one still unblackened faces. His shoulders slumped forward. His hand gripped the table for support. Something broke behind his wide brown eyes. A gasp escaped his lips before he choked the cry with his fist.

With a few ink droplets I had inflicted upon his soul a violence beyond anything my most loving portraits could have ever achieved. For art to be the chisel that breaks the marble inside us, the artist must first become the hammer.

"No more idleness," Maxim says. "Today we correct the dancer."

"You are too eager, Maxim. Personal ambition doesn't sit well on a socialist's shoulders."

He grunts. He may be science's fullest proof that man is descended from monkey.

A few days have passed since we received the photograph of the disgraced dancer. I've hoped she'd be overlooked in the influx of other offending images. The anteroom is a shoulder-high maze of boxes growing taller by the day. Best not follow this to its natural conclusion.

Maxim readies the photograph on the table. My brother's wife isn't a ballerina. This isn't her. This is no one I owe anything to. She is an enemy, a nonperson, she isn't even there. I've airbrushed out Trotsky so many times that I know him by every mood and gesture, know him with the familiarity of a family member and have never felt regret, yet at the thought of erasing this single stranger something in me collapses over a hollow sphere of sadness.

Collect yourself, man.

"May I borrow your lighter?" Maxim asks, holding up a cigarette. I pass it to him and he lights his cigarette without taking his eyes from me.

He primes the airbrush and I load a gray-scale paint canister. Beneath brief exclamations of smoke he observes as I airbrush the stage over the disgraced dancer's legs, the faces of the audience over the dancer's slender torso. She falls, I have decided, into her partner's hands. She looks away from the audience, to the camera positioned at the back of the stage, through the open aperture, to me, her final audience, as I erase her eyes.

It takes such artistry, such visual perception to disappear a figure into the backdrop. With a magnifying glass and a thin paintbrush, I expunge her waist from the furrows that widen between her partner's spread fingers. I airbrush her arms until all that remains is her left hand, stenciled in spotlight, like a windblown glove dancing with a lonesome man, and I leave it there while I finish.

There are moments of intense creative pleasure: The dancer's right leg obscures the face of an adolescent in the front row, and in its place I paint a postage-stamp portrait of my brother, Vaska, when he was that age. Over the last two years I have inserted him into hundreds of photographs and paintings. Young Vaskas. Old Vaskas. Vaskas in crowds listening to Lenin. Vaskas laboring in fields and factories. He hangs on the walls of courthouses, ministries, schools, prisons, even the NKVD headquarters, where if you look closely you will see Vaska glaring at Yevgeny Tuchkov, the man who made him disappear.

Do I worry I'll be caught? Please. My superiors are too focused on who I take out to notice who I put in.

The dancer's left hand still dangles in the air. My decision isn't decided so much as felt. I set down the airbrush as one might set down a fork when nauseous. I will leave the disgraced dancer's hand where it is, where it should be, right there, a single hand waving for help, waving good-bye, applauding no one, a single hand that may have once held my neck while a voice in my ear asked for help.

I slip the corrected photograph into a stack of a half-dozen others. Maxim flips through them as I clean the airbrush with an oil cloth. He grunts. Has he noticed?

"Is everything all right, Comrade?" I ask, unable to steady the shake in my voice.

He smiles warmly. Tusks of smoke slide from his nostrils.

"I was only admiring your work," he says. "It's so easy to overlook the beauty of what we do, isn't it?"

We spend the afternoon working through the most recent box. When Maxim plods to the anteroom, I slip the photograph of the dancer from the stack. It's irrational, a madman's instinct, but what if her hovering hand is noticed? Will I be punished for my carelessness?

Maxim returns to the office before I can correct or return it to the stack, and I hide it in my lap. "Are you well, Comrade?" he asks. "You look feverish."

I blot my forehead with my shirtsleeve. "Too much time underground, perhaps."

Maxim nods and suggests we end early today. I nod, gratefully. Not knowing what else to do, I fold the photograph into my overcoat pocket. I am a dozen paces into the tunnel when he calls. "Comrade, I think you have forgotten something."

The fever Maxim suspected suddenly feels real. There is no excuse for taking a photograph from the premises. The suspicion cast makes it a capital offense. I hold the doorframe.

"Yes, Comrade?" I manage.

Maxim eyes me. He knows. He knows.

"You're growing forgetful, Comrade," he says, and holds up my silver cigarette lighter.

As children in the years leading up to the Revolution, my brother and I played monarchists and revolutionaries, switching sides a half-dozen times before dinner. At night we rapped against the wall separating our bedrooms in the prisoner's code invented by the Decembrists. The code arranged the alphabet into a graph of five rows and six columns. The tap for each letter corresponded to its row and column number. We wrote with sound on a wall that divided us no more than a letter divides sender from recipient.

By the time we were old enough to mistake ourselves for men, I'd already turned toward Bolshevism. Vaska found comfort in the Orthodox Church. We idolized the dead martyrs of our respective causes. One evening my comrades beat Vaska with such ferocity he nearly became one. His left eye had swollen shut and his nose bent at an awful angle when he entered my grandmother's kitchen. I grabbed his hands. Only his knuckles were unbruised.

"You must run away when they come after you," I told him.

"No, I must stay," he said, glaring at me.

"Then at least put up a fight. This is shameful."

He leaned forward, offering his busted face as evidence, and said, "Do you think this shames *me*?"

It was the last time we spoke. For many years after that, I believed that I knew so little of his life I would never betray him.

In August 1931, agents of the OGPU told me that Vasily Markin would be arrested within a fortnight on charges of religious radicalism. They told me my brother had married, that his wife was pregnant. They gave me his address. It was a test. It must have been. So much was lost in communications between *raions* that had I warned Vaska, had he fled Leningrad, he might still be alive. Had I done that, had the agents raided his apartment in the early hours and found him missing, they would have come for me instead—I believe this, I must, because if I begin to wonder, if I begin to think maybe they tipped me off as a professional courtesy, so that I *could* warn Vaska, if I begin to think . . . all roads in that direction lead to darkness.

That October, after the arrest, trial, and execution, the agents returned with a brown envelope. "Have a seat, Citizen," the senior among them said, and gestured to my divan, where I'd just been eating dessert. I followed his extended hand, suddenly a guest in my own home.

The officers sat on either side of me, making the divan feel like the backseat of a Black Crow police van, and the senior agent opened the envelope and slid a photograph across the heat-ringed coffee table. If I gasped, it was from shock, from terror, from some dark thing rending inside me that might have been the birth pangs of remorse. I had corrected some thousand photographs in that year alone, but not one had I recognized, not one had I been part of.

The portrait the agent held out had been taken in 1906, on a Wednesday. My father, a haberdasher, had closed the shop that morning. He was well regarded, at least in haberdashery circles, having built his reputation on a pearl netting *kokoshnik* that had made a minor countess the talk of the Winter Palace ballroom. My mother did the bookkeeping, the restocking, the hiring of seamstresses—nearly everything, she felt, but placing the hat on the buyer's head. She had grown up on potatoes and made sure her children grew up on meat.

We dressed in our finest clothes that Wednesday in 1906 and took the train from Pavlovsk to Petersburg to the photographer's studio. It had been our mother's idea, as most good ideas were. A portrait, by camera rather than paintbrush, would convey in a single image the forward-looking optimism she had spent her life enacting. Peacock plumage roosted on my mother's head. In the photograph, it is dishwater gray. I stand in front of her with a faint smile. Not even the noose of my necktie strangled the excitement of having my picture taken. And beside me, wearing a matching necktie, a matching smile, his cowlick roughly brushed, his broad face whittling to a slender nose, my brother stood stiffly, gazing through the lens, through time, to meet my eyes as I sat framed between the agents who had executed him.

After leaving the photographer's studio, my parents had taken us to the Petersburg Zoological Gardens. It had been a terrible decade for the zoo—the grounds had been largely abandoned and many of the cages were empty—but I was a child, and didn't understand what the empty cages meant. What still lived in that zoo was a revelation. I had never before spied an animal larger than a milk cow, more ferocious than a hungry dog. Who could have imagined a beast as strange and melancholy as a giraffe? But of every animal we saw that afternoon, I remember none more clearly than the leopard. Loose-limbed and lanky. Nostrils spouting narrow triangles of steam. Claws clicking coded messages across the concrete floor. Eyes all pupil. Each step unfurling through the spine. An inconceivable creature at which Vaska and I first marveled, then threw bread crumbs.

"You recognize this, I'm sure," the senior agent said, nodding to Vaska in the portrait. "I trust you know who to correct."

By this point I had moved from India ink to airbrushing. It was no longer enough to obliterate a traitor's face; the inky mask acknowledged that a traitor *could* exist, an assertion that quickly becomes a traitorous act in itself. History is the error we are forever correcting.

The senior agent guided me to my workbench.

"Is it necessary to do this now?" I asked.

"The work of building socialism never ceases. It doesn't take leisure hours." He frowned at my dessert on the table. "It doesn't eat sugar plums."

I flattened the photograph, loaded the paint into the airbrush like a bullet into a pistol. With the patience of an Ottoman miniaturist, I corrected my brother. I began with his black leather shoes, slowly dissolving them into the floor they stood upon. Then his stockings and breeches. Our father stood behind him, and with slow, even strokes, I airbrushed an approximation of our father's trousers over my brother, so it seemed I was not erasing Vaska but folding him in our father's clothes, where he would stay safe and warm, his skin pressed to our father's. I remembered drawing him when we were children, paying him in sweets to sit for me when he was angry, tearful, exhausted, contrite, merciful, joyous. I had never felt closer to him than when I had felt some essence of his soul pressing its way through the pencil to the page.

When my brother's face disappeared into my father's dress shirt, I looked to the boy standing beside him, and wondered what judgments he cast as he stared through the lens and into the future where he met the gaze of the man he had become, and I knew then, beyond doubt, that I had sealed myself to the state, that my faith had become unshakable, my loyalty unimpeachable, because if this was wrong, if we did *this* in vain, all the water in the Baltic wouldn't be enough to cleanse us.

I passed the corrected photograph to the senior agent when I finished. He hadn't taken his eyes from me the entire time.

"You know what they're saying about you?" the agent asked, holding the photo to the light.

"What do they say?" I asked.

"That it takes less talent to dredge a face from oblivion than to cast it back. In that sense, you are a genius of a certain kind."

* * *

Three weeks have passed since I corrected the dancer. Several times I have tried to correct her hand, to slip the image back into its file, but Maxim's watchful eyes never leave me, I cannot retrieve the airbrush from our office, and what's more, the file has already been returned to NKVD headquarters.

There has been no mention of the missing photograph, and given the deluge of erroneous images, it has likely been overlooked and forgotten. But something *is* happening. People keep their eyes fixed roadward, afraid to speak or glance about. One evening at a restaurant, I pulled out my notebook to sketch an elderly man hunched over his soup bowl. Within two minutes everyone sitting at the poor man's table had quietly left. Twice this week I've woken to raids on the floor below me; the NKVD works at night, as is typically the case with murderers. The stacked boxes of erroneous images grow ever taller, threatening to topple and crush us as we work. I ask Maxim what he has heard.

"There is talk that the security organs have uncovered a Polish diversionist-espionage network."

"I salute the vigilance of our state police," I say. What a relief. I am not Polish. I have no relations or friends who are Polish.

"Saboteurs and kielbasa are Poland's only exports," he says, winking. "The NKVD will take care of the saboteurs, but you and me, we should take care of the kielbasa!"

"I have no desire for foreign sausages of any kind. If I ever hear another remark about Polish meat products I will report you."

Maxim's smile wilts and a surprised hurt sinks into his eyes.

We get to work. Over the past few weeks, Maxim has shown an interest in the mechanics of airbrushing, even asking me to explain linear perspective and my personal theories regarding the submersion of a subject into the background. To my pride and dismay, he's gotten rather good. The light of socialism burns bright enough to illumine even his brutish soul.

From our office, we hear the tick-tock of pickaxes, the gears of immense machines grinding forward. The construction never ceases. Working in twelve-hour shifts, the crews excavate the bedrock, cart-haul the debris, raise tunnel walls, lay ties and rail beams. At this rate, the entire metro system will be built before our work is finished. When Maxim and I break at lunch, I wander through the unlit tunnels. Each day I tell myself to walk farther, but in the darkness, with no unit of measurement but footsteps, distance becomes an increasingly futile concept. I doubt I will see the end.

When I return, Maxim is beaming. "I finally have a rendezvous with a certain blue-eyed secretary from the New Metal Institute this evening," he says. "I've been courting her for months."

"We'll be working late tonight," I inform him.

"But you said I could leave early tonight."

"New developments have arisen."

"But . . ."

"The work of socialism doesn't pause for secretaries of any eye color," I say. Poor Maxim. His misery is among the few indulgences I allow myself.

At twenty-two hundred hours, I surface to a tar-black night. December has come. If I maintain my current work schedule, I won't see the sun until April.

My cleaning woman has left my meal on the stove,

but I take only a glass of plum brandy and retire to the living room. I set a record on the gramophone and collapse into the comforting depression between the second and third divan cushions. I retrieve the rolled photograph of the dancer from the hollowed coffee table leg. A spot-lit hand, and below, her partner dancing onstage alone. I remove my spectacles and set them on the side table. Like ice cubes melting in a glass, the furniture loses its edges, and I nestle into the cushions, and sip plum brandy as the notes creak through the gramophone, and I feel fine, feel freed from the heaviness of sight, and a waddling oboe enters, and I imagine the dancer onstage, the whole of her, and I extend my hand but cannot see to the end of my wrist, see only a floating blankness that could be hers as easily as mine.

In my dream, I wander through endless train tunnels with a paintbrush and a jar of India ink. It is dark and I find the tunnel wall by touch, dip the brush head into the ink, and raise it to the concrete.

Two years ago: After I left my brother's wife and son, I went to work.

On my desk lay a pastoral by the nineteenth-century Chechen painter Pyotr Zakharov-Chechenets, perhaps the dullest work in his *catalogue raisonné.* An empty pasture in late daylight rises to a crest at the canvas's top third. A white stone wall cuts a quiet diagonal across the field. A dacha, a well, and an herb garden extending halfway up the pasture hill, foregrounded in shadow. There is no sign of life or movement, not even a lost goat.

I'd had the canvas for over a month and had put off my assigned task of inserting the Grozny party boss into the foreground. It says less about the state of my ego than it does about the state of contemporary art to admit I could improve upon any work of Socialist Realism. A nineteenth-century master, that's something else entirely.

When I painted in the toy soldier-size party boss, I gave him Vaska's face; or what Vaska might have looked like had he grown into a bloated party bigwig. The best my profession can do is convert from image to memory, from light to shadow, but the brushstrokes I erased were repainted in me, and I realized that before I was a correction artist, a propaganda official, a Soviet citizen, before I was even a man, I was an afterlife for the images I had destroyed.

That morning the last images of Vaska's face had been scratched into nothingness with a one-ruble coin.

That afternoon I began painting him into everything.

At first I was sure I'd be caught. In public buildings, I'd passed corrected landscapes with the pulsing certainty that everyone recognized Vaska's face pinpointed into the background. No one did. It was just like that silly fairy tale I told my brother's son; he was safe, in the background, beyond sight of those who would hurt him. I went on inserting him into every image I could, at every age, even, or especially, Vaska as an old man. The ledger will never be righted, and Vaskas added to art will never make up for the Vaska subtracted from life, but the act of multiplying my brother, of seeing him again each day, seeing who he was and might have become, the idea that I may have finally become a portrait artist, makes the rest of the work bearable.

I was never original enough to have my work shown in a café. Now my miniature portraits of Vaska hang everywhere: I'm told one has even made it into Stalin's living quarters.

I hung Zakharov's canvas in my office for several days before taking it down and shipping it back to Grozny. I never learned what became of it.

A loud splintering wakens me. I reach for my spectacles, but they are not on the nightstand. There is no nightstand. I have fallen asleep on the divan. Before I can sit upright, hands seize my shoulders and throw me, face first, to the floor. A kneecap presses against my spine and I am a pinched, gasping flail. I am not trying to escape, I want to say, I am trying to breathe, but the kneecap presses harder, making a home between my vertebrae.

"My spectacles," I mutter, as I am heaved to my feet.

The reply is the crunch of glass underfoot.

"I can't see." But if the man hears me, he doesn't care.

"What is this?" another agent asks, holding a gray image to my face. The dancer, I realize. I must have fallen asleep with it in plain view on the coffee table. A moment later he thrusts in my hands the frame that displays the portrait of Stalin on one side, and Rousseau's jungle cat on the other.

"There is more than one side," the agent marvels.

"True," the first agent says. "And like this picture, he will be pressed against the wall."

In the hall a third agent pulls a hazy crimson band—what must be the official state security seal—across what must be my closed door. They lead me down the staircase and place me in the backseat of a waiting car. The interrogation rooms of the Shpalerka jail have been full for weeks. We can only be going to Kresty Prison.

For a half hour we drive aimlessly, passing through half the city to arrive at the redbrick prison, on the far side of the Neva within view of my flat. The agents lead me through several doorways and depart. Someone takes my fingers, presses them to a damp pad and then to a sheet of paper, tells me to play the piano. From there I am taken to another room and given a placard to hold. A flashbulb goes off, a camera shutter snaps closed.

"What am I charged with?" I repeatedly ask, but I receive no reply. They are low-level functionaries to whom I am nothing. The fact of my arrest condemns me, everyone knows this; if I am a suspect then I am already a traitor, and traitors become prisoners, and prisoners become bodies, and bodies become numbers. The quota has taken my name and voice, so why dignify my question with an answer?

The man who searches me moves my limbs as if I am a collapsible bed. He checks between my toes, under my foreskin, inside my ears, beneath my eyelids. He searches my mouth for hollow teeth, pokes inside my nose with his pen, all with the gruff carelessness of the put-upon. He sighs and mutters, as if this charade pollutes his dignity alone.

When he finishes the search, I am allowed to dress. When I finish dressing, he unties my shoes and pulls out the laces, unbuckles my belt and rips it from the loops. "What are you doing?" I ask. In response he runs a blade down the front of my shirt. The buttons clink to the floor. He picks each up, then slices the waistband from my long underwear. "What is this?" I ask again, more urgently.

"Suicide is the enemy's final act of sabotage," the man says as he leaves. My shoes are falling from my feet, my trousers from my waist, and my shirt hangs open.

"How can anyone kill themselves with underwear?" I call after him, but the door has already closed.

One hand keeps my shirt closed, the other holds up my underwear and trousers. I take short, cautious steps into the gray murk and find the room empty but for two stools and a table. Was Vaska brought into a similar room in Kresty? An identical room? This room? It's not right: There should be a half-dozen other prisoners in here, twice that if the rumors of Kresty's overcrowding are even half true. I am no one special, no one at all.

Two sets of footsteps enter. Strong hands lift me by the armpits and guide me to a stool.

"What's wrong with him? Is he blind? What's wrong with you?" asks a voice from across the table.

Where to begin?

For nine hours, the interrogator asks me the same questions. *When did you and the disgraced dancer initiate contact? What does the severed hand signify? What other Polish spies are you in contact with?* We spin on a grotesque carousel—he makes the same accusations, I make the same denials—each of us mistaking our circling for progress.

"The dancer is a stranger to me," I explain. "Her hand, it was just a mistake at the end of a long day. It was just a mistake and I brought the photograph home to hide my mistake."

I'm exhausted and thirsty. The interrogator promises me a bed and water, a five-course meal, my freedom, all the world and a bottle of vodka if I will only confess the truth.

"But I have confessed the truth!"

The interrogator sighs, his disappointment palpable. In the silence I imagine him frowning at his paperwork, his frustration a blind mirror of mine. "We'll continue tomorrow," he says.

I ask for a pillow and blanket but the guard laughs and pulls me to my feet. If I try to sit, he kicks me. If I lean against the wall, he kicks me. "What time is it?" I ask. He kicks me. I had imagined steel laboratories, industries of pain, whirring instruments to uproot every nerve. Thirst, sleep exhaustion, a few kicks from a bored guard; it seems such an antiquated process. Effective nonetheless. My feet swell inside my laceless shoes. Nodding off, my grip loosens and my trousers and underwear fall to the floor. The guard, naturally, kicks me. It continues. Rounds of sleepless standing, punctuated by the guard's heel, followed by interrogation. The Kresty interrogators have no evidence, and so they will beat me until I build a case against myself. But they don't need evidence. They can invent whatever they want.

Three interrogation sessions pass and the interrogator begins to plead for my confession.

It is preposterous and strangely touching. The interrogator who until now has been a disembodied voice, an impossible question, becomes an afflicted soul. He needs my confession to confirm the infallibility of Soviet jurisprudence, to justify the descent from humanity we together share. I want to comfort him.

I've been awake for days, perhaps, when the minister enters. He relieves the current guard and waits until the door locks behind him before greeting me.

"My old friend," he says, sadly. "What have you gotten yourself into?"

"What day is it?" I ask. My stubble is the only measure of passing time.

"Friday," he says.

Of what week? What month? I try to visualize the six-day, five-week calendar month. Sundays were outlawed five years ago to discourage religious observance. On Friday evenings I buy a chocolate bar to celebrate the death of another week's work. I hold to the word like a rope. "Friday," I repeat, wrapping it around me, lashing myself to the life that was mine.

"You are an active builder of communism, Comrade," the minister says. "For as long as I've known you, you have been loyal to the Party, the People, the Future."

My head jerks up. My thoughts, diffused by sleep exhaustion, by torture, by the endless monotony of the same three questions, collect around the hope that I am still capable of being saved, that I haven't fallen beyond grace. "Yes, Comrade Minister, I have been loyal."

"And yet now, when you're needed, you become traitorous."

"They claim I'm involved with a Polish spy ring. It is a mistake. I have been loyal."

The table groans, and I feel him lean against it. "Would you give your life for the Revolution?"

"Yes."

"For the *vozhd*?"

"Yes."

"For our future socialist utopia?"

"Without hesitation."

"Then why deny your crimes?"

"Because I committed none."

My insistence on loyalty and innocence disappoints him. He coughs twice before lighting a cigarette and places the end between my lips. The first gasp of smoke leaves me woozy.

"I would think that you, of all people, would understand how little that means," he says.

"How little what means?" The tobacco leaf glows with the warmth of the Crimean sun under which it grew.

"What you did or did not do," he says. The words echo from some weary cavern within him. How many times has he entered the cells of Kresty Prison and explained what is obvious to all but the man across from him? "You think you narrate your own story, but you're only the blank page."

"But I did nothing wrong."

"What you believe to be true is a small muscle that exerts its strength only inside your head. You are involved in a Polish spy ring, Comrade. Whether you were before, you are now."

The verdict is handed down before the defense makes its case. Guilt and innocence do not determine judgment, but rather judgment determines all, including the definition of guilt.

"What should I do?" I ask.

The pale, pasty cloud leans toward me again. "You are a true revolutionary, are you not?"

"I have given my life to the party."

"No," he says. "You haven't yet."

Can I refuse? Must I renounce my loyalty to prove it? By refusing, I become the traitor whom I am accused of being. By acquiescing, the result is the same. But my allegiance to the party has superseded all other allegiances, even to Vaska; without it, I don't know who I am; without it, I die a stranger to myself.

"Will you prove your loyalty by confessing your betrayals?" the minister asks.

"But I don't speak Polish," I say.

He rises from the table and squeezes my shoulder. "I'm sure it will come back to you."

"It was Maxim, wasn't it?" I ask.

"What?"

"My assistant. He turned me in, didn't he?"

"I wouldn't know," he says and steps toward the door.

"Please, one more moment. There's something I can't figure out. I haven't been taken to the regular cells. I'm nobody, yet I'm in a private cell, subjected to endless interrogations. Trotsky would hardly receive such special treatment."

"What's your question?" the minister asks.

"My question is why bother?"

The minister loosens a satisfied sigh. "You're quite right, of course. You should be in the common cells and you should be tried, judged, and sentenced in under two minutes. But Comrade Stalin himself is a great admirer of your work, particularly your work on his cheeks. You've made him look years younger. Pity for you that he's not a vain man, or he might have interceded. But he's taken a keen interest in your case. You should be honored, Comrade. Through your work you've revealed the *vozhd*'s true face. Now he will reveal yours."

The minister leaves wordlessly and the whole cell sinks into an unfocused background.

I receive a pillow, a blanket, and each morning a new plate of stale bread. I consider asking for a new pair of spectacles, but I've grown accustomed to this half-blind state. The wall across the room and the wall beside me meld into a misty mantle. No distance, no linear perspective; the laws of my former domain do not exist here, and their absence is a perverse freedom.

Every night I have the same dream. I am walking through the dark train tunnel, paintbrush and India ink jar in hand.

Each morning, a woman with a lisp enters my cell to teach me Polish. She is patient and generous, a natural teacher. She teaches me an alphabet I can't write, words I can't read, her voice the thread stretching through my days, upon which all else hangs. She could be twenty as easily as forty, but I imagine her older, more maternal, a nurse as much as a teacher.

She straightens the labyrinth of language into passages through which I can escape. I picture the Polish alphabet—with its *ę*, *eł*, and *żets*—arranged not as an unbroken line, but as a periodic table, the upper- and lowercase letters written as elements—*Dd* and *Śś*—and the relationships between these elements, how and why they bond into words and clauses, require new theorems, new natural laws, and so it feels as if I am not learning a language, but the physics of a new universe.

For so long words have ceased to mean anything. If one were to compile a dictionary of Soviet Russian, the first definition of each entry would be *submit.* But *przyznanie się* means confession. *Jurto* means tomorrow. I repeat the Polish words, and the repetition has a restorative effect. Sometimes she asks a question, and I fumble, searching through the scant inventory of my new vocabulary for any offering, but there is nothing, and the face of that resounding emptiness is my future.

"We're going to fool them," I say one day.

"Yes, we'll have you proclaiming like a Polish prince," she answers.

"I want to know a word I will never have to use," I say.

"What do you mean?"

"A word that won't go into my confession. A word you don't have to teach me, that I'll never have to use."

"*Styczeń*," she says, after a moment. "It means January."

"But it's still early December."

"It's a word you will never have the occasion to use," she says, comfortingly.

I remember the Petersburg zoo, where my parents took Vaska and me after sitting for our portrait. Still dressed in our breeches and little leather shoes, we looked like the dignitaries of a shrunken realm. I remember approaching the cages of the big cats; behind the bars a black-spotted beast took long, slinking strides. The magic and shame of something so ferociously impotent. It was our first exposure to incarceration.

"Leopard," I say. "I want to learn the Polish word for leopard."

She hesitates. It's easy to forget she has more to lose than me.

"Don't joke around," she says. "We have serious work to do."

When I'm with her, and only when I'm with her, I wish for my spectacles. One night, the adjacent cell opens. A guard shouts, or maybe it's the prisoner, and the door slams closed. He prays aloud, a habit the guards will soon disabuse him of. My brother prayed on the other side of the wall that separated our bedrooms when we were children. I could hear him whisper long into the evening.

I tap against the wall. It was the first coded phrase that came to mind, the phrase my brother and I tapped to each other before we stepped away from the wall, climbed into separate beds, fell into our separate dreams. *you are loved.*

The praying pauses. He can hear me. I press my hand against the wall. He doesn't respond.

you are loved, I tap again.

Nothing. He must not know the tapping code. Why would he if he's innocent? I tap the alphabet out—1,1; 1,2; 1,3—hoping that he'll catch on.

He doesn't tap back. I repeat the alphabet several more times and sign off with *you are loved.* Every night I tap the alphabet to the prisoner on the other side of the wall. He never responds. I draft my confession.

Q: What is your history with the disgraced dancer?

A: The disgraced dancer recruited me as a covert spy in 1933. We met once a month in one of a rotating series of safe houses along with other prominent artists and intellectuals, all of whom disguised their traitorous nature within the guise of revolutionary fervor.

Q: What type of information did you provide the disgraced dancer?

A: Propaganda circulars, the internal memoranda of NKVD agents, the names of prominent officials that might be corrupted, the locations of sensitive sites of political and military value, anything that might be useful to her diversionist, defeatist, fascist-insurrectionist cabal.

Q: What does the disgraced dancer's hand symbolize?

A: The hand was left in the portrait as a signal to covert cells to commence diversionist sabotage.

Q: Why would you betray the great socialist future?

A: Because the future is the lie with which we justify the brutality of the present.

In my new language I recite the indignities of Soviet rule. I admit that I am guilty of condemning the censorship, the ideological inflexibility, the cult worship of Stalin, the sham laws, the broken judiciary, all of which, I must concede at the end of the confession, are vital to ensure the future of the communist mission. I become the dissident and wrecker the party needs me to be. The arguments are so convincing I fear that I am beginning to believe them.

One day, while we go over in Polish the contents of my confession, I ask the Polish teacher her name.

"You know I can't tell you that."

"Of course not," I say, unable to mask my disappointment. "I was just curious."

She says nothing.

We are on the verge of something. A border will be transgressed. "My name is—"

"Don't," she snaps. "Don't do that."

We are quiet for some time.

"What did you do before this?" I ask.

"I taught children Polish," she says warily.

"Will you go back to teaching children when you're finished with me?"

"Oh no," she says. "This is the only place I can teach Polish legally."

In my half-blindness, hers becomes the voice of my brother's wife, of the dancer, of anyone I have betrayed. "I'm sorry," I whisper. "I'm sorry," I say, and mean it, even if I cannot name what I am sorry for.

"In Polish," she commands. "Say it in Polish."

One night, like all the others, I tap the alphabet on the wall. The wall responds.

are you god? The taps are slow and cautious. The man in the next cell must have finally learned the coded alphabet.

no. why? I tap back.

you test my faith in you, but by testing me, you prove the extent of your grace.

i'm not god, I insist. It's a ridiculous thing to insist, but the religious don't surrender to reason without a fight.

you are, he taps.

i am roman markin. i worked in propaganda. i was arrested on december third. i am a party member.

who but god would reach me here? he asks.

there is no god, I tap. *not here nor anywhere.*

you were him. this i know.

how? I ask.

There is a long pause before the man begins to tap: *for so long i heard the tapping on the wall. first i thought it was mice. then i thought i was going mad. a trick of the devil. then i understood you were teaching me the alphabet in code. then i could read what you had been tapping for weeks. for months. forever. you are loved. who could you be but god? who else would find me here?*

I don't know how long it took him to tap this out. I don't know how he had mistaken me for anything more than a prisoner like him. The bitumen floor drains the warmth from my legs.

you are a believer? I ask.

a seminarian, he taps.

then you have the benefit of knowing why you're arrested, taps the Bolshevik in the prison.

this is the highest point in leningrad, he taps. *with the very best view.*

these are windowless rooms, I point out. *in a cellar.*

yet from here i see the kingdom of heaven.

* * *

On the day before my trial, I run through my confession for a final time with the Polish teacher, the minister, the procurator, and several others, judging from the density of cigarette smoke. It's a stage-worthy soliloquy. The procurator initially wanted me to recite a basic confession, once in Russian and once in Polish, but I convinced him that it would be more effective to merge the two. I begin in Russian, my voice soft and compliant as I describe the roots of my betrayal, but as I list the reasons for my perfidy, as I numerate Soviet crimes, my voice rises from submission to defiance, from Russian to Polish, lashing out as if Polish nationalism is a savage beast caged within me. When I finish, there are ten seconds of silence, broken by the minister's applause.

"Marvelous," he says. "You sound truly maniacal."

The procurator makes a few slight corrections to my testimony, and then one by one the officials file out of the room, until I am alone with the Polish teacher.

"That was quite a performance," she says. "You should have written for the theater."

I'm still elated from the minister's applause. "I'm so glad they approved."

"I've never met a man more eager to load the gun that will kill him," she says. "Tell me, honestly, for my own understanding, in your own words. Are you guilty?"

For a moment, I'm stunned. Her dissenting voice, so unexpected amid the chorus of approbation, moves through me as light moves through a lens. It is the last question I would expect to hear in an interrogation cell.

"You coauthored my confession," I tell her. I'd give anything to see how she looks at me, whether it is with disgust or anger, or with concern for how I will live my last days.

"They will shoot you, no matter what you say or do," she says.

You see what I am, I want to shout. You have seen how easily, how eagerly, I debase myself. Why now, when we have reached the end, do you expect me to be a better man?

"You should leave," I suggest. "Go back to Poland. Go somewhere."

"Why?"

"Because when they run out of students, they will start on the teachers."

She laughs. "They will never run out of students."

She gathers her papers. I want to ask if she will be at my trial, but I fear what I might do if I know she is watching. Before she leaves she places her hand on my neck. Her skin is warm and she gently kneads my flesh. It's the first time in many weeks that the touch of another has not inflicted pain. I try to remember the face of my brother's wife but it's gone.

"I've had several students in Kresty," she says. "You might be my favorite."

"I love you," I reply. Absurd, sentimental, maudlin, I know, but the warmth of her hand on my neck, the consolation in her voice, it makes me feel as if I'm still alive. Whatever pleasures or punishments that await in the afterlife, if there is one, must feel fainter than those that fill any given day here on earth. "We have built something real together here."

She gives my shoulder another squeeze. "*Kocur*."

"What?"

"*Kocur*," she repeats. "The leopards at the zoo."

Only once the door closes do I see the golden-haired, black-peppered cat sulking behind the bars of the

Petersburg Zoological Gardens. *Kocur.* I whisper the word—*kocur, kocur*—each iteration rattling the tin box inside my chest. I tap the word in code against the table with sharp raps of my fist. It's remarkable to know a new word to name such an old memory. A weary leopard in a zoo. What could be more simple? Yet this vision I shared with my brother has grown into mystery so unlikely and lasting I can only describe it as a mercy granted by some magnificent wholeness to the world that was already breaking between us.

Later I walk to the wall and sit down, my back to it.

tomorrow is the trial, I tap. *tell me what to do.*

i'm only a seminarian, he taps back.

then tell me how you keep faith.

i know that belief is the last thing I own.

even when everything is gone?

that's the point, the seminarian taps. *not everything goes.*

i've been a loyal bolshevik, I insist, tapping so furiously it's a wonder he can assemble the knocks into words. *i've given them my work, my devotion, my brother's life. they've scripted the confession. they want me to prove my allegiance by breaking it.*

you might question a belief that so readily betrays its believers.

this is no time to be clever, I tap.

He doesn't respond. I continue: *how do i confess when every word means what they tell it to mean?*

The seminarian answers with silence.

That night, like every night, I return to the tunnel. I trudge through with my brush and jar, but this time the dream is different. A light winks at the tunnel's end, growing larger and brighter. An approaching train. It careens toward me. Its headlight floods the tunnel. I turn and see for the first time what I have been painting for these months of night. Across kilometers of tunnel, I have painted every husband, wife, daughter, son, sister, and brother I have ever erased. In the flickering light they are cave paintings. Primordial. Before the edge of history. I try to touch the nearest face, a boy, but before I reach him the train slams into me and I wake.

It is morning. They feed me eggs and kielbasa, the best meal I have had since arriving. I am the eighth of twelve tried for espionage. The first seven traitors recite monotonous confessions of their crimes. In comparison, mine will be a work of brutal beauty, resounding with the vehemence and desperation of a true dissident. But when I am called before the procurator, I say nothing.

The procurator, assuming I haven't heard him, again asks, "What was your history with the disgraced dancer?"

Again, I say nothing.

Realizing my silence is intentional, the procurator stamps his foot, a gesture that will likely be repeated on my face when this is all over, and shouts the question.

I say nothing.

Imagine the judge turning to the procurator, the procurator to the minister, the minister to the bailiff, then all turning to me. What if my brother's wife could see me? Or the Polish teacher? Would they have watched with trepidation, with surprise, with approval that might one day deepen to pride? The procurator's voice trembles; with rage, yes, but also fear, because my failure to confess implicates him. He demands to know my relationship with the dancer, the extent of our saboteur network, what her hand, amputated and floating over the stage, signifies.

Her portrait is perched as evidence on an easel. In it Vaska must be staring out at the court, invisible to all, even me.

I say nothing.

Let the descendants of our glorious enterprise find my silence in the official record. Let them fall into the lacuna. Let them see my omission for what it is: a silence as pronounced as a hand hovering in midair, the error in the lie that is the truth. Let them know that here, on this day, a guilty man began living honestly.

I am not blind enough to believe anything I have done today will last. As the bailiff leads me out by my shackles, I can already hear the court stenographer typing into the official record a transcript of the confession I refused to recite.

A guard hits me with his truncheon again and again. He soon tires, leans back against the cell wall. I want to tell him: I understand why my pain is required. I want to tell him: The truncheon will break my rib just once, but it will go on breaking you.

The interrogation has succeeded; I am now an enemy of the state. My mouth is filling with blood. It's been so long since I've been given water that I hesitate to spit it out. The guard shakes his head, disgusted. I have become a violent act of reality inflicted upon the fiction of which we are both citizens. I want him to know that I understand this, that every thump of his truncheon hardens my resolve, that he has my permission. But I haven't the breath in me to speak.

He strikes me twice more, feebly, tiring from his exertions.

"There's more work to do," I say, as consolingly as I am able, and lift my unbeaten parts to him. Consent is my only available means of resistance, and it angers him further. He strikes another two times, harder.

The cell door opens, I don't know when, and fills with Maxim's heavy breaths. Has he already erased me from my family portrait? Have I been folded within the pleats of my mother's dress? Vaska and I now exist in dimensions just below the photographic surface, where we share the realm of ghosts.

"You should have been kinder to me," Maxim says.

"Be careful who you choose for an assistant," I warn him.

"I looked up to you. You made me feel like a fool for trying to learn from you. You should've treated me better."

"So it was you, wasn't it?"

Maxim just breathes these deep, hulking breaths.

"You were never any good," I tell him. "You have no talent, no appreciation for what the work requires. You think you can replace me? Please. You could learn my techniques and my craftsmanship and still your work will never be as good as mine. Do you know why? Do you know why!" The coins in his pocket tremble. My shouts are sandpaper against my throat. "Because you need a soul the devil wants before you can begin bargaining with him."

"I know," he whispers.

"If you know, then why? Why did you inform on me?"

"What?" he asks with slow-witted startle. "I didn't. I vouched for you. As much as I was able."

"Then why am I here?" I can't see Maxim. I may be shouting at an empty patch of wall. "Why am I here? Tell me! Why am I here? What have I done to deserve this?"

He's quiet for a while, then closes the door behind him.

are you there, I tap, when I am alone.

i am here, the seminarian taps back.

Every inch of my body aches. My knuckles feel like my only unbroken bones. I bring them to the wall and tap, *i have a confession to make.*

i am listening, the seminarian replies.

For a moment I feel as if I've fallen into the dream, the dark tunnel wrapped around me, my brush raised to the wall. But the brush is only my curled finger, tapping coded messages on a cell wall meant for someone far away.

if you get out, you must pass it on to my brother's son, I tap.

what is his name?

vladimir vasilyevich markin.

what is your confession? he asks.

his father's face, I tap. *you must tell him where he can see what his father looked like.*

where?

in the work i have censored. in the background. behind stalin and lenin. behind their heads where their eyes can't find him.

When the guards come, I stand quietly and without protest. They return my shoelaces and share a cigarette while I lace my shoes.

"Can I sew my shirt buttons back on?" I ask.

"A comedian," one of the guards comments. "He's the leopard guy?"

A second guard says yes.

"Where'd you hear that?" I ask.

"The NKVD agent, of course," the first guard answers. "Your Polish teacher."

"They liquidated all the leopards at the zoo," the second guard says. "To send a message."

"A shame what we do to animals," the first guard replies.

I am on my knees. I cannot stand. They will have to carry me from here. I hear something from the wall. The seminarian is a madman, why else risk tapping to me with two guards in the cell? First the faint rap of knuckles on the wall, then a pounded fist, then stomped feet. It gives me the strength to stand. The guards take me from the room, but it only grows louder, and they pretend to ignore it, but the floor and walls and ceiling are shuddering, every bar and bone in the prison resounds with the code I first sent him, the code Vaska and I would tap to each other before climbing into bed and going to sleep.

They lead me into the darkness where I take my first breath of cold air. I remember Vaska racing toward the leopard cage. I chased after him, but he was always faster than me. Even now, I don't know what that leopard was beyond an indefinable, nameless mystery.

They will put me in a car, take me to the edge of a pit not unlike those into which the disgraced dancer and Vaska fell, and with a bullet through my brain stem, I will also fall. Consider the disgraced dancer. Consider those who informed on her, those who relayed the information, those who approved the action, those who knocked on her door in the middle of the night, those who arrested her, those who photographed her, those who took her fingerprints, those who pulled out her shoelaces, those who interrogated her, those who beat her, those who engineered her confession, those who tried, judged, and condemned her, those who led her to the car, to the basement, to the pit, those who dug her grave, put a bullet in her head, buried her. And the countless others, like me, who destroyed her birth certificate and diploma, the newspaper clippings and photographs, the school and internal passport and ration voucher records, the near-endless documentation that proves she had lived. It takes nothing less than the whole might of the state to erase a person, but only the error of one individual—if that is what memory is now called—to preserve her.

And if that is true, perhaps someday, far from now, Vaska will be discovered. Perhaps the seminarian in the other cell is the error that preserves us both.

"A small favor," I say. "Please. Give me the mercy of a single question."

The guard sighs. "Yes?"

"The man in the cell next to mine, what was his name?"

"What man?" the guard asks, confused.

"The man in the cell next to mine. The seminarian."

He pats my shoulder with what feels like genuine pity. "There was no cell next to yours."

"Yes, there was. There was a man in it. I heard him. Please, just tell me his name."

The guard shakes his head. "There's only one solitary cell on the cellar floor and only you in it."

The car idles at the end of the walkway. The door opens and the guard pushes me in. We drive. Ahead, a light glows through the shadows. For a moment, it's the train approaching. I turn in my seat, hoping to glimpse something I have created before the end. The light expands as we near, as if we are entering. It rises in the windshield, disappears over the roof, fades behind us. It isn't the approaching train, but a streetlamp. The rest of the road is dark.

Granddaughters

Kirovsk, 1937–2013

BEST TO BEGIN WITH THE GRANDMOTHERS. Galina's was the labor camp luminary, while ours were the audience. Ours had been bakers, typists, nurses, and laborers before the secret police knocked on their doors in the middle of the night. It must be an error, they thought, a bureaucratic oversight. How could Soviet jurisprudence remain infallible if it failed to recognize innocence? Some held on to the misbelief as they stood pressed against one another in train cars heading east across the Siberian steppe, the names of previous prisoners haunting the carriage walls in smudged chalk. Some still held on to it as they were shoved aboard barges and steamed north on the Yenisei. But when they disembarked onto the glassy tundra, their illusion burned away in the glare of the endless summer sun. In distant cities, they were expurgated from their own histories. In photographs, they donned India-ink masks. We never knew them, but we are the proof they existed. A hundred kilometers north of the Arctic Circle, they built our home.

There we go, talking about ourselves again. Let's start with Galina's grandmother, the prima ballerina of the Kirov for five seasons before her arrest for involvement in a Polish saboteur ring. She was a long, lean splinter of beauty embedded in the gray drab of any crowded city street. Though she crossed the same rails and rivers as our grandmothers, she wasn't destined for the mines. The labor camp director was a ballet connoisseur as well as a beady-eyed sociopath. He'd seen Galina's grandmother perform *Raymonda* in Leningrad two years earlier and had been among the first in the theater to stand in ovation. When he spied her name on the manifest, he smiled—a rare occurrence in his line of work. He clinked shot glasses with his deputy and toasted, "To the might of Soviet art, so great it reaches the Arctic."

During her first year in the camp, Galina's grandmother was received as a guest rather than an inmate. Her private room was austere but clean, a single bed, a bureau for her wardrobe, a wood-burning stove. Several times a week, the camp director invited her to his office for tea. Across a desk cluttered with registers, quotas, circulars, and directives, they would discuss the Vaganova method, the proper femur length for a prima ballerina, whether Tchaikovsky really had been so afraid his head would fall off while conducting that he had held it in place with his left hand. Galina called the camp director "a loyal citizen of the People's Republic of Bullshit" for his insistence that *Swan Lake* contained Marius Petipa's most sophisticated *pas de deux*. No one but the camp director's six-year-old nephew spoke to him so bluntly, but he didn't cut her rations or put nine grams of lead through her head. He offered more tea and suggested they might reach a consensus the following week, to which she declared, "Consensus is the goal of the feebleminded." We can't help loving her just a little. Neither could the camp director.

The following year, he asked Galina's grandmother to create, train, and lead a small ballet troupe for his personal pleasure and for camp morale. The ensemble rehearsed for three months before making its debut. Some of its members had taken ballet classes as children and the rest were versed in peasant dances. After several long afternoons, the camp director and Galina's grandmother decided on an abridged treatment of *Swan Lake*. The ensemble rehearsed turns with questionably cosmopolitan French names until blisters pocketed their feet. Muscle memory was reeducated as Galina's grandmother browbeat elegance into these enemies of the people. It became increasingly unclear whether she was captive, captor, or both. After pulled muscles tightened and swollen toes deflated, after the curtain was drawn and a camp searchlight lit the far end of the canteen, it was evident to all that the stage was set for something extraordinary.

Our grandmothers sat on canteen benches in the audience, and the production was, as you can imagine, a fiasco. The nearest orchestra was eighteen hundred kilometers away, so the score played through the rusted horn of a gramophone previously used to store onions. The choreography required dozens of dancers; the ensemble had ten, and four of them wore charcoal-drawn mustaches to play Siegfried, Von Rothbart, and various footmen, tutors, and court gentlemen. The lake itself was rather thin on waterfowl; later some would joke that NKVD huntsmen had arrived first. There were slips and missteps, the music speeding past dancers left flailing in its wake. But then Galina's grandmother, alone onstage, slid into a pool of light. Her hair washed and laureled in feathers, her shoulders polar-summer pale, her feet laced in real silk slippers. In the crowd, our grandmothers went silent. Some were transported back to the concert halls, anniversaries, and champagne flutes of their former lives. Some used the reprieve to nap. But most, we suspect, were astounded. After working fourteen-hour shifts in the mines, inhaling so much nickel they sneezed silver glitter, none could have expected a private performance from the prima ballerina of the Kirov.

Despite the many mishaps, the camp director was thrilled. For the next eight years, he sponsored ballets on the summer and winter solstices; but he hadn't risen through the ranks by giving anything away for free. For a man determined to wring maximum productivity from his prisoners before they died, the ballet proved an effective coercion. Seats—and with them upgraded rations—were reserved for those who exceeded their ever-increasing quotas. Galina's grandmother helped shave years off the lifespan of her audience.

It all ended in the ninth year. Galina's grandmother had less than three months until her release date and the camp director had fallen in love. Can someone like him actually love another human being? We're pained to admit that yes, he might delude himself into believing so. We have some experience with this kind of man, not bureaucratic mass murderers, of course, but with alcoholic boyfriends, violent husbands, strangers harboring the misconception that their unwanted advances are compliments. Galina's grandmother was the only woman for thousands of kilometers who wasn't one hundred percent repulsed at the sight of the camp director. Perhaps he mistook her lack of utter contempt for infatuation? Whatever his reasons, he summoned her to his office eighty-five days before her release date. The office door closed behind her and what happened next we only know from rumors spread by the guards. There was a declaration of love followed by a moment that still astonishes, these many decades later, when Galina's grandmother refused the camp director. At this point in the story, our dried-up admiration for her floods back, and we feel a little bad about accusing her of collaboration. But the camp director was unaccustomed to rejection. The guards overheard a muffled struggle, a scream, the tearing of cloth. As the rest of the camp slept, the camp director became Galina's grandfather.

Or maybe they had been sleeping together the whole time. Who are we to say?

Years passed. Stalin's death and denunciation led to the decommissioning of the prison. Camp administrators transferred from the Interior Ministry to the Ferrous Metallurgy Ministry without even changing offices. The same people pulled nickel from the ground. Our grandmothers married miners, smelter techs, even former prison guards. They stayed for profit and practicality: The Arctic nickel mines paid among the highest wages in the country, and its former prisoners had difficulty obtaining residency permits to go back home. Galina's grandmother was among them. She raised her daughter and taught schoolchildren the tenets of communism. The camp director was demoted and replaced with a party boss. On her deathbed in May 1968, she clutched the arm of the attendant nurse and whispered, "I see, I see, I see." She passed before she could tell the nurse precisely what she saw.

But hers is the story of our grandmothers. Galina's story is ours.

* * *

She was born in 1976. The obstetrician didn't care for children, and so when he didn't frown at the sight of her, all took it as a prognosis of future beauty. As Galina grew, we all acknowledged the prescience of the doctor's early appraisal. Galina was more her grandmother than either of her parents.

She was born to a miner and a seamstress for a local textile factory, and yes, our mothers did approve of them in the early years of the girl's childhood. They managed to remain unremarkable in all the proper ways. They worked long days, adhering to the second principal of the Moral Code of the Builder of Communism: *conscientious labor for the good of society—he who does not work, neither shall he eat.* At home they spoke loudly enough for our mothers to hear through the wall that they harbored no perverse secrets. But strangely, they didn't allow Galina to play with us as children. They declined invitations to birthday celebrations, left early from International Day of Solidarity of Youth festivities. It raised our mothers' suspicion. "They are haughty at best, subversive at worst," our mothers whispered as they scooped jam into their tea. This was the late seventies, early eighties, and though the purges had receded into memory, glasnost was still years away. Our city was small and whispers easily became verdict. Who has forgotten the story of Vera Andreyevna, who unintentionally denounced her own mother, and was heralded in newspapers from Minsk to Vladivostok? Galina's mother might have suffered a similar fate, had not the lung cancer taken her first.

We didn't understand why Galina had been kept from us until our third year of primary school. We left for lunch after reciting our multiplication tables—no difficult task, for we excelled at memorization and recitation. Galina tripped over a loose shoelace and lurched, her books sailing through the air as she tumbled under them. We'd never seen a shoelace cause such a commotion before.

"Not quite living up to your grandmother's reputation," our teacher said. We laughed with the spite of those without legacies to honor.

"What do you mean?" Galina asked. She didn't know. We couldn't believe it. We gushed, speaking over one another, telling her about the ballet ensemble, the evil camp director, the remarkable fate of Galina's grandmother. She shook her head with confusion, incredulity, and, eventually, pride.

At home that evening, she demanded ballet lessons.

"Ballet?" her father asked, his voice a sore-throated rasp of nickel dust. He would die at the age of fifty-two, exceeding the life expectancy of a miner by three years. "You'll join Young Pioneers this year. You'll be busy with learning leadership and team-building skills."

But Galina was adamant. "I want to dance ballet like my grandmother."

Her father sighed and ran his hands through the scalding beam emitted from a reflector space heater. Over the years he had questioned why he and his wife had concealed the family celebrity, but the answer was simple: They were faithful communists, children of the labor camp, with a daughter who looked like her grandmother. Galina's father knew her best hope for prosperity would come from dulling all that made her exceptional until the plural voice accepted her as one of its own. No doubt he had heard Lenin's famous reaction to Beethoven's Sonata No. 23: *It is wonderful, ethereal music. But I am unable to listen to it. It moves me to stroke the heads of my fellow beings for being able to produce such beautiful things in spite of the abominable hell they are living in. It is necessary to smash those heads, smash them without mercy.*

But ever since his wife had passed, he had grown indulgent and rather fatalistic. "Of course, Galya," he said. The next day she told us all about it.

Gorbachev came to power the year Galina began ballet training, and brought with him glasnost, perestroika, and *demokratizatsiya.* Our mothers whispered a little louder, and, as we passed from early to late adolescence, we found our voices. We started softly and we were wise to be wary; the city party boss was every bit as cruel as the camp director had been, and like new pop songs, political reforms reached us long after they were first broadcast in Moscow. In the winter, when the sun disappeared beneath the three-month night, we gathered in parks and deserted lots, under the rusted metal limbs of White Forest, warmed ourselves in deserted apartment blocks and cafeterias where we passed around tattered samizdat pages of Solzhenitsyn and Joseph Brodsky, danced to the Queen LPs someone's second cousin's violin instructor brought back from Europe, and wore black-market Levi's that always looked better than they actually fit. We traded old *ryobra*—rib records, bone music, skeleton songs—banned fifties and sixties rock and roll inscribed by phonograph onto exposed X-rays that could be played on gramophones at hushed volumes. Radiographs of broken ribs, dislocated shoulders, malignant tumors, compacted vertebrae had been cut into vague circles, the music etched into the X-ray surface, the center hole punctured with a cigarette ember, and it was glorious to know that these images of human pain could hide in their grooves a sound as pure and joyful as Brian Wilson's voice. Our parents called the music capitalist pollution, as if the cancerous masses on the X-rays had been caused by a song recorded on the other side of the world, rather than by the pollution that flowed from the smokestacks just outside our windows, free for us all.

In the summertime, the devastation of the earth permeated the clouds. Yellow fog enshrouded the city like a varnish aged upon the air. Sulfur dioxide rose from the Twelve Apostles, the dozen nickel smelters ringing a lake of industrial waste. Rain burned our skin. The pollution congealed into a dense ceiling blocking the starlight. The moon belonged to the past our grandmothers spoke of. We made the most of our summers: days without school, nights without darkness. First dates, first kisses. We were so awkward, morning pimples in the mirror, hair where we never wanted it, and we thought of the lung cancer X-ray that was the album art for *Surfin' Safari*, considered the ways a body betrays its soul, and wondered if growing up was its own kind of pathology. We fell in and out of love with fevered frequency. We constantly became people we would later regret having been.

On clear days we trudged through White Forest, a man-made woods of metal trees and plastic leaves constructed in the boom years of Brezhnev when the party boss's wife had grown nostalgic for the birches of her youth. By the time we trudged beneath them, however, the years had ravaged both the forest and the party boss's wife, and the plastic leaves above were as sagging and liver-spotted as her face. We went on. The mud was a mustard we plodded through. On the forest's far side we looked across the expanse of sulfurous waste stretching to the horizon. We shouted. We proclaimed. We didn't need to whisper out here. For a few short weeks in July, red wildflowers pushed through the oxidized waste and the whole earth simmered with apocalyptic beauty.

But the only color belowground was a silvery metallic luster. Our fathers blasted the ore in the most productive nickel mine in the world in twelve-hour shifts. Mine shafts ran a kilometer and a half into the ground below us, and at the bottom the air was so sticky that even in January they stripped to undershirts, and hours later when they came home they'd stumble toward the shower, shedding their overcoats, sweaters, shirts, trousers, and the nickel dust that had dried onto their chests, their backs, their legs, and for a few moments before they showered our fathers were indestructible, men of metal, men who gleamed.

Other metals were mined—gold, copper, palladium, platinum—but northern nickel was our lifeblood. The Twelve Apostles burned it from the ore in two-thousand-degree heat and the falling snow was tinged with color depending on what had been in the furnaces the previous day: the red of iron, the blue of cobalt, the eggy yellow of nickel. We measured economic prosperity by the spread of rashes on our exposed skin. Even those who had never lit a cigarette had a smoker's cough. But the mining combine took care of us: vacations at mineral spas, citywide festivals on International Workers' Day, and the highest municipal wages of any city in the six time zones. When our fathers fell ill, the combine provided hospital beds. When they died, the combine provided coffins.

Through it all, Galina disappointed our expectations faster than we could lower them. The ballet instructor's initial excitement at seeing her name on the class list turned to dismay. Despite inheriting her grandmother's beautiful figure, Galina danced with the subtlety of a spooked ostrich. Basic barre exercises upended her. During performances, she was, thank goodness, relegated to the most minor ensemble role. But we really shouldn't be so harsh: If she were anyone else's granddaughter, we wouldn't think twice about her dancing like the victim of an inner ear disorder. Besides, we're free from the burden of expectation—no one has ever predicted that we would distinguish ourselves in any way—therefore we can't understand what it's like to fail where one might seem destined to succeed. So stop prodding us. We really do want to be kind.

With our newfound spirit of generosity, let's talk about something Galina was good at: making herself the center of attention. She arrived to a party our first year of secondary school wearing an olive-green miniskirt stitched together from the ugliest of her mother's head-scarves. We had never seen anything like it—this most demure of garments transformed into a scandal wrapped around her hips. The skirt ended mid-thigh, hardly larger than a washcloth, and goose bumps covered the rest of her legs. Boys stared with open-mouthed thanksgiving, then turned away, as if acknowledging Galina's presence was an unlawfully lewd act. No one knew what to say. There was no precedent for miniskirts in the Arctic. We whispered among ourselves that Galina had become a prostitute, but when we arrived home, we began stitching miniskirts of our own.

The miniskirt attracted the attentions of Kolya. If we

could we would airbrush him from our story as thoroughly as the censors airbrushed Galina's grandmother from photographs she had once populated. You see, Kolya was a hundred meters of arrogance pressed into a two-meter frame, the kind of young man who makes you feel inadequate for not impressing him. He was forever leaning, slanting, sidling, his existence italicized down to his crooked hat. In another country, he might have grown up to be an investment banker, but here he grew up to be a murderer, the worst kind of murderer, the kind who murdered one of us.

Galina couldn't have foreseen this. None of us could. For his first date he invited Galina for a romantic stroll around Lake Mercury. Yes, that Lake Mercury. The man-made lake that holds toxic runoff from the city's smelting facilities. For a first date. No kidding. But this is too sad to think about. Forget Kolya, even if we haven't.

Though her scarf miniskirt scandalized the school, it didn't prevent Galina from dancing at the fifty-year anniversary of the mining combine. Kremlin officials arrived by prop plane to celebrate our party boss. Our most inept bureaucrats received medals and commendations. Gorbachev's men told us that we lived atop the globe so that the rest of the world could look up at us. Our fathers beamed as the general secretary himself thanked them by video recording. *You not only mine the fuel of the Soviet Union*, he proclaimed, *you are the fuel of the Soviet Union*. The final night of celebrations ended with an outdoor ballet performance in the city center. Dancers from the Bolshoi and Kirov flew in for the leading roles. Against all expectations, Galina was chosen for the backing ensemble. The Twelve Apostles had been turned off two weeks earlier, and the July sun pierced the remnant cloud cover, spotlighting Galina for us.

A wall fell in another continent and soon our Union of Soviet Socialist Republics dissolved. Oleg Voronov, a "new Russian" and future oligarch, replaced the party boss. For the first time in seventy years, our city opened and some of us left. One found work as a ticket collector on the Omsk-Novosibirsk rail line, eventually marrying an engineer and having three boys. One received a scholarship to study physics in Volgograd. One left for America to marry a piano tuner she'd met online. But most of us remained. The world spun the wrong way around. It was no time to stray from home.

Kolya—like most of the boys in our year who couldn't bribe their way into university—was called up for his mandatory military service just as the conflict in Chechnya was beginning. Before he left, he'd proposed to Galina in the grocery store vegetable aisle, which tells you all you need to know about his idea of romance. Also, she was pregnant. The army granted deferments to fathers who bore sole responsibility for one child, and to fathers of two or more children, so this gave Galina and Kolya a few options: They could marry immediately and then get divorced to work the sole responsibility angle, or they could get married and hope for twins. We urged Galina to do neither. She was only eighteen years old. She had the rest of her life to make rash, irrevocable decisions. Do the sensible thing. Take care of the pregnancy and the deadbeat boyfriend with a single trip to the doctor. But despite all our well-reasoned advice, she still loved Kolya. The television dramas we grew up on, stories of star-crossed lovers, stories of love overcoming all obstacles, well, they're all fairy tales, obviously, like the television news; but the obvious is only obvious when it happens to someone else. We've all ended up with men we'd pity others for marrying. After Kolya's deployment, Galina seemed diminished, strained, just *less*. Could we have misjudged the seriousness of their relationship? Galina had been as vivid as stained glass, but we hadn't imagined that Kolya might have been the sunlight saturating her.

We had walked her to the clinic and had walked her home afterward. We were proud of her. We were sorry for her. We were there for her.

Galina worked as a telephone operator for the nickel combine and took computer classes on Tuesday evenings. She was with us when we saw the first poster for the inaugural Miss Siberia Beauty Pageant plastered on the wooden bus stop. It called for women of youth, beauty, and talent for a nationally televised event. We looked to Galina. She looked to her waist.

Auditions were held two weeks later in the events hall of our old school. We climbed onstage one at a time, our makeup layered, our legs bare. The casting director circled us, patting our thighs, squeezing our hips, testing out the firmness like a babushka at the beet bucket. Most of us were dismissed after he made a single revolution. Not Galina. When the casting director saw her in her headscarf miniskirt he gave a relieved sigh. He circled her again and again, grazing the hem of the skirt without touching her skin. "What is your talent?" he asked. "Ballet," Galina replied. He nodded. "Bring your toe shoes to Novosibirsk."

Soon Galina was everywhere. Her name appeared in the newspaper for fifty-seven consecutive days. She was not only our representative in Novosibirsk, but also one of three contestants selected to advertise the Miss Siberia competition, and we encountered her face more frequently than the faces of our parents and boyfriends, we saw her face more often than we saw our own in the mirror; it was our flag.

Galina may have still loved Kolya, but it didn't keep her from climbing into the nickel-silver Mercedes every Friday night. "She's done well," our mothers said, and though we had never seen the two together in public, we agreed. At thirty-five, Oleg Voronov was young to be the fourteenth richest man in Russia. When the nickel combine was auctioned, he purchased a majority stake with funds cobbled together from foreign investors, crooked officials, and gangsters. The auction lasted all of four and a half seconds. He paid $250,100,000, just one hundred thousand dollars over the opening bid. How could a state industry that yielded several billion dollars annually be bought for two hundred and fifty million? Its ownership had been converted to stock and divided among the combine employees. The stock, however, could only be sold or traded at full value in Moscow, in person. Our fathers had no choice but to sell their shares at kiosks on Leninsky Prospekt manned by Voronov's underlings who bought back the shares at a fraction of their stock price. It was enough to cover the hospital visits for chronic respiratory ailments. Soon after we heard the rumors of Voronov's silver Mercedes waiting outside Galina's apartment block, Miss Siberia advertisements began appearing in the windows of the share-buying kiosks.

Given that we were standing in the background of Galina's life, the spotlights fell on us as well. A newly opened salon gave us free manicures, hoping the presence of Galina's former classmates would give it an aura of success and sophistication. Ex-boyfriends called, apologizing. Our mothers began eavesdropping on us. We hope we don't sound petty saying we relished it while it lasted.

No one worked the evening of the beauty pageant. We huddled around television sets to watch Galina take the stage with young women from Siberian towns better known for closed military sites and uranium mines than for beauty. It was mid-September and frost filled the outer pane. Sugary champagne chilled in the refrigerator, vodka warmed in our glasses, and we drank and shushed each other as the orchestra began "The Patriot's Song." We hummed along, but didn't sing. Our country was three years old and the lyrics to the national anthem weren't yet composed. The host strode across the stage and welcomed the audience to the first annual Miss Siberia Beauty Pageant. His rosy-cheeked optimism suggested that he hadn't spent much time in Siberia. He introduced each contestant, but we saw only Galina.

The show broke for commercials and when it returned the contestants wore high heels and swimsuits; the minority among us who saw the event as glorified smut pointed out that only in pornographic films are swimwear and stilettos paired together. We hissed at the other contestants, willing them to trip, break a heel, spontaneously combust, wishing them nervous breakdowns, emotional collapse, dismemberment, decapitations, Old Testament torments, and this eruption of barely submerged cruelty felt appropriate, even proper because we shared it together. When the swimsuit contestants crossed the stage without breaking a heel or tripping, we decided they must have had much practice as pornographic actresses. Only on Galina was the outfit as graceful as an evening gown.

In the interview section, we derided the rehearsed eloquence of the other contestants and quieted when Galina approached the microphone. The host introduced her and consulted a set of green index cards with a long downward stare that drew out the suspense of the moment and made him appear illiterate. "What does the Miss Siberia Beauty Pageant mean to you?" he finally asked.

With a demure smile Galina turned to the nearest camera. "It means a great deal to represent my hometown on a national stage. I am pleased this pageant is bringing attention to the rich cultural heritage of Siberia. For centuries European Russia has used Siberia as a prison for its criminals and exiles. But we are not criminals and we are not prisoners. We are the citizens of a new country and soon the world will recognize that Siberians not only mine the fuel of the Russian Federation, we are the fuel of the Russian Federation."

The host flashed one of those peculiar frowns that express both approval and surprise. "And what will you do if you are chosen as Miss Siberia?" he asked.

"I will become famous, of course," Galina said and winked at the camera. For the two-second pause before the audience cheered and the backing band trumpeted, Galina didn't need a tiara because she had already crowned herself with that wink.

During the talent portion a withered cornstalk from Vladivostok played Rachmaninoff on a balalaika. Fake nails, breasts, eyelashes, and hair extensions alchemized into the real woman from Barnaul who donned a blindfold and solved a Rubik's Cube. Who were these bombshell savants? The judges were as surprised as we were. When it was announced that Galina would dance Odette's solo from *Swan Lake*, we fell silent. What was she trying to prove by selecting the solo from the first ballet her grandmother had performed on the canteen stage sixty years earlier? Why would Galina, our icon of the new Russia, dance from the USSR's most widely performed ballet? Photoflashes detonated. White tulle swathed her waist. Her head rested between the parentheses of her raised arms, and rising to her toes, noosed in spotlight, she began.

The cellos trilled. Galina stood en pointe, her waist ringed in a white tutu. She lifted her left leg and traced a parabola in the air with her slipper. Her foot landed just as the violins came in, and oh, how we wished our grandmothers had been alive to witness it. For the two and a half minutes she danced, all the city was silent. Seventeen hundred kilometers from the auditorium and we'd never felt closer to our friend. The attendees from Moscow, Petersburg, and Volgograd only saw the woman flapping her arms onstage, but we saw her in her first ballet auditions when the instructor had given a spirit-sapping sigh. We saw her jaw slacken when we told her stories about her grandmother. We saw her fly through the air when she tripped on her shoelace in third-year arithmetic. But we couldn't blame any shoelace for the fall Galina took in the final fifteen seconds of her routine. It could only be attributed to a series of formidable *grand jetés*, the polished stage floor, excessive ambition, and insufficient talent. She leapt from the ball of her right foot but landed on the side of her left. The microphones didn't pick up the fracturing of her medial malleolus above the orchestral din. We only heard the host's exclamation, a short scream from Galina as she slammed to the floor, and the stubborn melody of a viola player who continued playing to the end of the page, long after his colleagues fell silent. When Galina pushed herself upright, her face was red. Her tutu spread around her on the stage, filling every centimeter of spotlight, and she looked at the camera with a beseeching whimper of defeat so familiar, so intimate we could feel it in our own throats.

Galina received medical treatment while the other contestants demonstrated their talent through song, acrobatics, and party tricks. We slouched, too bereft to do Galina the honor of ridiculing her rivals. She was pushed onstage in a wheelchair for the crowning ceremony, her ankle packed in ice. We couldn't not watch her not win. We'd come too far. The night had given us something to talk about for years. Already we'd begun criticizing her poor preparation, her arrogance, her hubris for not consulting us when we could've warned her that she was destined to fail. The host received an envelope from the judging panel and opened it onstage. He frowned. It wasn't one of his suspenseful pauses; he was reading and rereading the name in genuine disbelief. Though we would later learn that the oligarch had been one of the chief financiers of the contest, and that the winner's name had been written on the stationery and sealed in the envelope three days before the pageant began, it wouldn't dilute the memory of the joy that rushed through us when the host smirked at the camera and said, "It gives me great pleasure to announce that the Miss Siberia tiara goes to none other than Galina Ivanova." We clapped and we shrieked. We stomped on the floorboards and danced in the halls. We'd known she could do it. We'd never had a moment of doubt. Photoflashes sparkled back from Galina's wet eyes. She couldn't climb to the podium so stagehands lifted her and the host set a golden tiara on her head. Within a month the gold leaf would chip to reveal alloyed nickel underneath.

Fame followed. Galina received roles in film and television shows, and for a number of years we only saw her on cinema screens and in grainy tabloid papers. Kolya returned from Chechnya to a city where he was only employable as a hoodlum, and soon we forgot there had been a time in Galina's life when she wasn't the oligarch's woman. She lived in Petersburg and Moscow in the penthouses of Voronov's luxury hotels. Even in their most scintillating speculations, the newspapers were always respectful of the oligarch. A generation or two ago, men like him would have sent troublesome writers to Siberian labor camps. Now, they simply had troublesome writers shot.

We had little time for celebration. Our fathers died of lung disease and our brothers and husbands replaced them. They returned from the mines glinting as our fathers had, but quiet, joyless, hollowed by existential worry. They'd only begun working when they began losing their jobs. The benefits the combine had once provided its employees had gone the way of the sickle and hammer. No more sanatoriums or hospital beds. The rubles received for combine shares had long been spent and we no longer had legal claim to the mines our grandparents had died excavating. And it stung, this hard slap of realization, when we understood that our mothers had been right: Teenagers yearn for freedom;

adults yearn for security. Our country had been powerful. The world had feared us. A paternal state had provided. Now what did we have? Epidemics and addictions. As teenagers we had seen ourselves pitted against the strength of the state, but it was this very strength that had propped us here at the top of the earth.

And yet there was joy. We had children. They came into the world screaming, pale, and slick with placenta. They came coughing and sputtering and we received them into our arms and taught them to laugh. We applauded first birthdays and first steps. Our children forever changed our relationships with our mothers. Pity replaced the mild contempt with which we had previously regarded them, and we loved them as we never had before, as we could only love ourselves, because despite our best intentions we had become them.

When Galina's first film came to the cinema, we went with our children and their grandmothers. Galina seemed even more incredible when stretched two stories tall. She played a heroine trapped in a web of mystery and intrigue. She was held hostage by the CIA and escaped. She used her mental and physical agility to her advantage. She acted with cool cunning and even in moments of great danger she summoned withering one-liners. Critics lambasted *Deceit Web* as implausible, but we didn't care. Our former classmate, our best friend, starred in a feature film, and here we were, watching it.

We didn't hear from Galina for several years. After she gave birth to a girl, she faded from public scrutiny, replaced by newer Miss Siberia winners, younger starlets. Her films went from theaters to television, then vanished from the airwaves altogether. We stopped talking about her. We had our own lives to worry about.

The layoffs began shortly after the first war in Chechnya ended. Automated machines mined nickel with greater efficiency than our husbands. Pensions vanished in the fluctuations of foreign stock exchanges. Even those who kept their jobs struggled. With the collapsing ruble, the payments of wages and pensions delayed for months, no one could afford the imported products that replaced familiar Soviet brands. We considered moving to a milder climate but couldn't manage relocation costs. Besides, our children were the fourth generation to call the Arctic home. This meant something even if we didn't know quite what.

Amid the misfortunes of the late 1990s, one in particular stands out. It is the story of Lydia, who had been one of us until she moved to Los Angeles to marry the piano tuner she had met online. The marriage ended—we had all called it—and Lydia returned to Kirovsk and moved in with her mother, Vera Andreyevna. Surely you remember Vera, who as a child denounced her own mother to the NKVD? She was well provided for during the Soviet years, but her fortunes fell with the red flag. By the time Lydia returned, Vera had become involved with the same drug dealers that had given Kolya work after the war. Lydia was shocked and horrified to discover that her childhood home had become a criminal haven. It was only natural that she vent her anger and disappointment to us, her closest friends. She swore us to secrecy, but how could she expect us to keep gossip like that to ourselves? Within a week, word reached the city crime boss, who passed down the sentence of execution. But guilt, like nickel, is a finite resource divided and parsed in so many ways, with Kolya and the hoodlums who pulled the trigger taking the largest share, then the crime boss who passed down the verdict taking the second largest share, then Vera who went into business with these gangsters, then the police chief who conspired with these gangsters, then Lydia herself who should have never trusted us with such good gossip. We are somewhere far down the list, accepting only a fragment of guilt, and that fragment itself is divided by six, so no single one of us will ever feel personally responsible for spreading the rumors that led to the murder of Lydia, who had once made us seven.

When the KGB man won the presidency in 2000, we celebrated.

Our children were assigned new history textbooks in school and we helped them with their homework. They read about Peter the Great, whose magnificent city on the Neva cost the lives of a hundred thousand serfs, and yet the whole world agrees that St. Petersburg is among humanity's marvels. They read about the tsars, the reach of imperial power, the discontent of workers, and the October Revolution. They read about Stalin and we read along with them, surprised that the new textbook offered a more generous perspective of him than our own did. According to the text, Stalin was an *effective manager who acted entirely rationally* and *the most successful Soviet leader ever.* Arctic labor camps were *a vital part of his drive to make the country great.* We reconsidered our grandmothers. Perhaps theirs was a necessary suffering, an evil justified by a greater good. They had sacrificed themselves for us, after all. When our children read aloud that *the collapse of the Soviet Union was the greatest geopolitical catastrophe of the twentieth century* we nodded and told them, "This is the truth."

There was another war in Chechnya—or perhaps it was the resumption of a singular war waged for centuries, we'll leave that to the judgment of the textbook historians—and Galina's story took a turn, though we only heard of it later, after she had become one of us again. When the counterinsurgency forces replaced major combat operations, and the republic showed its first signs of revitalization, Galina accompanied the oligarch on a business trip to Grozny. Voronov had built his fortune in mineral mining, but he was merely the fourteenth richest man in Russia, and eager to expand into oil. The Chechen fields, untapped during the decade-long unrest, provided an ideal starting point. While Voronov met with various ministries, Galina sought news of Kolya. He had reenlisted as a contract soldier after the horrible business with Lydia. Years had passed since she had last seen him. By the time he completed his two-year military service, impenetrable layers of publicists, managers, and agents shielded her from men like him. She wondered if he had tried to contact her, if her silences had pushed him down the path that ended in Lydia's murder.

For the wife of an oligarch, military officials were all too happy to hand over medical and service records, because at the heart of the military's famously incompetent bureaucracy lives an efficient adjutant class reserved for oligarchs, politicians, and crooks too wealthy and powerful to know by name even one soldier fighting their wars. Within an afternoon, a petty bureaucrat and *Deceit Web* fan had given Galina Kolya's file, which identified him in descending taxonomy that began with brigade and ended with blood type.

"The good news is that his company is stationed five kilometers from here," the petty bureaucrat said. "The bad news is that Kolya has been declared killed in action."

Galina nodded solemnly.

"Don't look so glum!" the petty bureaucrat said. "We declare perfectly healthy soldiers KIA all the time. You don't have to pay a dead man a living wage, after all. KIA is more a clerical than existential state. In fact, we had a patient from Kolya's platoon who was declared KIA along with him."

The patient's name was Danilo. He had been discovered some months earlier in the mountains near Benoi, the petty bureaucrat went on to say after further study of the file folder. He had been missing for months and would have been court-martialed as a deserter had he not already been declared dead. By the time he arrived at the hospital, his wounded foot had grown gangrenous, and it had to be amputated, a specialty of the resident surgery team. Danilo had lost much of what little mind he had, but from what the military police had gathered he had been held by insurgents at the bottom of a well.

The petty bureaucrat produced a photograph from a file. The photograph had been folded and unfolded so many times that its image looked superimposed on graph paper. He handed it to Galina and she saw a woman in a leopard-print bikini standing between two boys in leopard-print bikini bottoms. In the background yellow smoke drifted from the Twelve Apostles. The photograph had been taken several years before Galina had met Kolya. She recognized him as the taller of the two boys.

"The episode has an added peculiarity, one which an artist such as yourself might find intriguing," the petty bureaucrat continued, blithe to the grief building on

Galina's face. "The alpine meadow where the two soldiers were held captive is well known, locally at least, because it was the subject of a landscape painting that once hung in the Grozny Museum of Regional Art."

Galina still hadn't looked up from the photograph. She still looked at Kolya as if back through time, which of course is the only way to look at a photograph, and we've done so with photographs of our teenage boyfriends killed in Chechnya or at home, by land mines or gunshots, by drug overdoses or alcohol poisoning, by mining accidents or maniacal drivers, by tuberculosis or HIV. Galina must have felt the sorrow we are familiar with, a sorrow so commonly experienced it has become a touchstone for our generation, the sorrow that begins the moment you learn your teenage boyfriend died violently, prematurely, senselessly. Their deaths have aged us, as if their unlived years have been added to our lived years and we bear the disappointments of both the lives we have and haven't lived, so that even when we are alone, brushing our teeth in our quiet bathrooms, lying awake in our empty beds, even when our little ones are tucked in, when our friends are brushing their teeth in their quiet bathrooms, lying awake in their empty beds, even when the door is shut and no one can see or hear us, we are not alone, we still think in the plural voice.

Galina asked if Kolya really had been killed in action. The petty bureaucrat scanned the rest of the file.

"Technically, no. He was likely killed in captivity. But dead all the same." The bureaucrat delivered the news in the same tone he used to greet an orderly good day. "We haven't recovered a body, but in hostage situations like this, when one soldier makes it out, the other one, well, he often doesn't. Danilo said he died on the mined meadow itself."

"I want to see where he died," Galina said.

The petty bureaucrat explained, at considerable length, his uneasiness in declining the request of an oligarch's wife, and the star of *Deceit Web*, no less, but that the mountainous region was still an active war zone, even if given the euphemism of *zone of counterterrorism operations*.

"What about the painting you mentioned? The one that shows the place where Kolya died?" Galina asked later that afternoon. "I want to see that."

Three days later, Galina met the former deputy director of the Museum of Regional Art. The museum had been destroyed several years earlier, and the deputy director had begun a second career as a tour guide.

We've been told that Galina was never the same after returning from Chechnya. She ate little. She turned morose. Even when she took her daughter for afternoon walks in the park, she returned to the penthouse pallid and weary. Whatever she'd seen in Chechnya had changed her—and we don't really know what she saw, our story is rumor and hearsay, which when applied to a figure like Galina quickly becomes myth.

In short, she was stupid enough to become a dissenter. Had she educated herself on the situation in Chechnya, she would have seen that the president was correct in his approach, as he is in all things. Don't valorize her: She only wanted to create enough distance to enjoy the luxuries of the ruling class without feeling morally complicit in its actions. They were only whispers, of course. Galina wasn't a protester. Yet anyone who has gone to see one of Galina's films knows that a single whisper can be quite a disturbance when the rest of the audience is silent.

No one paid heed to her off-color comments at dinner parties and art gallery openings. But when we heard Galina as a phone-in guest on a radio show we knew from her breathless first words that she hadn't thought through her entire course of action. What could have prompted her? How could she be so ungrateful to the government that had given her so much? She had no right! She had everything! Later we learned that the radio station was the subsidiary of a media holding company, which in turn was the subsidiary of a conglomerate whose primary shareholder was none other than the now thirteenth richest man in Russia, our dear oligarch. Had she known it when she mocked the prime minister's love of sport by calling him a *bare-chested barbarian*? It is unlikely. After all, as the newly minted thirteenth richest man in Russia, the oligarch was a primary shareholder in just about everything. For a man like the oligarch whose fortune and freedom relied on good relations with the Kremlin, political marriages would always trump romantic ones.

In the ensuing weeks, her films disappeared from DVD kiosks and she was quietly but officially stripped of her Miss Siberia title. She wasn't airbrushed from photographs, as her grandmother had been; instead, she was Photoshopped from Miss Siberia publicity materials. We didn't blame the oligarch. The Khodorkovsky affair was still front-page news. Galina lost the Petersburg and Moscow condos, the chauffeured black sedans, the pearls and furs. Everything for which she did not possess a title, deed, or receipt was taken away.

The oligarch, who didn't think much of children, particularly his own, granted Galina one surprising concession, giving her their daughter to raise in Kirovsk.

Now we see Galina all the time. Not on billboards or cinema screens, but in the market, walking down the street, waiting at the bus stop. Her face is the same size as ours. Still prettier, we'll grant her that, but we've long outgrown such jealousies. In general, we're happy. The rising price of oil and natural gas has stabilized the ruble. The mining combine profits grow in correlation to the Chinese economy. Ninety-five percent of the world's catalytic converters are made with Kirovsk palladium and our town prospers beneath denser layers of pollution thanks to the efforts of American and European environmentalists hell-bent on keeping their skies clean. From time to time we hear stories not unlike those of Galina and her grandmother; people who speak too loudly tend to find themselves charged with corruption and sentenced to Siberian prisons. Their lives are small sacrifices.

Look across the street. That's Galina's girl on the jungle gym, playing with our girls, laughing and shouting down the slide. A beautiful girl, we won't deny it. Usually Galina sits on this bench with us while we reminisce and vent our frustrations and share our joys. Mainly, we talk about our children. How they infuriate us; how they make us ache; how our fear of failing them startles us from our sleep. No one likes a braggart, and to praise your children is to curse them with misfortune, but we admit it, if only in secret, if only to ourselves: We are proud, we are so proud of them. We've given them all we can, but our greatest gift has been to imprint upon them our own ordinariness. They may begrudge us, may think us unambitious and narrow-minded, but someday they will realize that what makes them unremarkable is what keeps them alive. In a few years, they will be married and having children of their own. We wonder what stories our grandchildren will tell of us and if their stories will sound at all like ours.

The Grozny Tourist Bureau

Grozny, 2003

THE OILMEN HAVE ARRIVED FROM BEIJING FOR a ceremonial signing over of drilling rights. "It's a holiday for them," their translator told me, last night, at the Grozny Eternity Hotel, which is both the only five-star hotel and the only hotel in the republic. I nodded solemnly; he needn't explain. I came of age in the reign of Brezhnev, when young men would enter civil service academies hardy and robust, only to leave two years later anemic and stooped, cured forever of the inclination to be civil or of service to anyone. Still, Beijing must be grim if they're vacationing in Chechnya.

"We'll reach Grozny in ten minutes," I announce to them in English. The translator sits in the passenger seat. He's a stalk-thin man with a head of hair so black and lustrous it looks sculpted from shoe polish. I feel a shared camaraderie with translators—as I do with deputies and underlings of all stripes—and as he speaks in slow, measured Mandarin, I hear the resigned and familiar tone of a man who knows he is more intelligent than his superiors.

The road winds over what was once a roof. A verdigris-encrusted arm rises from the debris, its forefinger raised skyward. The Lenin statue once stood in the square outside this school, arm raised, rallying the schoolchildren to glorious revolution, but now, buried to his chin like a cowboy sentenced to death beneath the desert sun, Vladimir Ilich waves only for help. We drive onward, passing brass bandoliers and olive flak jackets, red bandannas and golden epaulettes, the whole palette of Russian invasion painted across a thunderstorm of wreckage. Upon seeing the zero-two Interior Ministry plate dangling below the Mercedes's hood, the spies, soldiers, policemen, and armed thugs wave us through without hesitation. The streets become more navigable. Cement trucks can't make it from the cement works to the holes in the ground without being hijacked by one or another shade of our technicolor occupation and sold to Russian construction companies north of the border, so road crews salvage office doors from collapsed administration buildings and lay them across the craters. Attached to the doors are the names and titles of those who had once worked behind them. *Mansur Khalidov: Head of Oncology; City Hospital Number Six. Yakha Sagaipova: Assistant Director of Production; Ministry of Oil and Gas Industry.* Perhaps my name is written over a crater on some shabby side street, supporting the weight of a stranger who glances at the placard *Ruslan Dokurov: Deputy Director; Grozny Museum of Regional Art* and wonders if such a person is still alive.

"A large mass grave was recently discovered outside of Grozny, no?" the translator asks.

"Yes, an exciting discovery. It will be a major tourist attraction for archaeology enthusiasts."

The translator frowns. "Isn't it a crime scene?"

"Don't be ridiculous. It's millions of years old."

"But weren't the bodies found shot execution-style?" he insists.

I shrug him off. Who am I to answer for the barbarities of prehistoric man?

The translator nods to a small mountain range of rubble bulldozed just over the city limits. "What's that?"

"Suburbs," I say.

We pass backhoes, dump trucks, and jackhammers through the metallic dissonance of reconstruction that comes as a welcome song after months of screaming shells. The cranes are the tallest man-made structures I have ever seen in person. I drive to the central square, once the hub of municipal government, now a brown field debossed with earthmover tracks. Nadya once lived just down the road. The oilmen climb out and frown at each other, then at the translator, and then finally at me.

Turning to the northeast, I point at a strip of blue sky wedged between two fat cumuli. "That was Hotel Kavkaz. ABBA stayed two nights. I carried their guitars when I worked there one summer. Next to that, picture an apartment block. Before ninety-one only party members lived there and after ninety-one only criminals. No one moved in or out."

None of the oilmen smile. The translator leans to me and whispers, "You are aware, of course, that these three gentlemen are esteemed members of the Communist Party of China."

"It's okay, I'm a limo driver."

The translator stares blankly.

"Lloyd from *Dumb and Dumber*?"

Nothing.

"Jim Carrey. A brilliant actor who embodies the senselessness of our era," I explain.

The interpreter doesn't bother translating. I continue to draw a map of the square by narration, but the oilmen can't see what I see. They see only an empty square demolished by bomb and bulldozer.

"Come, comrades, use your imagination," I urge, but they return to the Mercedes, and I am talking only to the translator, and then he returns to the Mercedes, and I am talking only to myself.

Three months earlier, the Interior minister told me his idea. The proposition was ludicrous but I listened with the blank-faced complacency I had perfected throughout my twenty-three years as a public servant.

"The United Nations has named Grozny the most devastated city on earth," the minister explained between bites of moist trout.

I wasn't sure of the proper response, so I gave him my lukewarm congratulations.

"Yes, well, always nice to receive recognition, I suppose. But as you might imagine, we have an image problem."

He loomed over his desk in a high-backed executive chair, while across from him I listened from an odd, leggy stool designed to make its occupant struggle to stay upright before the minister. The minister's path had first crossed mine fifteen years earlier, when he had sought my advice regarding a recently painted portrait of him and his sons, and I had sought his regarding a dacha near my home village. He'd had two sons then. The first emigrated before the most recent war to attend an American pharmacology school, now worked at a very important drugstore in Muskegon, Michigan. I don't know what happened to the second, but the lack of ministerial boasting serves as a death knell. The portrait, which still hung on the far wall, depicted the minister and his sons in tall leather boots, baggy trousers, long woolen *chokhas*, and sheepskin *papakhas* heroically bestriding the carcass of a slain brown bear that bore a striking resemblance to Yeltsin.

"Foreign investment," the minister continued. "Most others don't agree with me, but I believe we need to attract capital unconnected to the Kremlin if we're to achieve a degree of economic autonomy, and holding the record for the world's largest ruin isn't helping. Rosneft wants to sink its fangs into our oil reserves, but the Chinese will cut a better deal. Have you heard of Oleg Voronov? He's on the Rosneft board, the fourteenth richest man in Russia, and one of the hawks who pushed for the 1994 invasion. The acquisition of Chechen oil is among his top priorities."

The minister set down his silverware and began sorting through the little trout bones on his plate, reconstructing the skeleton of the fish he had consumed. "If we're to entice foreign investment, we need to rebrand Chechnya as the Dubai of the Caucasus. That's where you come in. You're what, the director of the Museum of Regional Art?"

"Deputy director, sir."

"That's right, deputy director. You did fine work sending those paintings to Moscow. A real PR coup. Even British newspapers wrote about the Tretyakov exhibit."

With a small nod, I accepted the compliment for what was the lowest point of my rut-ridden career. In 1999, Russian rockets had demolished the museum and with my staff I'd saved what I could from the ensuing fires. Soon after, I was ordered to surrender them to the Russians. When I saw that I'd been listed as co-curator of an exhibit of the rescued Chechen paintings at Moscow's Tretyakov Gallery, I closed my lids and wondered what had happened to all the things my eyes have loved.

The minister tilted the plate over the rubbish bin and the ribs slid from the spine of the skeleton fish. "Nothing suggests stability and peace like a thriving tourism sector," the minister said. "I think you'd be the perfect candidate to head the project."

"With respect, sir," I said. "I did my dissertation on nineteenth-century pastoral landscapes. I'm a scholar. This is all a bit beyond me."

"I'll be honest, Ruslan, for this position we need someone with three qualifications. First, he must speak English. Second, he must know enough about the culture and history of the region to show that Chechnya is much more than a recovering war zone, that we possess a rich cultural history unsullied by violence. Third, and most important, he must be that rare government man without links to human rights abuses on either side of the conflict. Do you meet these qualifications?"

"I do, sir," I said. "But still, I'm entirely unqualified to lead a tourism initiative."

The minister frowned. He scanned the desk for a napkin before reaching over to wipe his oily fingers on my necktie. "According to your dossier, you've worked in hotels."

"When I was sixteen, I was a bellhop."

"Well," the minister beamed. "Then you clearly have experience in the hospitality industry."

"In the suitcase-carrying industry."

"Then you accept?"

I said nothing, and as is often the case with men who

possess more power than wisdom, he took my silence for affirmation. "Congratulations, Ruslan. You're head of the Grozny Tourist Bureau." And so my future was decided, as it often is, entirely without my consent.

Office space was a valuable commodity given how few buildings were still standing, so I worked from my flat. I spent the first morning writing *Tourist Bureau* on a piece of cardboard. My penmanship had been honed by years of attempting to appear productive at the office. I taped the sign to the front door, but within five minutes it had disappeared. I made a new sign, then another, but the street children who lived on the landing kept stealing them. After the fifth sign, I went to the kitchen and drank the vodka bottle the minister had sent over in celebration until I passed out in tears on the floor. So ended my first day as Tourist Bureau chief.

Over the following weeks, I designed a brochure. The central question was how to trick tourists into coming to Grozny voluntarily. For inspiration, I studied pamphlets from the tourist bureaus of other urban hellscapes: Baghdad, Pyongyang, Houston. From them I learned to be lavishly adjectival, to treat prospective tourists as semiliterate gluttons, and to impute reports of kidnapping, slavery, and terrorism to the slander of foreign provocateurs. Thrilled by my discoveries, I tucked a notebook into my shirt pocket and raced into the street. Upon seeing the empty space where an apartment block once stood, I wrote *wide and unobstructed skies!* I watched jubilantly as a pack of feral dogs chased a man, and wrote *unexpected encounters with natural wildlife!* The city bazaar hummed with the sales of looted industrial equipment, humanitarian aid rations, and munitions suited for every occasion: *unparalleled shopping opportunities at the Grozny bazaar!* Even before I reached the first checkpoint, I had scribbled *first-rate security!* The copy wrote itself; the real challenge was finding images that substantiated it. After all, the siege had remapped the city. Debris rerouted roads through abandoned warehouses—once I found a traffic jam on a factory floor—and what was not rerouted was razed. A photograph of the present city would send a cannonball through my verbiage-fortified illusion of a romantic paradise for heterosexual couples. But I couldn't find suitable photographs of prewar Grozny within the destroyed archives. In the end, I forwent photographs altogether and instead used January, April, and August of the 1984 Grozny Museum of Regional Art calendar for visuals. In the three nineteenth-century landscapes, swallows frolic over ripening grapevines and a shepherd minds his flock beneath a sunset; they portray a land untouched by war or communism and beside them my descriptions of a picturesque Chechnya do not seem entirely inappropriate.

I return home after depositing the troika of Chinese oilmen at the Interior Ministry. The street children vanish from the staircase landing as I approach, but leave behind the instruments of their survival: a metal skewer to roast pigeons, a chisel to chip cement from the loose bricks they sell to construction crews for a ruble each.

I knock on the door of the flat adjacent to mine and announce my name. Nadya appears in a headscarf and sunglasses. Turning her unscarred side toward me, she invites me in. "How was the maiden voyage?"

"An excellent success," I say. "They dozed off before we reached the worst of the wreckage."

Nadya smiles as she takes measured steps to the Primus stove. She doesn't need her white cane to reach the counter. I scan the room for impediments but everything is in order. Nothing on the floorboards but the paths of kopek coins I'd glued down so her bare feet could find their way to the bathroom, the kitchen, the front door in her early months of blindness. At the end of one of these paths is a desk neatly stacked with black-and-white photographs, once the subject of her dissertation on altered images in the Stalinist era. I sift through a few while she puts the kettle on. Nadya has circled a single face in each. The same face, or rather, same person is painted into the background of each photograph, from his childhood to his elderly years, the signature of the anonymous censor.

The kettle whistles in the kitchen. We sip tea from mismatched mugs that lift rings of dust from the tabletop. She sits so I can't see the left side of her face.

"The tourist brochures will be ready next week," I say. "I'll have to send one along to our Beijing comrades, if the paintings come out clearly. I'm skeptical of Ossetian printers."

"You used three from the Zakharov room?"

"Yes, three Zakharovs."

Her shadow nods on the wall. The Zakharov room, the museum's largest gallery, had been her favorite too. The first time I ever saw her was in that room, in 1987, her first day working as the museum's newly hired restoration artist.

"You'll have to save me one," she says. "For when I can see it."

Her last sentence hangs in the air for a long moment

before I respond. “I have an envelope with five thousand rubles. For your trip. I’ll leave it on your nightstand.”

“Ruslan, please.”

“St. Petersburg is a city engineered to steal money from tourists. I know. I’m in the industry.”

“You don’t need to take care of me. I keep telling you,” she says with a firm but appreciative squeeze of my fingers. “I’ve been saving my disability allowance. I have enough for the bus ticket and I’m staying with the cousin of a university classmate.”

“It’s not for you. It’s for movies, for videocassettes,” I say, a beat too quickly. Slapstick and romantic comedies have become my favorite genres in recent years. “Find some that are foreign.”

She’s looking straight at me, or at my voice, momentarily forgetting the thing her face has become. She was with me when rockets turned three floors of art into an inferno she barely escaped. The third-degree burns hardened to a crevassed canvas of scar tissue wrapped over the left side of her skull. She might feel with her fingers what had been her face, but she can’t see it, and in that sense her blindness is a gift the fire gave as it took everything else. Her left eye isn’t there. She could point it at the noon sun and it would remain midnight in that bare socket. But her right side was partly spared. There the scar tissue opens onto valleys of smooth skin. In the heat her right eyelids fused together, sealing her eye from the worst of the flames. In it she can at times sense the flicker of light, the faintest movements. There is the possibility, an ophthalmologist told her, that sight could be restored to her right eye. But any optical surgeon clever enough to perform such a delicate operation was clever enough to have fled Grozny long ago. Nadya hasn’t any appointments, but she'll try to meet with a half-dozen eye surgeons in Petersburg next week. If there is an operation, and if that operation is successful, she says she will move to Sweden. I fear for her future in a country whose citizenry is forced to assemble its own furniture.

"If it happens, the surgery, if it's successful," I say. "You don't need to leave."

"What I need is sleep."

When I return to my flat, I scoop the hardened residue of the morning's kasha onto a slice of round bread. The granules wedge into my molar divots, rough and folically acidic, suggesting the kind of rich, fibrous nutrients that uncoil one's intestines into a vertical chute. I rinse my hands in the sink and let the water run even after my hands are clean. Indoor plumbing was restored six months ago. Above the doorway hangs a bumper sticker of a fish with *WWJCD?* inscribed across its body, sent by an American church along with a crate of bibles in response to our plea for life-saving aid.

I take a dozen scorched canvases from the closet and lay them on the floor in two rows of six. They were too damaged for the Tretyakov exhibition. Not one was painted after 1879, and yet they look like the surreal visions of a psychedelic-addled mind. Most are burned through, some no more than mounted ash, more reminiscent of Alberto Burri's slash-and-burn Tachisme than the Imperial Academy's classicism. In others the heat-melted oils have turned photo-realistic portraits into dissolved dreamscapes.

My closet holds one last canvas, the Zakharov I rescued. I set it on the coffee table and examine the brushwork by the light of an unshaded lamp. The seamless gradation of color, the nearly invisible brushstrokes;

classic Zakharov. Not even the three years I spent writing my dissertation on Pyotr Zakharov-Chechenets could diminish my fascination with his work. Born in 1816, during the Caucasian War that Lermontov, Tolstoy, and Pushkin would later memorialize in their "Prisoner of the Caucasus" story cycle, he was a war orphan before his fourth birthday. Yet his brilliance so exceeded his circumstances that he went on to attend the Imperial Academy of Arts in St. Petersburg and despite exclusion from scholarship, employment, and patronage due to his ethnicity, he eventually became a court painter and a member of the Academy. Here is a Chechen who learned to succeed by the rules of his conquerors, a man not unlike the Interior minister, to be admired and pitied.

A meadow, an apricot tree, a stone wall in a diagonal meander through the grasses, the pasture cresting into a hill, a boarded well, a house. In 1937, the censor who would become the subject of Nadya's dissertation painted the figure of the Grozny party boss beside the dacha. For more than fifty years the party boss occupied the bottom left corner of the painting like a mislaid statue of Socialist Realism. Soviet dogma had already pervaded the whole of the present, and here was a reminder that the past was no less revisable, no less susceptible to alteration than an unfinished canvas. In 1989, when the Berlin Wall fell and Soviet satellite states began breaking away, when the politicians and security apparatus had more pressing concerns than nineteenth-century landscapes, I asked Nadya to restore the Zakharov. She was well trained, intuitive, a natural restoration artist, and over the course of several weeks, she expunged the party boss from the painting. We didn't take to the streets; we didn't overthrow governments or oust leaders; our insurrection was ten centimeters of canvas.

It's among the least ambitious of all Zakharov's work. Here is an artist who painted the portraits of Tsar Nicholas I, General Alexei Yermolov, Grand Duchess Maria Nikolaevna, and the famed depiction of Imam Shamil's surrender, and this, in my hands, portrays all the drama its title suggests: *Empty Pasture in Afternoon*.

I grew up in the southern highlands, just a few kilometers away from the pasture. Illiterate villagers who knew nothing of art proudly claimed this strip of soil worthy of Zakharov's paintbrush. Though the land was technically part of a state farm, nothing was ever planted, and flocks were banned from grazing because no one liked the idea of sheep relieving themselves on Zakharov's pasture. In secondary school, my class took a trip to the Grozny Museum of Regional Art and I finally saw the canvas that existed more vibrantly in village lore that it ever could on a museum wall.

More than anything, it was that painting that led me to study art at university. There I met and married Liana. We lived with my parents in cramped quarters well into our twenties, and found the privacy to speak openly only in deserted public areas: on the roof of the village schoolhouse, in the waiting room of the shuttered village clinic, in Zakharov's pasture. After I received my doctorate and a position at the museum, we relocated to a Grozny flat, where we learned to talk in bed.

The USSR fell. We had a son. With the assistance of the Interior minister, I purchased the dacha on Zakharov's pasture amid the frenzied privatization of the post-Soviet, prewar years. When the first war began, I stayed in Grozny and did my best to protect the museum from the alternating advances of foreign soldiers and local insurgents. My wife and son lived in the dacha, far from the war.

In my tourist bureau research, I've learned that the first and second Chechen wars have made the republic among the most densely mined regions in human history. The United Nations estimates five hundred thousand mines were planted, roughly one for every two Chechen. I didn't know that number when I visited the dacha during the first war, taking what provisions I could cull from the ruined capital, a few treats for which I paid dearly, tea leaves for my wife, sheets of fresh drawing paper for my son. But I knew enough to warn them never to venture into the pasture. Until May 1996, they heeded my warnings. I don't know how it happened, why they walked into the pasture, if they were pursued, if they fled masked men, if the mined field was a sanctuary compared with the depredations of their pursuers, if they were afraid, if they called for help, if they called for me. Those questions have been unanswerable from the moment they swung open the back door, descended the stairs, and ran across that fallow garden. I'd like to believe it was a day so beautiful they couldn't be kept from the crest of the hill, the open sky, that radiance. I'd like to believe that my wife suggested a picnic on the hill. I'd like to believe that the moment before their last moment was one of whimsy, charm, anything to counter the more probable realities at the edge of my imagination. With terror or joy, with abasement or delight, they remained my wife and child, right to the end—I must remind myself because in the mystery that subsumes those final moments, they are strangers to me. I was in Grozny, at the museum, and never heard the explosion.

For the two weeks Nadya is in Petersburg, my evenings stagnate. Russian dignitaries, potential investors, state-approved journalists, and the omnipresent oilmen fill my mornings and afternoons, but when I return to my flat I'm reminded I am, at the end of the day, alone. Twice I go to Nadya's flat to clean her bedroom closet, the back corners of shelves, behind the toilet, the little places that even in her fastidiousness she'd miss. I'm uncomfortable with the neediness that underlies my decision to insert myself into her life under the pretext of concern. I am concerned, of course. Some nights I wake from nightmares that she has tripped over a chair, a shoe, a broomstick I could have moved. But in rare moments—like now, as I scour the mildew from her bathroom tiles—clarity surfaces through the murky soup of daily life, and I know I have purposefully made myself into a crutch she cannot risk discarding. What I don't know is whether I've done so out of love or loneliness, or if in this upside-down world where roofs lie on streets, intentions have lost their moral weight altogether.

One Wednesday, feeling unusually alert given the hour, I contemplate Zakharov's pasture. It's the least ruined of the canvases, stained with ash and soot, but still the damage is minor. Most severe is the burn hole at the center of the canvas, upon the hill, and even though the hole was burned into the canvas during the museum fires, I see it as the crater left by the land-mine blast, the hole through which everything disappeared. A few years ago, Nadya could've restored it in days.

An idea. I let myself back into Nadya's flat to retrieve her restoration kit. It's at her desk, amid the black-and-white photographs censored by the propaganda officer who had painted the Grozny party boss into the foreground of the Zakharov. Nadya became fascinated with the propaganda officer after she had expunged the party boss from the painting, particularly when she discovered that he had inserted a portrait of the same person into hundreds of the censored images, from boyhood to elderly years. If you lined up all the photographs, you might see this stranger's entire life unfold before you in the background. I pause on one, identified as Leningrad 1937 in pencil on the back. Here he's just a boy, chubby face and gray eyes below the accent mark of a cowlick, hardly noticeable in the crowd. I feel him staring up at me with an intensity approaching sentience, and for a moment I can't move: His gaze has pierced and pinned me to a present space we share. How did he die? The question has looped through me on a ticker tape these past five years, but I have never before asked it about a boy who was not my son.

Back home I set the contents beside the Zakharov canvas. Plastic bottles of emulsion cleaner, neutralizer, gloss varnish, conditioner, and varnish remover. A tin of putty. Eight meters of canvas lining. A depleted packet of cotton-tipped swabs. A dozen disposable chloroprene gloves. I'd taken a yearlong course in conservation at university, but my real education came from Nadya, when, in the months after my family died, I neglected my duties as deputy director and spent most afternoons in her office, watching her work.

Every evening for the next week I snap on the chloroprene gloves and wash away the surface dirt with cotton balls dampened in neutralizer. The emulsion cleaner smells of fermented watermelon, and I apply it with the swabs, running small circles until the cotton tips gray and the unadulterated color of Zakharov's palette is revealed. Using the repair putty as sealant, I patch the burn hole with a square of fresh canvas. Then, for the real challenge, I paint.

The patched hole is the size of a halved playing card in the center-right of the painting, near the cresting hill. The grass, turned emerald by sunlight, must be flawless, the gradation beyond reproach, and I spend several hours testing different blends of oils before coloring the canvas patch with delicate brushstrokes. As I work, I realize that even in his rendering of a distant field of grass, Zakharov is beyond imitation. I lean back, search the painting for two familiar figures, as I have for years, but this time is different. Nadya would never forgive me had she been here and been able to see me paint, upon the patched hole on the hillside, a woman and a boy.

With quick, strong lines, I draw them as silhouettes. The boy's arms are raised, his body elongated as he makes for the crest, his hands thrown open. The woman, a step behind, follows him up the hill. Their backs are to me. The sun rakes the grass and ripe apricots bend the branches. No one chases them. They run from nothing.

Nadya has returned and the white tea has cooled in our cups and still she hasn't mentioned the Petersburg eye surgeons.

"Good news," she says and feels across the floor for her suitcase. She hands me two VHS tapes. "These are the two you wanted, right?"

I examine the two VHS cases. Soviet comedies, sadly.

"Yes, these are precisely the ones I wanted."

"I was afraid the street vendor had swindled me."

"What did the eye surgeons say, Nadya?"

The pause was long enough to peel a plum.

She delivers the news with a downcast frown. “Reconstructive surgery is possible.”

I force as much gusto into my congratulations as I can muster, slapping my palm on the table while my spine wilts. What will I be if Nadya no longer needs me, what if she moves to Sweden and assembles bookcases in a living room I will never see? This is good news, though, of course it is, but Nadya’s face is joyless. “What’s wrong? Is there a long wait for the operation?”

“There won’t be one.”

“What? Why not?”

“Too expensive.” She’s still facing the empty chair across the table, thinking that I’m still sitting there. “It’s one hundred and fifteen thousand.”

One hundred and fifteen thousand rubles. A huge, but not impossible, sum. Years to save for, but within the realm of possibility, like a vacation to Belarus. I’m already scheming ways to defraud the Interior Ministry when she says, “Dollars.”

My heart spirals and crash-lands somewhere deep in my gut. At thirty-three rubles to a dollar, the number is insurmountable. Nadya reaches for her purse and pulls out an envelope.

“What I owe you for the trip. Help me count it out,” she says. For a moment her instinct to trust anyone, even me, is infuriating. Isn’t suspicion the natural condition of the blind? Haven’t I warned her, told her to be careful, that she can’t rely on anyone? But by some perversion she’s become more trusting, more willing to believe that people aren’t by nature hucksters and scoundrels, which is why, I suppose, my VHS collection is rounded out with *Gentlemen of Fortune*.

“It’s nothing,” I say.

"I'm paying you back."

"If you want to be a martyr go join them in the woods."

"Help me count it out," she insists, her voice stern, cool, serious. "I still have money left from the disability fund. I'm not a charity."

Of course there's no disability fund. Of course the government isn't sending her a monthly payment or subsidizing the flat adjacent to mine. The cash sealed in the Interior Ministry envelopes I bring over on the first of the month comes from me, as does her monthly rent.

"I'm waiting," she says. We both know this is a farce. But I sit beside her. I play my part in the lie that preserves the illusion that our friendship, our romance, whatever this is, is based on affection rather than need. I count out the bills that I will return to her in an Interior Ministry envelope on the first of the month, and when I finish we shake hands as if our business is concluded and there is nothing left that we owe each other, no debt unpaid, no obligation unfulfilled.

In bed I run my fingers through what remains of her hair, press my fingertips to her cheeks, slowly scrolling, as if I am the blinded of us, to decipher the dense Braille scrawled across her face. I slide my hand down her torso, over the bulge of her left breast, the hook of her hip bone, to thighs so smooth and unmarked they're hers only in darkness. She rolls away.

Lying here in bed, you nearly forget the falling rockets, the collapsing museum, the air of the clean sky impossibly distant, the cinder blocks shifting like ice cubes in a glass. The Zakharov was in your hands when you found her, her face halved by burns, her teeth chattering. You nearly forget how you lifted her cheek to cool it with your breath, how her broken eyes searched for you as you held her.

You nearly forget the many times you have warned her of monsters as though they are a people apart: lurking beyond her doorway, ready to prey on the blind and vulnerable. As she turns from you, tucking the sheets beneath her hip, you nearly forget to ask yourself, "What monster have I become today?"

In the morning I return to my flat and find the canvases on the floor where I left them. Daylight grants the scorch and char an odd beauty, as if the fires hadn't destroyed the artworks, but revised them into expressions of a brutal present. I pick up the nearest canvas, a family portrait commissioned by a nobleman as a wedding present for his second son. The top third of the canvas has been incinerated, taking with it the heads of the nobleman, his wife, the first son, and the newly betrothed, but their bodies remain, dressed in soot-stained breeches and petticoats, and by their feet sits a dachshund so fat its little legs barely touch the ground, the only figure—in a canvas commissioned to convey the family's immortal honor—to survive intact.

I hang the canvas on the wall from a bent nail and step back, marveling that here, for the first time in my career, I've hung a work of modern art. After pulling the furniture into the kitchen, I hang the remaining canvases throughout the living room, finally coming to the restored Zakharov, which I consider taking back to the closet, shelving in the darkness where it will exist for me alone, but my curatorial instincts win out, and I hang the Zakharov on the wall where it is meant to be. The street children long ago stole the last of my door signs. I scrawl one more on a cardboard shingle and nail it to the door: *Grozny Museum of Regional Art.*

Now for guards. I toss a crumpled hundred-ruble note down the stairs, thinking that they, like the Sunzha trout, are too hungry to pass up a baited hook. A small hand reaches around the corner, and I grab it, yanking on the slender arm to reel in the rest of the child. He squirms wildly, biting at my wrists, until I shake him into submission and offer him a job in museum security.

He stops squirming, perhaps out of shock, and I close his hand around the hundred-ruble note. His fingernails look rusted on. His shirt is no thicker than stitched-together soot.

"Bandits are stealing the signs from my door," I tell him. "I'll pay you and your friends three hundred rubles a week to keep watch."

Over the following weeks, I bring all my tours through the museum. A delegation from the Red Cross. More Chinese oilmen. A heavyweight boxing champ. A British journalist. *This is what remains*, the charred canvases cry. *You cannot burn ash! You cannot raze rubble!* As the only museum employee besides the street children, I give myself a long overdue promotion. No longer am I deputy. As of today, I am director of the Grozny Museum of Regional Art.

The newly installed phone rings one morning and the gloomy Interior minister greets me. "We're properly fucked."

"Nice to hear from you, sir," I reply. I'm still in my sleeping clothes and even for a phone conversation I feel unsuitably dressed.

"The Chinese are out. They traded their drilling right to Rosneft for a few dozen Russian fighter jets."

I nod. It explains why China hadn't sent their most shrewd or sober representatives. "So this means Rosneft will drill?"

"Yes, and it gets even worse," he heaves. "I may well be demoted to deputy minister."

"I was a deputy for many years. It's not as bad as you think."

"When the world takes a dump, it lands on a deputy's forehead."

I couldn't deny that. "What does this mean for the Tourist Bureau?"

"You'll have one more tour, then it's safe to say you'll need to find new employment. Oleg Voronov. From Rosneft."

It took a beat for the name to register. "The fourteenth richest man in Russia?"

"Thirteenth now."

"With respect, sir, I give tours to human rights activists and print journalists, people of no power or importance. I'm not qualified to give a tour to a man of his stature. Why does he even want a tour?"

"My question precisely! Apparently his wife, Galina Something-or-other-ova, the actress, has heard of this art museum you've cobbled together. What've you been up to?"

"It's a long story, sir."

"You know I hate stories."

"Yes, sir."

"Well, do show him our famed Chechen hospitality. Be sure to offer him a glass of unboiled tap water. Let's give the thirteenth richest man in Russia an intestinal parasite!"

"Don't worry, sir. I'm a limo driver."

"I'll land on my feet, Ruslan. Don't lose too much sleep over my future. Perhaps I'll visit America. I'd like to see Muskegon while I'm still young and healthy enough to really experience it."

Three weeks pass and here he is, Oleg Voronov sitting in the backseat of the Mercedes with his wife, the actress Galina Ivanova. Up front is his assistant, a bleached-blond parcel of productivity who takes notes even when no one is speaking. But try as I might, I'm unable to properly hate Voronov. So far he's been untalkative, inattentive, and uncurious; in short, a perfect tourist. Galina, on the other hand, has read Khassan Geshilov's *The Origins of Chechen Civilization* and recites historical trivia unfamiliar to me. The office doors of dead administrators clatter beneath us and she asks thoughtful questions, treating me not as a servant, or even a tour guide, but as a scholar. I casually mention the land mines, the street children, the rape and torture and indiscriminate suffering, but Voronov and his wife shake their heads with sympathy. Nothing I say will turn them into the masks of evil I want them to be.

The tour concludes at my flat. I'm hesitant to allow a man of his stature into the small world of my museum, but his wife insists. As we ascend the stairwell, Voronov checks his watch, a cheap plastic piece of crap, and in that moment I know I will not hate him as he deserves to be hated.

"This is what remains of the Grozny Museum of Regional Art," I say as I open the door. Voronov and his assistant circle the room. I glance to the kitchen sink, but a glass of unboiled tap water is a fate I wouldn't wish upon even a Russian oligarch.

Voronov and Galina pass the burned-out frames to the pasture painting. "Is this the one?" he asks her. She nods.

"A Zakharov, no?" he asks, fingering his lapel as he turns to me. "There was an exhibit of his at the Tretyakov, if memory serves."

Only now do I see clearly the animals I have invited into my home. "The fires destroyed most of the original collection when the museum was bombed. We sent what was saved to the Tretyakov."

"But not this?"

"Not this."

"Rather reckless, don't you think, to leave such a treasure on an apartment wall guarded only by street urchins?"

"It's a minor work."

"Believe it or not, my wife has been looking for this painting. It has special meaning for her. I know, I know. I married a sentimentalist."

"Could I offer you a glass of water?"

"You could offer me the painting."

I force a laugh. He laughs too. We are laughing. Ha-ha! Ha-ha! It's all a joke. "The painting is not for sale," I say.

He stops laughing. "It is if I want to buy it."

"This is a museum. You can't have a painting just because you want it. The director of the Tretyakov wouldn't sell you art from his walls just because you can afford it."

"You are only a deputy director and this isn't the Tretyakov." There's real pity in his voice as he surveys the ash flaking from the canvases, the dirty dishes stacked in the sink, and yes, now, at last, I hate him.

"Come now, I have a penthouse gallery in Moscow. Temperature and moisture controlled. First-rate security. No one but Galina, and a few guests, and I will ever see it. You must realize I'm being more than reasonable." In a less than subtle threat he nods out the window to the street where his three armed Goliaths skulk beside their Land Rover. "What is the painting worth?"

"It's worth," I begin, but how can I finish? What price can I assign to the last Zakharov in Chechnya, to the last image of my home? One sum comes to mind, but it terrifies me. Wouldn't that be the worst of all outcomes, to lose both the Zakharov and Nadya in the same transaction? "Just take it," I say. "You took everything else. Take this too."

Voronov bristles. "I'm not a thief. Tell me what it's worth."

My gaze floats and lands upon the bumper sticker of *WWJCD?* inscribed within the body of a fish. What would he do? Jim Carrey would be brave. In the end, no matter how hard, Jim Carrey does the right thing. I close my eyes. I don't want to say it. "One hundred and fifteen thousand dollars. U.S."

"One-fifteen?"

I nod.

"That's what, three-point-seven, three-point-eight million rubles? Let's make it an even four," Voronov says with a single fleshy clap. His wife still hasn't looked away from the painting. He turns to his assistant who has followed him around the room, taking notes all the while. The assistant unyokes herself from a mammoth purse, pulls out eight stacks of banded five-thousand-ruble bills, and lays them on the floor. "Never trust banks," Voronov says. "You can have that advice for free. It's been a pleasure." He slaps my back, tells the assistant to bring the canvas down with her, and heads for the door.

Then he's gone. Galina remains at the Zakharov. Even now as I'm losing it, I'm proud my painting can elicit such sustained attention.

She nods to the stick-figure silhouettes of my wife and child, smiling as she dabs the corners of her eyes. "You wouldn't understand, but someone I once loved died in this field."

She pats my shoulder and walks to the door.

Then she's gone and I'm left alone with the assistant whose saccharine perfume smells of vaporized cherubs. I close my eyes and try to imagine the darkness extending into permanent night, to imagine our lives as dreams we tumble through, but I can't imagine, because even at night I know morning will come, and even with my eyes clamped I know I will open them. What will Nadya see when she opens hers? Who will she see when she sees me?

"And you'll have to give us a curatorial description," the assistant says. "Something we can mount on a placard."

She passes me the notepad and I stand before my painting for a long while before I begin. *Notice how the shadows in the meadow mirror the clouds in the sky*, I write. *Or the way the leaves of the apricot tree blow in the same direction as the grass on the far side of the meadow. For such a master, no verisimilitude is excluded. Notice the wall of white stones cutting an angle across the composition. It both gives depth and offsets the horizon line. On the left side of the canvas, running up the hill, you will see channels of turned soil. One could assume they are freshly dug graves, or recently buried land mines, but look closer and see they are the furrows of a newly planted herb garden. The first shoots of rosemary already peek out. In this painting, Zakharov portrays all the peace and tranquility of a spring day. The sun shines comfortably and hours remain before nightfall. Toward the crest of the hill, nearing the horizon, you may notice what look to be the ascending figures of a woman and a boy. Pay them no mind, for they are merely the failures of a novice restoration artist. They are no more than his shadows. They are not there.*

A Prisoner of the Caucasus

Chechen Highlands, 2000

THEY CREST THE RIDGE WITH A THUMP AND roll onto a green terrace as the Shishiga engine gasps twice and dies. Danilo, a contract soldier, body built like a flour sack and brain wired like a bargain firecracker, curses the Shishiga, then Jesus's mother, and doubles down on both by shooting three at the engine block and three at the clouds. Their bad luck began years before they broke down in rebel-controlled territory, but no luck is so bad that Danilo can't make it worse: Flames flutter through the hood's bullet holes. Still, part of Kolya is relieved to climb down from the truck and that part is his stomach. The closest paved road lies fifty kilometers behind them, and the boulder-strewn path they've summited has more dips and swells than a tempest. Three thousand meters above ocean level and Kolya's doubled over with seasickness.

"You are a disgrace to your people!" Danilo shouts as he upends his canteen on the smoking engine block. "Engines like this, engines made of tin cans and sheep shit, are the reason Putin drives a Kraut car." He ticks off Teutonic inhumanities inflicted on western civilization: Karl Marx, Adolf Hitler, Claudia Schiffer. "A country whose main export is bad ideas and they still manage to build better engines than us."

Folded at the waist in mid–dry heave, Kolya watches the scene upside-down through his spread legs. It's the only way to look at the world that makes much sense to him these days. Danilo, son of a mechanic, has a history of abusive relationships with most of the unit's vehicles, so Kolya isn't surprised when he begins sweet-talking the shot-up engine. With no small effort, Kolya rights himself and looks around. A green staircase of terraces ascends the ridge. Far below, a ragged trail of white rocks tapers into a backwash of muddied branches. They're in fuck-knows-where Chechnya, on an operation that might be the stupidest Kolya has ever encountered in a career that's been a highlight reel of futility. Behind one of these jade lumps is a block-headed colonel in need of body bags. Not in itself an unreasonable request. But Kolya knows the colonel wants to build a *banya* and in terms of insulation, nothing invented by God, man, or Germany can contain steam better than the heavy black plastic of a Federal Army body bag.

Kolya returns to the truck. Danilo moves back behind the wheel. He coaxes the ignition, pumps the gas. The starter motor gags. Danilo gives Kolya a slow shake of his head. "It won't start."

"Because you shot it," Kolya says.

"Your point?"

"No point," Kolya sighs. Sometimes his expired faith in rational logic revives itself long enough to believe in points. It's as comforting as believing in Ded Moroz, but in the end he always ends up feeling like an asshole for thinking any of the pain he either inflicts or endures has meaning beyond the senseless fact of its existence. "No point at all."

"Once I got shot while I was jerking off and you know what I did?"

"Depends where you got shot."

Danilo gives him a don't-doubt-me glare. "I manned up and I finished, Kolya. It was easy with that photo of your mom in the leopard-print bikini."

Kolya elbows him in the kidney.

"Don't worry," Danilo says. "I folded it so you and your little bro were out of view. And I didn't get a drop of blood on it."

"It's not blood I'm worried about."

"Point is, I finished my mission. Unlike this goddamn engine." Danilo slams his fist into the steering column and Kolya waits it out before suggesting they reevaluate their options. They climb out from the truck and unfold their map on the ground. Kolya had made it by taping sheets of notepaper over command's computer monitor, tracing pictures of antique maps of Chechnya, and then pasting the sheets together in what he hoped was the right order.

"Which way's north?" Danilo asks.

Kolya pulls out a compass that points north no matter which direction he holds it. "Which way do you want it to be?"

"We should check the map," Danilo surmises.

They check the map. Having forgotten to include a legend within the map itself, they examine the map, squint at the horizon, quarter-turn the map, frown at the horizon, and repeat a half-dozen more times without discovering any of the map on the land or any of the land on the map.

"We can't find north on the map and we can't find north where we are. We are more than fucked," Kolya says.

"The map's fucked. We're fine." Danilo scans the ridge. "That fat old bastard's got to be here somewhere. It's supposed to be a day's drive, right? We've been driving, what, five hours? That's a day, right?"

Kolya's from the wrong side of the Arctic Circle, from Kirovsk, where a winter day is a fifteen-minute glow on the horizon. "Sure," he says.

It's clear they'll have to set out on foot. They have a radio, but it hasn't worked in several years and they carry it as a good luck charm more than anything; even in that capacity, it isn't working. They pack up as many of the body bags as they're able, to prove they aren't deserters in case a patrol picks them up. With two body-bag-stuffed parachute duffels, and whatever provisions and extra ammo they can pocket, they set off.

They only make it fifty meters when Danilo drops his parachute bag. "Hold up," he says and jogs back to the Shishiga to empty the rest of his clip into the engine block. The eight staccato blasts multiply off the valley walls in a brief but thunderous applause for Danilo's coup de grâce. When Danilo returns, he looks much more chipper.

"Was that necessary?" Kolya asks. He should be irate with Danilo for wasting the ammo, but more seriously, for announcing themselves to any rebel in a ten-kilometer radius. It's April 2000 and the army has sealed the bulk of the Chechen insurgents within the topographical confines of the southern mountains, an area into which generals issue demands with the ineffectual bluster of zookeepers shouting into a cage. But Kolya can't summon the appropriate anger. Whatever life-preserving instincts evolution endowed him with have been war-blunted to an amused disregard for all mortality, particularly his own.

"Don't you worry yourself," Danilo says. "We know two things about our revered colonel. First, that he loves his *banyas*. Second, that he's a cur-hearted coward less likely to see action than my left hand. If he's around here, then here is as safe as my grandmother's lap."

Kolya wouldn't put much trust in anyone involved with raising Danilo. But he shoulders his parachute duffel and his Kalashnikov and follows Danilo into the valley.

They spend the night zipped inside the body bags. In the morning Kolya drinks from a stream that runs clearer than any faucet he's ever known. Upon closer inspection, it's not a stream but an ancient irrigation canal that continues to water the terraces a century after the soil was last tilled. They decide to march downhill and Kolya points the busted compass toward the valley to officially make it the right direction. Trees prosper on the valley floor and dwindle to waist-high grasses as they climb another ridge. Vertical seams of white stone split the green slopes at haphazard intervals. The soreness in Kolya's heels is less a physical pain than a physical fact he's as familiar with as the color of his eyes.

Beyond the next ridge an emerald field gradually unrolls, dead-ending into trees. With binos, Danilo scans the straight edge of woodland cutting across the meadow. They go quickly and somewhat ridiculously, bent at the waist in a crouched shuffle as if the open field has been rolled into a tight tunnel. Discrete packets of panic burst in Kolya each time the wind shifts the grass, or the shadow of a bird cuts over the ground. He focuses on his breathing to delay an oncoming anxiety attack. Over the past year he's developed a deep mistrust of open spaces and now can't cross anything wider than a doorframe without wondering if he's walking into a sniper's scope.

When they reach the tree line, Danilo snaps up his arm with tight-lipped alarm.

Kolya freezes.

Danilo farts.

"Devil," Kolya mutters, cuffing Danilo on the shoulder. "You'll give me a heart attack before the rebels ever get me."

"Oh no," Danilo says. His face, often formed of diagonals—slanted eyebrows, sneered lips, sloped cheeks that together resemble a crudely drawn demon—completely wilts.

"Fuck off," Kolya says.

"It won't be a heart attack." Danilo nods into the forest, where Kolya catches sight of a dozen rebels gathered around the remains of a campfire. They hold their rifles in their right hands, bowls of kasha in their left, apparently alerted by Danilo's flatulence. Twelve barrels stare up at Kolya, and the fear that had loosened its grip in his chest since he crossed the field now crushes his heart with both hands.

They drop their parachute bags and raise their arms as they are relieved of their weapons, ammo, and boots. The man patting Kolya down misses the cassette tape buttoned into his shirt pocket. The rebels sport full beards, slender waists, and mud-spattered plastic and leather sandals. One wears a green headband squirming with Arabic script. The one patting Kolya's calves for concealed sidearms has the straightest, whitest teeth he's ever seen. The scrawny kid with almond eyes doesn't have the beard of an insurgent yet, but Kolya knows that's what he is, deep down, just as he'd feared himself capable of murder long before he ever picked up a gun.

"*Kontraktniki*," the rebels whisper. From their tattoos and black sleeveless shirts, Danilo and Kolya are obviously mercenaries rather than conscripts. The rebels deal with captured conscripts—all poorly trained and terrified teenagers—more leniently than contract soldiers, who collectively conduct themselves like Russian Rambos with less discriminate aim.

A tall, silent man in a Tesco T-shirt kicks Kolya's legs from under him and binds his wrists from behind with wire. He lies on the ground beside Danilo. Behind them, younger insurgents sift through their belongings. The tall one doesn't leave their sides. We'll die today, Kolya realizes, but rather than horror or surprise, the realization hits him like the first breath after a long, dark dive under water.

The tall man spreads open two body bags in front of Kolya and Danilo. "Get in," he orders.

Danilo begins to protest, but a swift rifle butt to his temple interrupts the plea. Kolya watches two younger rebels fold Danilo into the black plastic body bag like a poorly tailored suit into a garment bag. The second bag lies open on the ground, and with a sigh, he climbs in legs first and is zipped up.

They lie there for an indeterminate interval while the rebels talk in Chechen. The body bag traps all of Kolya's heat. The whole goddamn thing smells like the inside of his boot. There's a two-centimeter gap in the zipper and he puts his mouth to it as if to a nipple and sucks. He keeps waiting for the sifting of dirt, the ring of spade on rock, and when several strong hands lift the corners of the body bag, his throat clenches and he thinks: *this is it, this is it, this is it.* But rather than falling, he is raised. Rather than dirt, he feels the ribbed plastic of a truck bed slide under him.

The ignition thrums to life. German make, no doubt. The truck jolts forward.

The seconds unspool and in the dank darkness Kolya finds himself wondering what Danilo's wife is doing at that moment. Where she is, what she's wearing, what thoughts are dreaming their way through her mind. Only four men in the unit are married and their wives have become communal. In small Siberian towns, those four wives will never know that in Chechnya they're polygamous, that soldiers they'll never meet yearn for and wish after them. Some compose long love letters, never sent. Others rewrite their wills to bequeath their modest possessions—a hunting knife, an ammo belt—to women known only in their imaginations. Danilo's wife had grown up in Irkutsk as the granddaughter of a barber rumored to have once trimmed Stalin's mustache. As a child she'd wanted to play the violin, but the violin teacher had taken one look at her cigar-stub fingers and told her to take up the trombone instead, even though she was a girl. That trombone might've saved her life when grain shortages hit the city: Party bigwigs wanted a healthy horn section on call for fanfares in case someone from Moscow visited, so she received upgraded ration coupons while the violin teacher went hungry. She has wet-grass green eyes and a Prometheus disco light set. All throughout childhood her father told her that only a mousetrap offers free cheese, but she'd already left home and couldn't repeat the proverb back to him when he decided to invest his life's savings in a bank account that promised a five-hundred-percent annual return. She can still perform patriotic fanfares when required, but prefers big-band jazz, and when she plays "When the Saints Go Marching In," her single trombone sounds like a twelve-piece band. From the raw materials of Danilo's stories, Kolya has built himself a life with her. Believing in the unconditional love of a woman he's never seen, never met, is the closest he's ever felt to God's grace.

He rolls over and speaks through the two-centimeter gap. "You there?"

Danilo rolls over too. They're lying side by side, bagged bodies nearly touching, passing a single breath back and forth through the small slit in their zippers. The truck lurches beneath them.

"I guess I am," Danilo answers. They both know better than to speculate on what's to come.

"Hum that song about the marching saints for me," Kolya whispers. But whatever Danilo hums is lost in the wind-whipped velocity of the accelerating truck.

They don't speak again, but the muggy lightless coffin becomes less oppressive to Kolya when he thinks of Danilo suffering too. Minutes and hours lose their edges inside the body bag, and Kolya has no idea how much time has passed when the truck stops. With a heave, Kolya is carried thirty paces. "One, two, three," a voice counts in Chechen, and then Kolya is weightless, aloft, and falling. Two seconds later the impact knocks the breath from his lungs and his left shoulder from its socket. His breath finds its way back a few moments before his shoulder. He lies there in the body bag, paralyzed with pain, waiting for the first clump of dirt to scatter over him. A descending scream and a hard thump announces Danilo's arrival. Kolya goes to work on the zipper with his teeth and eventually pulls it far enough to fit his head through.

"Where are we?" Danilo asks. They're in a pit, what might have once been a wide well. The stone walls rise six or seven meters to a tight circle of sky. It's wide for a well, but not wide for a prison, two and a half meters across, he guesses. He squirms out of the body bag and unzips Danilo's. Sitting back to back, they untie each other's wrists.

The weeks shrink from seven days to five, counted first on Kolya's left hand, then his right, then Danilo's left hand, then his right. Each morning a pair of sun-browned hands appears at the lip of the pit to lower jugs of water that become latrines by noon. Disks of bread fall from the sky and plop into the dirt with disorienting irregularity. At two weeks, Kolya and Danilo are nearly as bearded as the rebels who tossed them in here. At three weeks, a matchbook-size soap bar drops. It's from a Saudi hotel. Kolya dips it in a water jug but can't summon a single bubble from the stupid thing. Danilo grabs it from him. Peeling off his shirt, Danilo shows Kolya the bullet hole in his left shoulder where he'd been shot mid-jerk. It's hardened to a pink coin of scar tissue. Danilo has six others scattered over his torso and legs and surrounding each are homemade tattoos of irises, lids, and lashes. When Danilo bends to try the bone-dry bar on his feet, his back stares up at Kolya.

On cold nights Kolya climbs into his body bag and zips it to his chin. Although the two body bags are demonstrably identical, Kolya has grown attached to his. He's tried to personalize it, to tear through the sealed seams, to write his name in mud on the canvas carry handles, all token efforts to inflict enough change on his one possession to convince himself that he's actually alive, that this isn't some metaphysical holding pen, because a few days in the bottom of a pit with Danilo has taught him all he needs to know about eternity. Sometimes Kolya thinks of his captain, Feofan, a man who always wears his uniform, even to sleep. Behind his back the soldiers would joke that he'd collapse on the ground like loose straw without his fatigues to give him shape. The body bag has begun to feel to Kolya what the uniform must feel to Feofan.

When he's exhausted all other memories, he thinks of home. The lake of industrial runoff ringed by gravel where one summer he had sunbathed with his mother and younger brother, pretending they were on a Black Sea vacation. The nickel furnaces blurting endless exclamation marks of smoke. The pollution so dense nickel is extractable from snowdrifts. The raw-fish pinks and reds of dusk, where clouds of sulfur and palladium clot the sky. Here starlight domes the open pit. Kolya was eighteen when he saw stars for the first time. It had been his first night in Chechnya.

He still has the mixtape his brother gave him before his first tour. *For Kolya. In Case of Emergency!!! Vol. 1.* Searching for a cassette player down here is as pointless as hoping for an electrical outlet on the moon, but he keeps the gift close, wondering what his brother has spooled on its gears. It's the only question he has that he might someday answer, his reminder to live long enough to hit play.

One morning the leathery hands appear at the pit lip, this time holding a yellow rope knotted with handholds.

In training, Kolya climbed a rope twice its length in thirty seconds. It takes him two minutes to summit this one. The two brown hands that mean to Kolya both captivity and nourishment are attached to a squat elderly man with a ferocious mustache. In one hand he holds a black Makarov, the handgun favored by Kolya's own superiors. In the other he holds two sets of leg cuffs.

"A gift from one of your generals," the old man says, eyeing the gun proudly. He tosses the leg cuffs between them. Kolya closes his eyes and focuses on the sun's saturating warmth. The bottom of the pit receives only a half hour of direct sunlight a day and Kolya feels he has emerged from a long Arctic winter and stepped directly into June's bright beam.

The old man leads them past a white stone house, past a collapsed toolshed, to a sloping field. Without boots, the field is their best avenue for escape. "Land mines," the old man says, snuffing Kolya's dim hope. A blast hole is sunken halfway up the hill. "You're welcome to try."

He takes them to a bed of weeds a little way off where two shovels angle from the ground. "Begin," he commands.

This is it, Kolya thinks. We're digging our graves. Should they run? Should they try to overpower the old man? They could hit him in the face with the shovel before he could shoot them both. He tries to catch Danilo's eye, but Danilo harbors no great zeal for staying alive, and come to think of it, neither does Kolya. The leg cuffs make it difficult to get much leverage on the shovel, but he manages to get three decent scoops before the old man stops him.

"Russian," the old man mutters as if the language,

culture, and people are a curse word. He takes the shovel from Kolya, kicks it into the ground, and goes to one knee to yank weeds from the loosened soil. He extracts the green clumps and then sifts through the dirt for their white veiny roots. When finished, he pulls a few seeds from his tunic and scatters them in the hole. Realizing that only seeds will be buried here, Kolya sighs, loud enough for the old man to glance up and smile.

That night, Kolya gets hard for the first time in weeks. "Did your wife send you any photos of her yet?" Kolya asks Danilo, pointing to his crotch with both index fingers. Some mornings Kolya sizes Danilo's wife's nipples to the coins in his pocket, and then slips the one- or two-ruble coin between his lips, closing his eyes and tonguing the coin vertical against his front teeth while he jerks off, hearing Danilo's wife moan, telling him to lick faster, suck harder, and he always complies, because this is the closest he will ever come to the woman he loves, and the sharp brass sweating from the coin is a taste to remind him of who he is, to remind him that he is loved, a taste to savor and preserve by forgoing food and water for the rest of the day. Kolya has never seen Danilo's wife, but Danilo claims she's pretty enough to do porn, which as far as Kolya knows is the highest compliment you could pay someone from Irkutsk.

"Nope, but I still got that picture of your mom in the leopard-print bikini," Danilo says.

Kolya looks to the pyramid in his lap. His dick feels like the densest of all his calcium-starved bones. It's been so long since he's seen a woman that any would do. Danilo passes Kolya the wrinkled photograph, still folded so Kolya and his younger brother are out of view. Kolya shakes his head. If someone had told him he'd one day be living in a pit and jerking off to a photograph of his mother, well, he'd probably have tried harder in school. In fact, he'd rethink just about all the choices he'd made if only to ensure access to a clean bed and some decent pornography.

"No shame to it," Danilo says, seeing Kolya's hesitation. "The ancient Greeks were always trying to fuck their own mothers. And those sickos invented civilization."

For a moment Kolya feels so far gone he could do it. But he's two hundred clicks from anywhere he'd call civilization and the moment passes. He folds the photograph and slips it into his pocket. "Tell me a story about your wife instead," he says.

"I'm not telling you about my wife while you get off. We've got to have some kind of boundaries."

"No, tell me something nice. Tell me again about when you met her."

Danilo sighs and tells the story Kolya's heard so many times it's become a song he knows by heart. Danilo had already dropped out of his final year of school when he met the young woman who would one day become his wife. She was with one group of friends, he with another, and their quick glances were invitations to an event both were too nervous to attend. After she left, Danilo learned that she'd moved to Irkutsk from some corner of Siberia even colder and more remote. He started going back to school just to talk to her. He kept asking her out and she kept saying, "Another time," and he kept going to school to keep asking her. Danilo had wanted a date and ended up with a high school diploma. She said, "Yes," just before the graduation ceremony. Kolya is there beneath the auditorium's shadow-faded heights. Kolya follows her onstage. The audience applauds. He smiles, bows, and falls into a dreamless sleep.

As the weeks pass, Kolya and Danilo wire-walk the line between captives and guests. The leg cuffs they donned the first time out of the pit are still fastened, though looser given the weight they've lost, and brittle enough to break with a good hammer strike. But the old man has granted them greater freedom. In the mornings they work the garden, weeding, planting, fertilizing, according to the old man's instruction. They sow the herb garden that extends to the base of the mined hill. The single crater, halfway up the hill, sucks into it lingering fantasies of flight. Sometimes Kolya seats his hand in an unearthed clump of soil and watches earthworms and roller-upper bugs, an unnameable underworld of blind little bastards that rise through the dirt to promenade on his open palm, and he's drawn back to that time in his life when he still had the chance to become someone else and is momentarily freed from who he is. At midday the old man brings him a bucket of water and greasy flatbread. Sometimes they talk for a few minutes, finding common ground in the institutional incompetence of both their respective armies.

In the afternoons, he and Danilo rebuild the collapsed shed or the white stone fence. The evenings are theirs. Escape is a vague, undefinable goodness, and they discuss it abstractly, as they would God. Sure, they could easily handle the old man, but then what? Then they're just two bootless idiots lost in the mountains. At least with the old man alive, they're prisoners of war. Danilo finds a length of fishing line among the debris of the shed and fastens it to the end of the yellow rope. When the old man pulls up the rope each evening, the fishing line dangles into the pit like a rip cord they'd only use in a genuine emergency.

One day while harvesting *kalina* berries for the old man's sore throat, they spot a Shishiga trundling through the forest toward the dacha. As it approaches, they make out the bullet holes in the hood where Danilo had shot it. They sprint for it, as much as one can sprint in leg cuffs. When the old man emerges from the dacha with his hands raised not in surrender but in greeting, Kolya's ballooning hope ruptures. When a soldier jumps from the truck and clasps the old man in friendship, it deflates entirely.

"Vova?" Danilo calls when they're close enough to recognize the soldier. The soldier takes two steps forward, cocks his head, and frowns. Behind him the old man fiddles with his prayer beads, unconcerned.

"It's me. Danilo."

Vova is the type of Omskman remembered for his weak chin and little else. He'd started as a conscript, leaping to contract soldier only six months earlier, which made him the runt of the unit and the target of Danilo's bullying. Vova smiles. "That's you under all that beard, Danilo?"

"What is this? You're here to rescue us, right?" Danilo asks.

"No, not this time," Vova says with so much pleasure he turns to the truck bed to conceal it. There he hoists a bucket of bullets. "We didn't know what happened to you. Found the truck, but no Danilo or Kolya. Give me a hand with these, will you?"

Kolya and Danilo each carry two buckets of loose ammo to the shed they've rebuilt over the past several weeks. They're Russian army bullets, manufactured in Russia, where they'll one day return sealed first inside dead Russian soldiers, then inside black body bags.

After watching them hump rifles and red petrol jugs to the shed with a cheerful smirk, the old man gives Vova an envelope stuffed with green currency. Vova quickly counts the bills. "Anything you'd like me to pass on to Captain Feofan?"

Danilo stares, dumbfounded. "Tell him to get us the fuck out of here!" He pauses, for a moment unable to find the words to liberate them from the curlicue of logic that imprisons as totally as their ankle cuffs. "The captain can't evacuate his bowels without first putting in paperwork to Moscow. You better contact my wife too."

While Danilo writes his wife's details on one of the mint U.S. bills, Vova asks the old man for a ransom price. The old man leans against his cane, stroking his mustache thoughtfully. He looks to Kolya. "This one is very good in the garden. He works with care and diligence. The garlic will be wonderful this year. A thousand U.S. for him. As for the imbecile," he says, turning to Danilo, "you can have him for a barrel of cooking oil."

Danilo raises his index finger in objection to the price disparity before thinking better of it. "Can you lend us the money, Vova? So we can buy ourselves now?"

The weak-chinned Omskman beams. Apparently he hasn't forgotten the drunken night when Danilo made him wear a dead woman's dress. "The slave trade is unlawful," he says. "As your comrade, I cannot allow you to engage in it."

"We didn't ask Vova if the colonel ever got his *banya*," Kolya says that evening at the bottom of the well.

“I bet they sent two more idiots in a truck full of body bags the day we didn’t arrive. He’s probably steaming the fat from his ass right now.”

“Why did you sign the contract?” Kolya asks, a few minutes later. Danilo frowns at the question. With reason. You don’t ask questions about life before the war unless you already know the answer, and the answer better involve drunken antics and irresponsible sex.

“First time was to get out of jail,” Danilo answers plainly. “Ten years in prison or two down here. After those first two years, my wife and I married and moved into this tiny studio flat. I wanted to stay up late drinking and she wanted to get up early to practice trombone. You just can’t do both well in a studio flat. So I signed on a second time. I told her it was so we’d have enough to afford a place with two rooms, but really I just wanted some peace and quiet. Don’t know why I thought I’d find it in a war. Never the brightest pennant in the parade, as my dad liked to remind me.” Danilo closes his eyes and a quiet expression of yearning irons the wrinkles from his face. “I told myself so long as she insists on blowing her horn before noon, I’ll keep signing whatever these brass-button motherfuckers push in front of me. That’s just how love works.”

“You think?”

“I know it, man,” Danilo explains. “Some people need at least a thousand kilometers between them to stay happily married. But I don’t think I’m that husband anymore. Living in a pit changes the way you look at things, you know? I mean, to think that once my biggest grief was waking up to music.” Danilo doesn’t seem to realize he’s crying. “But everything’ll be all right if I can just get back. We can live in a broom closet and the entire Irkutsk Philharmonic can squeeze in to practice. But enough about that. Why'd you sign on?"

"It was this army man," Kolya begins. "He told me about this guy he knew who stepped on a land mine. Both legs missing, but it's okay, he likes sitting, he's got a nice divan, he comes home. But right quick he learns no woman wants to get with a cripple. And that was the only thing he had any talent for. Tragedy."

"Like the Greek kind. Speaking of which, you've been holding that photo of your mom real close. You sure you're not part Greek?"

"No way," Kolya says. He pulls the photo from his pocket and gives it back to Danilo. "But anyway, this army man tells me it's okay. What the army takes away, the army gives back. They pay for the cripple to see a sex surrogate."

"What's a sex surrogate?"

"My question to him. He says it's a doctor you fuck."

"Like in a porn movie? Like, we need to take her temperature and your dick is the only thermometer?"

"No, like the kind of doctor that speaks Latin."

A supernova of disbelief lights up Danilo's eyes. "Wait, wait, wait. *Doctor*, doctor? Like he's fucking a woman Doctor Zhivago?"

"Well, yeah. He's fucking a woman Doctor Zhivago."

"You believed him?"

"What can I say? I'm a romantic. Who wouldn't want to believe that somewhere a cripple's out fucking a woman Doctor Zhivago on the army's ruble? Who wouldn't want to believe that the world could be that just and right-sided? So here I am, getting fucked every which way but the way I signed on for." Kolya isn't sure if the conversation ever actually took place, or if the lunacy governing his present life is so omnipotent it's changed his past. He lights one of the cigarettes Vova had given them. "You know what, I'm glad we got captured. I mean, we spend our days planting gardens."

"You crazy? We're slaves, Kolya."

"Come on."

"What word would you use? We wear chains. We do field labor. Doesn't matter if we're planting gardens, we're living in a hole in the ground."

True, but Kolya doesn't care. The past few months have been the most serene of his adult life. The megalopolis in his mind has quieted to a country road. He does his work, he eats his bread, and he sleeps with the knowledge that today hasn't added to the sum of human misery. For now at least it's peace of a kind he hadn't imagined himself worthy of receiving. "We don't have to shoot people here," he says simply.

Danilo bats at the fishing line rip cord, then spits a sunflower seed husk at Kolya's head. "Someone like you? You're born a killer. The army doesn't make you shoot people. They make you shoot the right people."

Kolya tries to remember how many people he's killed. A baker's dozen maybe, but who knows? It's a moral failure that keeps him awake even after he's forgotten the faces comprising the lost figure. It began with Lydia, back home, but he tries not to think about that. What modest pay and war loot he has gathered, he's sent home to bribe university officials on his younger brother's behalf. Now his brother is just starting a philology degree. He won't ever have to keep count.

"My brother read a story about us a while back," he says. "Two assholes in Chechnya. They get captured and tossed in a pit."

"There are literates among the Kolya clan?"

"Shocking, I know."

"How did that story end?"

In Kolya's recollection, one of the men escapes and the other stays behind. But that isn't the kind of story he wants to tell tonight. "They got some sex surrogates."

Danilo laughs. "My kind of fiction."

"I think Tolstoy wrote it."

"He did, Pushkin did, Lermontov did, all those old bastards wrote about two assholes in a pit in Chechnya."

"How do you know?"

"We read them in school," Danilo answers. "My last year, in fact. When I started going back to school to ask out my wife. She wasn't my wife then, but I knew she would be."

"Tell me something new about her. What's her favorite book?"

"No," Danilo says softly. "Tonight, she's mine."

Summer clots the air to a moist spoonable heat. In Kirovsk, summers were twenty-four hours of sweater-weather light, and Kolya has grown fond of Chechen Julys with the languid green color scale, the birds without Russian names, the humidity heavy enough to drown you if you breathe too deep. He spends hours planting seeds and tending to the little green stems that spurt from the soil. He has no idea what any of them are. Growing up, food came in cans delivered to the Arctic by transport truck and ice-breaking barge. He still can't say what goes into a loaf of bread. He rakes the dirt, amazed by its looseness, its warmth. The one time he buried a body back home, he had to empty a clip into the frozen ground to break it up enough to begin digging.

When the head of the blue-handled trowel comes loose, he flings it toward the trees. From then on he does all garden work with his hands and at the end of the day they are so dark with dirt he no longer recognizes them as his.

Summer is fighting season and rebels arrive every few weeks to resupply from the munitions stockpile Vova left in the rebuilt toolshed. When he spots the rebels in the distance the old man hurries Kolya and Danilo toward the pit, his stout little legs miraculously cured of whatever affliction makes necessary his cane. He smears mud on their faces, ruffles their hair, and sends them down the yellow rope with instructions to hold their hands behind their backs and moan from time to time.

"Why?" Kolya calls up.

"Russians," the old man laments, as if their ethnicity is the most pitiable aspect of their current state. He's peering over the lip of the pit, his face an inky sun-silhouetted pool. "If they think I'm beating you, they won't feel they have to."

Two rebels look into the pit an hour later. Garbed in bandannas and fat-framed sunglasses, they look more like members of a late-Beatles cover band than of a jihadi insurgency. Kolya and Danilo moan and writhe on cue and they nod with satisfaction.

The following morning the old man orders Kolya into the dacha to clean up. Refuse from the rebels' visit—tea-stained mugs, bread crust, dried rice kernels, bandannas streaked with gun lubricant, fuses of homemade Khattabka hand grenades—are strewn in a manner suggesting that the old man doesn't rank highly within the insurgency. A multitude of overlapping woven rugs cover the walls and floor, so many that Kolya at first can't tell where the floor ends and the walls begin. Some of the patterned arabesques resemble sabers, others the daydreams of a meticulously warped mind, but all display a painstaking artistry as antiquated as the rugs themselves. Kolya fingers the rug at his feet, unable to remember the last time he touched something so fine.

Bookcases line the living room's far wall. The cracked-leather spines look bound in the same century the rugs were woven. "Any of these good?" Kolya asks.

"They belong to the previous tenant," the old man says. A heavy sadness is anchored to the word *previous*. With a sigh the man hoists himself from the divan and pulls a brown tome from the bottom shelf. Its pages are rimmed with gold, like those of a holy book.

The old man splays the book on his lap and points to a photograph of an oil painting stretching across two glossy pages. It's a landscape you wouldn't look at twice from a car window, the type of monumentally dull painting that adds to Kolya's general suspicion that artists are always trying to pull one over on him. "Recognize it?" the old man asks.

It does look familiar. A moment and the sense of familiarity upgrades to recognition. The field cresting two-thirds up the canvas, the well, the toolshed, the white stone wall Danilo is now repairing. It's the very landscape that stretches outside. "Where's our pit?"

"Right there," the old man says, tapping the painted well with pleasure. "See how there is no pail or winch? The well had probably already run dry and was already converted for prisoners when this was painted." He huffs on his spectacles and cleans them with a pinch of his white tunic. Without his glasses, his face looks made of loose skin that had once, maybe, belonged to a larger man. When's the last time Kolya has seen an old man? Average male life expectancy in Kirovsk hovers somewhere in the high forties and while elderly men aren't mythical creatures, they aren't quite of this realm.

"So our fieldwork is to make the land look like it did back when this was painted?"

The old man nods with apparent admiration. "You are not one hundred percent idiot," he says. Kolya takes it as an expression of great respect. "The property looked peaceful, didn't it, before all of this awful business? We'll make it look like this again. This is the blueprint."

In the painting, the garden extends halfway up the left side of the hill that is now mined and punctured with a blast crater. The garden Kolya has planted and cultivated stops far short. "The garden, we won't get it the rest of the way up the hill, will we?"

"No, not with the mines there." The old man falls silent and dips an almond into an ashtray of honey.

"Who lived here before you?" Kolya ventures.

"My daughter and grandson."

"I'm sorry," Kolya says after a long, uncomfortable moment staring into the ashtray of honey to avoid the old man's eyes. It hits him that this is the first time he's ever said those two words in relation to a killing. And he had nothing to do with this one.

A week later Kolya is tending the garden when the asthmatic heave of the Shishiga announces Vova's return. The suspension sags beneath the mass of Kalashnikovs, rocket launchers, RPG rounds, an armory so large half the roof has been cut away to accommodate it all. Steam shoots through the bullet-holed hood as the truck summits a knobby incline to reach the dacha.

"Well?" Danilo asks.

With procedural solemnity befitting a papal pronouncement, Vova unfolds a note, sits a pair of reading glasses on his steeply sloped nose, takes a deep breath, clears his throat, takes another deep breath, and reads. "'Dear Nikolai Kalugin and Danilo Beloglazov. I hate you. May the devil take you both. Respectfully yours, Captain Feofan Domashev.'"

Danilo grunts but nothing follows. Vova folds the letter, then his reading glasses, and returns both to his shirt pocket.

"The colonel's *banya* was built three weeks late because of your little excursion," Vova explains. "The colonel gave the captain a barrel of shit, which the captain's now pouring on your heads. Chain of command, I'm afraid."

"What about my wife?" Danilo asks. "Can she come up with the ransom?"

"Danilo. Man, I'm the bearer of bad news," Vova says with a grin. Never has bad news been more happily borne. "I had to remind her who you were."

"She's forgetful," Danilo snaps.

"Brother, she doesn't *know* you."

Danilo leaps forward and Kolya instinctively holds him back with one arm, like a parent to a child in a car stopping short. "Vova," Kolya says. "I know you've got grudges to settle with Danilo, but this isn't the time or place. What did his wife really say?"

"Believe whatever you want. I called her and she thought I was playing a prank. It took her a few minutes to remember some creep named Danilo Beloglazov who kept asking her out her last year of school."

"She's ly—" Danilo's voice breaks. "She's lying."

"She said she's been married to an electrician for five years. They have a four-year-old son."

Danilo holds his cheeks in his large hands. His red eyes radiate substratum pain, an ache so deep and unyielding that Kolya witnesses it as a geologic event. And Kolya, he's reeling. In a unit stocked with more liars, crooks, and bullshitters than the Duma, no one had once doubted the existence of Danilo's wife. A half-dozen soldiers have survived the war thanks to their imaginary marriages to her. The hope she's given the unit is real and unequivocal and in that sense she's an act of generosity that Kolya had assumed extinct in Chechnya. Kolya recalls the painting the old man showed him and he's a little disgusted that some nineteenth-century syphilitic so unambitious he merely reproduces reality should be venerated while at the bottom of that meticulously painted well lives a half-literate, borderline lunatic maker of miracles. Meanwhile, the miracle maker is shaking like an anesthetized thing slowly coming to life.

"Take us back with you," Danilo pleads in a voice whittled to a whimper. Kolya wants to reach out and take his friend in his arms and sway side to side as he did when his younger brother woke from nightmares of dark, endless forests. He hadn't known Danilo was still capable of shock, of disappointment, and he envies and pities him for it. The old man emerges from the dacha with a blue cellophane cookie bag bulging with money. "Please. Right now," Danilo says. "Put one between his eyes and we'll just go."

"I can't do that," Vova says. "These are our business partners."

"They're our enemies."

"They're our counter party. But I do have some good news. You two have officially been declared dead."

"How is that good news?" Kolya asks.

"Before you were listed as deserters."

Kolya leads Vova a few meters from tear-streaked Danilo. "Don't tell the unit about Danilo's wife," Kolya says and holds Vova's gaze until he's sure the weak-chinned Omskman will obey.

"Okay. And I'm sorry," Vova says, frowning from Danilo to Kolya, unsure where to direct his condolences. "I'm sorry for your loss."

Kolya and Danilo, widowers for all of three minutes, bow their heads and stare at the dirt.

Rebels arrive later that afternoon to pick up the new stock of munitions. Their voices, coming from the dacha long into the night, are still audible when Danilo announces his intent to escape. "I got to get back. My wife needs me," he says.

A half-moon sits low in the star-buttoned sky. An ache relays down Kolya's vertebrae as he sits up, from his neck to the base of his spine. "We need to prepare. Need a map, provisions. More than anything we need boots," Kolya points out.

Danilo gives Kolya a deadened stare. "I'm leaving tonight." Without further explanation, he begins filling his body bag with handfuls of dirt. When Danilo has filled it with a narrow body of soil, he stands and assesses his work. "Good enough. You should do the same, Kolya. They'll think we're just sleeping in tomorrow."

Kolya is zipped in to his waist. He presses his head back against the white stone wall, draws meaningless shapes in the dirt floor. This well, this pit has become for him a burrow. He considers the endpoints of escape—reenlistment, death, home—and the happiest outcome he can envision is this, right here, recaptured and resentenced to work a peaceful plot of land. It's as much as he can hope for right now. He's lived longer than he ever expected, longer than he has any right to live, and he's tired. His twenty-third birthday is still three weeks away.

"You'll have to take this mission solo," Kolya says. Danilo studies Kolya for a long moment, then pulls the photo of Kolya's bikini-clad mother from his pocket and offers it. Kolya unfolds the two wrinkled wings where he and his brother stood, shirtless and swimsuited, arms locked around their mother's pale, fleshy waist. He can't remember who had taken the photo, or when, or where, or why. He can barely recall that little family, that three-citizen-republic bordered by the Polaroid frame. If he were to unbutton his pants right now, he wouldn't feel the faintest twitch of shame.

"Don't give that picture too much of a workout," Danilo says. He pulls the fishing line rip cord with a dramatic flourish and the knotted yellow rope flops over the edge of the pit. Kolya folds the photo into a tight pellet and tosses it to Danilo when he reaches the top. "Send that to my brother. Tell him you're the asshole who escaped."

He keeps the mixtape, *For Kolya, In Case of Emergency!!! Vol. 1*, buttoned in his breast pocket. There's still time, he tells himself, to hear what it has to say.

Danilo catches the folded photo, gives Kolya a half-cocked salute, and wades into the India-ink night with his shirt wrapped around his leg cuffs to muffle the clatter. His escape routes are limited. He could try the hill, and whatever lies beyond its crest, but it's mined. He could try the stone path the rebels drove up on, but that would be the first place they'd search for him. The woods, he decides, are his best bet. He's nearly reached them when something slashes from the ground into his right foot. Pain pulsates from the ball of his foot, up his leg, through his chest, exiting through his throat in an involuntary gasp. It must be a land mine, he thinks as he buckles into the grass. But there is no explosion, no flame, just silent agony enveloping his foot. He bites down on his wrist to steady his breathing and examines his foot. Blood spits from the wound and drips down a deeply lodged trowel blade. He takes the blade in both hands. With a terrific wrench, he withdraws the blade and the void fills with an agony so searing that white light flashes on the backs of his closed eyelids. Before his adrenaline expires, he crawls to the tree line.

Under a screen of floppy green leaves, Danilo collapses. His foot has been replaced with some awful instrument whose only purpose is to hurt. A breath rises from the cellar at the center of his chest and leaves his lips in a shrill, unfamiliar cry. He lifts his hands to the trees in surrender. "I give up," he announces, no longer caring if the rebels hear him, no longer caring about anything. When did he begin telling people that his secondary school crush was his wife? There must have been a moment of deliberate deception, but his mind has been so jumbled for so long he can't discern now. He can see his wedding so clearly. He wore a thirty-thousand-ruble suit. She couldn't stop kissing him. They honeymooned in Moscow, posing for photographs in front of the Kremlin and Saint Basil's and GUM. His father emerged from wherever he had disappeared to ten years earlier and shook Danilo's hand saying, "I was wrong about you."

The night is a sweat-slick fever dream. His wife stands at the well-scrubbed sink, wearing the paisley apron he bought her one spring day four and a half months after New Year's and four and a half months before her birthday, the day of the year when she was farthest from presents, and thus, the day Danilo most wanted to give her one. She's wearing the paisley apron that had made her flush with happiness when she unwrapped it from pink tissue paper, not that the paisley apron was itself responsible for the lovely glow within her cheeks, no apron wrapped in pink tissue paper has ever brought anything but disappointment to the recipient, rather Danilo was responsible for the lovely glow within her cheeks because he had counted the days from New Year's and then counted the days to her birthday, and calculated the day in her annual orbit at which she was farthest from presents, and surprised her with a paisley apron that on New Year's or her birthday would have disappointed her, but on that particular day, in that particular pink tissue paper, made her feel unbelievably loved. She's wearing the paisley apron and she's standing at the well-scrubbed sink and her back is to him so he cannot see her face. She's standing at the sink in an apron and carving dark bruises from a potato with a paring knife. She carves away the dark bruises until so little potato remains it could fit in a teaspoon. "Even these rotten ones have a little good in them," she says and tosses the nub into the boiling pot, standing at the well-scrubbed sink, her back to him so he cannot see her face, wearing the paisley apron all the while.

A single gunshot launches him from dreams of his wife and into stark morning light. His pulse leaps with jungle-cat acceleration. He's just behind the tree line, where he passed out in the night. When he figures out that the gunfire isn't directed toward him, he examines his foot. The wound has clotted into a black slit from toes to arch. Another spurt of gunfire. He drags himself until he can see a half-dozen rebels standing at the bottom of the mined hill. The spindly one angles his Kalashnikov skyward and fires another shot. Beside him, the old man smooths his rebellious mustache with one hand and holds a large, unwieldy book in the other. Marooned alone in the middle of the hill, thirty meters up, Kolya kneels.

For a moment, Danilo assumes the rebels are firing at Kolya, but the gunman has his rifle pointed at the morning sun and shoots to encourage Kolya, rather than kill him. On his knees, Kolya claws at the ground. He seems to take direction from the old man, who uses the fat art book as a map. They're making him dig for mines, Danilo realizes. But no, that's not it either, because Kolya pulls a handful of something from his pocket—dill seeds?—sprinkles them over the holes he's dug, and begins repacking the dirt.

A cement-thick heaviness hardens in Danilo's stomach as he realizes that Kolya is being made to extend the herb garden up the mined hill. As punishment for Danilo's escape? He doesn't want to know. He bandages his foot with folded green leaves. During the next spray of gunfire, he slams the trowel head into his leg cuffs. The rusted metal chain snaps on his third try. He spreads his legs for the first time in months and a wonderful relief seeps along his tendons. The undergrowth cushions his wounded foot and he hobbles away as fast as the pain allows. The scent of butter-fried potatoes hangs sweetly in the air. His wife is setting the table for lunch. An explosion echoes from the mined hill and enters the forest, but it's nothing, only a plate falling from the table. Little pieces of flowery porcelain lie everywhere. His wife tucks in her apron and drops to one knee. With open arms she gathers them all.

Intermission

The Tsar of Love and Techno

St. Petersburg, 2010; Kirovsk, 1990s

1

GALINA CALLED TO SAY SHE HAD BOUGHT ME a first-class ticket to Moscow, and then she said that my brother was dead. I couldn't believe my luck. I'd never even received first-class mail since the postal service introduced it six years ago, let alone a first-class train compartment. As for Kolya, well, he'd been dead for years.

She lived in a top-floor penthouse with a chest-tightening view, lined with thick white carpets that may have been polar bear pelts. Wealth announces itself with what's easy to break and impossible to clean. The chairs were all curvy works of art that turned sitting into yoga exercises. Jasmine and plum perfumed the air. A crooning tenor went into histrionics on the Bose. Dozy bronze Buddhas meditated on the bookshelf. I was wondering if artsy-fartsy types in Tibet fetishize crucifixes when Galina returned, her loosely tied kimono yawning at the chest and knees.

"My. God. *Who* is your hairstylist?" she asked.

In truth, I've never had a haircut that's fit my head. One-Eyed Onegin used to give my head the once-over with the clippers, but depth perception isn't his strong suit. Plus I'm pretty sure he uses them to shave his pubes.

"I don't really have one."

"Whatever you're doing, keep doing it. Very avant-garde."

If a stopped clock is right twice a day, a bad haircut is right twice a decade.

It had been longer than that since I'd last seen Galina, since my brother left for his first tour and she became a celebrity and they never saw each other again. It's easy to forget what someone really looks like when you see them everywhere. On billboards her face is airbrushed as smooth and shiny as an inner organ, and she has a bust-waist-hips ratio that is found in nature only inside the mind of a Dr. Frankenstein with Adobe Photoshop training. But the Galina standing there in a slab of noon light, made up and manicured, in a fancy kimono that ten million silk worms gave their lives for, looked more person-like than the Galina of the billboard, tabloid, or screen.

"It's been the most brutal morning, Alexei," she said. People who have it easy are always telling you how hard it is.

"You've been following the earthquake in Indonesia?" I asked.

"What? No, a trollop from the Royal Shakespeare Company landed the Russian seductress-spy role in the new Bond film. Probably shagged Leo the Lion to get the part."

"I'm sure you'd have gotten it if anyone in

Hollywood had seen *Deceit Web*," I offered encouragingly. Her gaze dive-bombed to the floor. Some people you just can't cheer up.

"I know I should count my blessings, but that's what accountants are for."

"Must be weird being you."

"It's a strange thing, Alexei. When we were teenagers, I'd never even imagined living in a penthouse with a chauffeur and a chef and a butler. But now that I have it, it's nothing. Am I *aw*ful for saying that?"

"Just a little."

"Life's a little awful, I'm afraid. Pitiful creatures spinning on a senseless rock around a dying sun in a cold and uncaring cosmos and they *still* won't give me the Bond movie. Fighting over matches while the world burns, no?"

"Sure," I said. But I was trying to decide if it was rude to take a fifth *konfeti* when she still hadn't taken one. Nope, definitely not.

"So how've you been? You're not still in university, are you?"

"I am," I beamed. Through sheer grit and tireless effort, I'd managed to stretch a five-year philology degree into its tenth annum. It was a loaves-and-fishes variety of miracle. The universe may be cold, dark, and indifferent, but in university you get to take club drugs all night and sleep all day. "I'm working on my thesis paper. On *Odessa Tales*. I have my title, 'Babel's Babbles,' but that's about it."

"Any good?"

"I haven't read it," I said. "I don't want the text to influence my interpretation."

A sixth confection dissolved into a starchy paste that

sopped the saliva from my tongue. We were quiet for a little while.

"You heard about Lydia?" I finally asked.

All the blush in a beauty box wouldn't've brightened Galina's cheeks. "Yes," she said. Her eyes fixed on a safe, vacant patch of wall over my left shoulder. "Alina told me about her and her mother, and of course your brother. Then Olga told me. Then Lara. Then Darya. Then Zlata. And Tamara must've told me a dozen times"—the six-member gaggle that feasted on crumbs fallen from the table of Galina's celebrity; Lydia had been their seventh member—"I don't even know how they get my number. I change it every few months, mainly to avoid them, and they still somehow find it. The Americans should hire them to track down Al Qaeda. Ten minutes on the phone with Tamara is enough to make anyone disavow their most sacred beliefs"—she lit an incense stick that smelled of lavender fields doused in sunshine—"but anyway, Lydia. Let's be honest, never the sharpest bayonet in the battalion, was she? I'm not saying she should've known better than to confide in them. But, come *on*. You could confide a secret to a megaphone and it would stay quieter. I've tried to make a film of her murder, but it's easier coaxing a mouse down a cat's throat than a decent script into production."

"It's a tragedy," I said. "For Lydia, for Vera, for Kolya, for—"

"You don't need to tell me. It's a national embarrassment, really, our film industry. If there is an afterlife, then the circle of hell just below the Satan-Judas-Brutus gang bang is reserved for development executives, I mean—"

"Why am I here?" I shrank a little in the cross-hairs of her narrowed eyes. She wasn't used to being interrupted.

"A good question, Little Radish, taking us to the heart of the matter—though why those with the most free time are the stingiest with it, I'll never know." She scooted her chair toward my side of the table. She even made *scooting* sound sexy. I was pretty sure she wanted me to become her paramour. I'm flattered, I'd tell her, but I can't do that to my brother, Kolya, even if he's dead. She'd dissolve into inconsolable weeping, saying if she couldn't have me she had no reason to go on. Buck up, I'd tell her. I'd kiss her right on the lips—*with* tongue—and she'd swoon, obviously. Then I'd walk out the door without looking back.

"So listen," she said, sliding her hand across the table until the space between her fingers and mine was as thin as a butterfly wing. "I went to Chechnya a few years back. With Oleg. He had some business there, drilling oil and his assistant. The tart. While he was out doing that, I visited a few army hospitals and bases. I thought starring in a Great Patriotic War biopic was enough, but no, my publicist *insisted* that I had to actually talk to the poor devils. A pair of jackboots away from being a *wunderbar* stormtrooper himself, my publicist. Anyway, I asked an army official about your brother."

"I've asked after Kolya with every army official in every army office with a listed address and phone number. No one knows anything."

"You're just the sweetest, aren't you?" Her eyes iced over. "When you're an important person, you can ask a question and even an army bureaucrat will answer."

She reached across the table and sealed my fingers within the warm envelope of her hand. Her pulse clicked against my wrist like a telegraph message her heart had sent me to decode. My nerve endings gasped.

"I was told that he was taken prisoner and died on that field"—she nodded to the wall where a frame of golden dollops and curlicues wrapped around a simple painting of a pasture—"The field is something of a local landmark because it was the subject of this painting by some nineteenth-century artist. Rather dreary place if *this* is its most majestic vista. But it used to hang in a museum, so it must be important. I bought it."

I left a trail of footprints in the plush white carpet as I approached the painting. It wasn't much to look at, which is about all you can do with a painting. An empty pasture cresting into a hill. A small house. An herb garden. A waist-high wall of white stone meandering at a diagonal. But in a patch of plugged-in canvas the size of a halved playing card, two slender shadows ran up the hill. One was a head and a half taller than the other. A slender bar of green grass separated their dark hands, and I couldn't tell if they were reaching for each other or letting go.

"Kolya died here? On this hill?" I asked.

"That's what the army adjutant said."

I turned back to the painting, to the two stick figures running up the hill, limbs unfurled. "Who are they?"

"I'm really not sure. I should've asked the prior owner when he called last year, asking for it back for a retrospective on Zakharov. Up in your stretch of the forest, actually. The Teplov Gallery, in Petersburg? I told them precisely where they could stick their request, and it wasn't in their mailbox, mind you. The nerve. Sell you a painting one day, then ask you to donate it back the next. No more than vipers in ascots, these academics."

A placard hung to the side of the painting. The final lines read *Pay them no mind, for they are merely the failures of a novice restoration artist. They are no more than his shadows. They are not there.*

My palms had dampened when I returned to the table. "You remember the mixtape we made for Kolya, before he went to Chechnya the first time?" I don't know what prompted me to ask, but I've often thought about that tape.

She gave the widest smile. It was the first genuine sentiment she'd expressed that morning. "Devil, I'd forgotten. Then again, I try to forget about everything from Kirovsk. I was a mess back then, wasn't I?"

She wanted me to say *no*, so I said, "Yes."

"Let's hope there're no extant copies. If that made it online, I'm not sure I'd ever live it down. Probably as damaging as a sex tape, that."

Nothing demystifies the glamour of celebrity like hearing one talk. I plopped an eighth confection onto my saucer. "He told me that he'd put off listening to the mixtape as long as possible. That he'd wait until he really needed it, like the last sip of water in his canteen. Do you think he ever heard it before, you know?"

I wanted her to say *yes*, so she said, "No."

"Yeah, you're probably right." Confections nine and

ten landed on the saucer in tiny detonations of powdered sugar. I swear I just didn't want them to go to waste.

"Oh, one other thing," she said, crossing the living room to an antique desk constructed of a jillion drawers too small to hold anything larger than paper clips and stamps. She returned with a folded Polaroid I'd given to Kolya before he left for his first tour. I couldn't risk unfolding it in front of her. "The army adjutant in Grozny gave me that."

"Why'd you wait so long to tell me all this?"

She gazed at her dim reflection in the teacup, and then quickly broke it with the turn of the spoon. "I didn't invite you here to talk about your brother. You see . . . my husband is divorcing me. Some people think I've been a bit too frank in my public comments on the state of modern Russia in recent interviews. You begin criticizing the casting choice of a certain director, and you end up comparing Putin, unfavorably, to Lord Voldemort. Who knows how these things happen?"

"What's this have to do with me?"

"The painting, you idiot. The Zakharov. Oleg's hired suit-jacketed leeches for lawyers. They'd claim my toes if they weren't attached to my feet."

I still didn't understand.

She stared dismally. "I'm giving you the painting. Better you have it than the lawyers."

Then I understood.

I wrapped the painting in enough bubble wrap to mummify a mastiff. She followed me into the hall. I'd sweep her off her feet and we'd waltz out the door. Never mind the daughter sleeping in the other room. The tabloids would call me heartless, but I won't raise another man's child as my own. We'd buy a mansion on the Riviera, and I'd learn how to do all the things the nouveau riche do, like buy cuff links and belittle the work ethic of the poor. I'd leave her heartbroken in Marseilles. She'd never recover. The tabloids would call me a cad, but I wouldn't play by society's rules. Everything in my life would be different. I just had to kiss her.

I shook her hand.

"It's been good to see you, Alexei," she said as she closed the door, and I knew she meant it. She's not a very good actor.

2

A parachute of yellow smoke, tethered by thick billows to the smokestacks, hangs permanently over Kirovsk. The twelve smokestacks, the tallest edifices for five hundred kilometers, are known locally as the Twelve Apostles. They encircle Lake Mercury, a man-made lake of industrial runoff whose silvered waters are so veined with exotic chemicals they lap against the gravel-pocked banks year-round, unfrozen even in February. Behind the brainy folds of smoke, the moon is a dim ghost. Kirovsk is in annual competition with Linfen, China, to hold the title of the world's most polluted city. When the nickel burns, it produces sulfuric soot so dense it stains the ground, accumulating in such concentrations that snowdrifts are mineable. And surrounding Kirovsk is White Forest. Constructed at the behest of the party boss's wife to counter Kirovsk's reputation as a frozen cesspool, the forest looks very fine in photographs circulated among engineering departments in Moscow and Leningrad to deceive their most promising students into taking jobs with the nickel combine. In person, however, you realize this is an unusual forest. The trees keep their leaves through winter. They neither grow nor die. No animals hibernate in their trunks. In a triumph over reality, the city commissioned an entire forest of fake trees. Over time the wind has stripped much of the plastic foliage from the steel limbs, and now White Forest is a field of rusted antennas, harboring the city's de facto garbage dump beneath its naked branches. It is in White Forest, where Lydia's story ends, that mine begins.

I must have been ten, Kolya thirteen, on the afternoon we watched two men kill a third. But I'll come back to that. We woke in the room we shared to the dueling cries of my father and the teakettle. Kolya climbed from bed. His hair was a typographical error someone had scribbled out. He hit me, as he did most mornings, to toughen me for my own good, but it's difficult to muster much brotherly gratitude while getting slapped. We skated across the floorboards and into the kitchen in our woolen socks.

My father had begun lending sweaters to Kolya. As Kolya grew, the neck and shoulders of the sweaters slowly stretched, giving my father the appearance of a man incrementally disappearing when he wore them once again. But that morning, my father looked years younger, taller, larger. His eyes were bloodshot rivets of inspiration. He paced before the charred stove top.

"This is it, boys!" he exclaimed. "The exhibition that

will send the Moscow Museum of Cosmonautics to the dustbin of museum history."

My father was an outer-space freak in a city roofed by pollution so dense he'd have to drive a hundred kilometers to see starlight. A few years earlier, in what was a moment of either personal courage or mental collapse, he had quit his comfortable position as a furnace technician to pursue his dream of opening a cosmonautics museum. His passion was rivaled only by his ineptitude, and he presided over the Kirovsk Museum of Inner and Outer Space as its founder, director, docent, archivist, press secretary, ticket inspector, and janitor. Quartered in an abandoned warehouse adjoined to one of the city smelting complexes, the museum was not only the kingdom of my father's unfulfilled ambition, but my playground, my classroom, and, in the lofted flat above it, my home.

If you haven't seen the museum, let's say it's one of the world's most unique science museums and just leave it at that. If you have seen it, my apologies. You could say my father built a Potemkin space station, that he forged every exhibit, that he had an intensely one-sided rivalry with the Moscow Cosmonautics Museum. You could also say that compared with the greater inhumanities of our city, my father's misdemeanors are so trivial they seem virtuous.

"What's he on about?" Kolya asked my mother, the family bilingual who translated my father's ravings. She stood at the sink. A postcard of the Black Sea had been pasted above the tap. As the discolored water softened her fingertips, she stared into the breakers unfurling over a sandy strip. Perhaps she strolled along the white-painted promenade, a slender leash wrapped around her wrist, a lady with a lapdog. Perhaps she imagined a summer romance, the thrill of unfamiliar hands, the unknown warmth of sunlight on her shoulders, the gasp of seawater on her toes. Sealed within the worn postcard edges was a sunlit world where my mother splintered into thousands of imagined selves, none of whom answered Kolya's question.

"The End!" my father declared. He punctuated the declaration with a blow to the kitchen table that scattered the silverware.

"The end of what?"

"The end of everything. An exhibit on all ends, from the end of a day to the end of a life, a civilization, a planet, a universe. It will put the museum in the guidebooks."

The museum had opened the previous year with my father christening the front door with a thrown bottle of saccharine Soviet champagne. It had hardened into a puddle of frozen glass that had resulted in the broken hip of our third visitor. My father dropped to one knee and clamped his hands on our shoulders. As we huddled together, linked through the chain of his grip, the current of his fervor sank into our muscles. "Go to the forest. See if you can find anything we might use."

The floor of White Forest had filled with waste in the decades since its construction. Over the years Kolya and I had found a collection of refrigerator doors, a dozen leaky barrels of toxic waste, a file cabinet filled with classified documents, knives and bullet casings in police department evidence bags, a cat caged in a kennel, a drunk driver sobbing in the car he had somehow skewered to a steel tree limb, and an electric heater in perfect working order. Most of the displays in the Hall of Inexplicable Phenomena came from the debris.

The last house we passed before crossing a wide field to reach the forest edge belonged to Lydia's family. She was the same age as Kolya, twelve or thirteen then. The metal skeletons held on to late spring snow. Broad plastic leaves wilted from a few barbed branches. Like the sky, the snow, and the insides of our lungs, these too had yellowed. They sagged over us like the spineless skins of a nuclear people.

"What are we looking for?" I asked. Except for a few hypodermics we poked each other with, we hadn't found anything worth keeping. "This is stupid. Where are we even going?"

"We'll know what we're looking for when we find it," Kolya answered loudly and slowly, as if I were both deaf and dim-witted. A note of vexation pulsed beneath the equanimity of his logic. I was afraid I'd disappointed him. You're probably thinking that I'm a high-density, dehydrated slab of manliness, a testosterone prune, if you will, but as a boy I was a plum. My family nickname was Little Radish: Even as a taproot, I didn't rise to the stature of greatness. I was terrified of nearly everything, from atomic war to other people's belly buttons, Kolya's displeasure most of all. When he was annoyed, he'd look just over my head when speaking to me. It made me feel shorter than I already was and embedded the conversation with an expectation I failed to meet unless I stood on stilts. We carried on. Ten minutes later, we heard voices.

"You're not scared, are you?" The rasped question carried the ghosts of ten thousand cigarettes.

"Scared of sharks," answered a second, younger

voice. Through the gaps in the trees, we saw the two men standing a dozen meters ahead. We crouched to get a better view. The first man must have been in his early thirties, wearing the circular spectacles and pressed trousers of a gulag-bound academic. A deep cleft made his chin look like a small dog's testicles. The other man wasn't even a man, a fifteen- or sixteen-year-old in a tracksuit, his hair slicked into an aerodynamic wedge, his upper lip feathered with a mustache as useless as a brush missing half its bristles, his little teeth swallowed by gummy arches.

"Sharks?" the older man asked.

The younger one shuddered at the word. "Those bastards just swim around the ocean eating kids, biting turtle heads, fighting giant squids and shit. The messed up thing is that they can't even stop swimming and fighting squids and eating children. They don't have hot air balloons shoved up their asses like normal fish."

"Good thing you were born a land mammal," the older man mused.

"Only good luck I've ever had," the young man agreed. He kicked at the pile of clothes lying at his feet.

A moan rose from the pile. Then the clothes began to move. A man was in there, his mouth expurgated with a strip of black tape, his hands bound behind him within the buttoned overcoat. When he shook from side to side his empty coat sleeves slapped the ground in a hapless dance. I wanted to run, but Kolya held my shoulders.

"If we move, if we make a sound, they'll put us right next to him," Kolya whispered. His eyes locked on mine for the first time that day. That little acknowledgment of my existence quieted the terror that clambered in my chest like a kitten locked in a suitcase.

The two men went on debating the dangers of sharks. The younger one asked if *Jaws* was a documentary.

Kolya held me in a bear hug; in a lesser brother, it would have conveyed false comfort, but Kolya made it feel like the moral obligation of possession: *You will be saved because you belong to me*. Daily push-ups and pull-ups had built out his once spindly arms and he wrapped them around me and pressed me in and held me. "Shush, Little Radish," he whispered. He didn't shake, he didn't tremble, not a single spasm of concern. His preternatural mental calm seeped down into his body and hardened into a second skeleton. Everything about him suggested a psychosomatic impenetrability so dense a bullet couldn't pass through him.

A dozen meters away the overcoat went on waving its sleeves in an agonized semaphore. The two men looked away uncomfortably.

"I saw the open ocean in a movie once," the older one said. He pulled a handgun from his waistband and passed it to the younger man. With a sickeningly slick *cha-chunk*, the younger man chambered a round. It sounded too smooth, too glib, an ease and efficiency unsuited to the brutal task before them.

The younger man closed his eyes and pointed the gun at the man lying at his feet. The prisoner turned his head slightly and through the upside-down V of the older man's legs his eyes met mine.

"He's looking at me," I whispered.

"Who is?"

"The guy on the ground."

Kolya glanced over. The condemned man's eyes widened. He was furious. Maybe our presence was a greater transgression than his impending murder, or maybe we were one indignity too many, the only one he had any chance of alleviating before he departed. The duct-tape strip swelled with his muted screams.

"He's trying to warn them," Kolya muttered disbelievingly. "He's trying to warn the people about to kill him."

But neither of the murderers noticed that their prisoner's anger had been redirected to the clearing a dozen meters away. The younger man tightened his lips, but when he pulled the trigger, nothing sounded but a hollow clack.

"You never make it easy, do you?" the older man asked the clouds. The two of them stared at the gun, clicking the trigger, tapping it on a corroded branch, inspecting its darkly oiled insides. They disassembled the gun and put it back together. I imagined myself buttoned in the overcoat, squirming on the far end of the barrel, lungs laboring to strain air through mucus-clogged sinuses, pleading with buffoons too stupid to pull a trigger in the right direction. I'd never imagined that something as solemn and final as death could be this idiotic. It was the keyhole through which I first glimpsed life's madness: The institutions we believe in will pervert us, our loved ones will fail us, and death is a falling piano.

"Maybe we should ask him," the younger man suggested, nodding to the ground. "He's the one who usually shoots people."

The older one considered it for a moment and leaned over to tear the duct tape from the condemned man's lips. The tape uprooted his brown whiskers with the soft plucks of a tiny harp. His eyes never left mine.

"Please," I mouthed. My vertebrae had tightened to a single, inflexible bone. His eyes drilled into mine. I was certain he would alert them. But he nodded once and silently looked up at his captors. It was a last act of mercy in what I imagined was an unmerciful life. Whatever needless suffering he brought to the world, I forgave him, from all of us, for it all.

With soft-spoken resignation, the condemned man explained how to properly load the clip. "Now turn the gun around so that it's pointing at your face," he instructed the younger man. "You want to be looking inside the barrel to see if there're any obstructions. Then click the trigger a few times to make sure there's nothing stuck in the chamber."

The younger man pointed the gun at his face, peering into the blind telescope of the barrel, but before he could pull the trigger the older man grabbed his arm.

"Wait, wait, wait," the older man said. "He's trying to get you to shoot yourself."

The younger man's shoulders slouched under the weight of the betrayal. "Really?"

The condemned man smiled and closed his eyes. The barrel stared back, unblinking.

Click click. Click click. "Goddamn thing's still—"

I recoiled into Kolya's arms. The blast thundered through the forest and fell into silence. There are more ways to remember one person than there are people in the world. No matter what Kolya went on to do, I remember him as the hand on the back of my neck, the shoulder beneath my cheek, the voice in my ear promising safety.

The murderers turned and stepped over the coat sleeves. What had been a skull was now a leaky bowl of borscht. Ruby spatters ran to the thighs of the younger man's navy track pants. The older man patted his protégé encouragingly. He had a limp chicken neck, downturned lips, shadowy crescents beneath his eyes, all of which seemed to hang a little lower, as if buried in his skull a slackening winch barely held his face together.

Kolya flung me from his arms when he realized the two men would pass us. "Play dead," he whispered. The cold earth seeped through my bones. We lay paralyzed. Our fingers rooted us to the glassy ground until the footsteps faded. The older of the two men was named Pavel, and he was on his way to becoming a leading figure in Kirovsk's organized crime. In eight years, my brother would begin working for him.

Kolya helped me to my feet. "You're going the wrong way," I called when he stomped toward the body.

The man had died with his legs splayed in his loose trousers, his wrists bound behind his back, his torso torqued so that his left shoulder wedged into the frost and his right jutted up.

"What are you doing?"

"Just waiting till they're gone." Kolya nodded toward the ellipses of footprints leading away from the body. He dropped to one knee and rolled the corpse into a more comfortable position. Kolya straightened the man's legs, uncoiled his wrists, returned his arms, at last, to his coat sleeves. For a man whose head had been shot off by incompetents, he looked surprisingly peaceful.

A patter at the far end of the clearing. Two eyes, the color of windshield-wiper fluid, met mine.

"Kolya," I called. He had found a dirty sheet and was pulling it over the body. "Kolya," I repeated.

He turned as the wolf trotted into the clearing. A scar ran the valley between its perked ears. The fur darkened down the length of its snout, the white graying until it dead-ended at the black period of its nose.

"Keep calm." Kolya backed away from the body. "Don't run."

"You keep telling me that," I snapped. "You keep telling me to keep calm and we keep almost getting killed."

Drawn by the gunshot or the scent of blood, the wolf beelined for the corpse. Its lips peeled and a yellowed row of incisors sank into the dead man's neck, making a mess of Kolya's funerary attempts. We stood a few meters away. Fear had locked our feet to the ground. The wolf lodged its teeth into the overcoat and tore through wool with a terrific twist of its head. It wasn't very large, as wolves go, more like a Labrador skeleton assembled inside matted wolf's hide.

When we began taking tentative steps backward, its head swung toward us. Its mollusk-like nose flared rhythmically. I held out my hand in peace, as I would to a dog. Only when it opened its maw and its ruddy tusks shone in the sunlight did I realize I was offering the beast its next meal! Its tongue shot past its black rubbery lips to coat my fingers in gore. I was too afraid to retract my hand. For a moment we stood there as the wolf slathered every centimeter of my hand with the dead man's masticated remains. When finished, it lifted its hind leg and a yellow stream splattered across my shoes, soaking into my socks. Then it started wagging its tail. Then it barked.

Kolya lodged his fist in his mouth to hold in his laughter, then he took me by the shoulder and led me home.

We sat between our two beds on legless chairs propped on book boxes (our father had used the screws that had held together the legs to mount a clock). Rugs draped over the wallpapered walls. Sometimes they slipped from their nails in the middle of the night, falling over us as we slept as second, stifling blankets. A poster of the periodic table hung between our two beds. I had changed my socks and washed my feet. My insides felt pureed.

Kolya hunched forward with his elbows pinned to his knees and his mouth drawn into a tight expression of concentration. Whenever he thought deeply, he looked constipated.

"What's it like being dead when everyone else is still alive?" I asked.

"Like being alive when everyone else is dead," Kolya answered. His back stiffened. He shot to his feet. "That's it! One of the exhibits can be about the last person alive. You know how Dad told us he'd foiled an American plan to nuke Kirovsk? That wasn't the whole story."

He dropped to a knee beside me.

"Tell me," I pleaded.

Kolya leaned back and his shoulders sank into the blubbery mattress. "Dad didn't tell you about the backup plan. The last resort. The answer to the question: What if the world ends today?"

"He told you?"

"Of course. I'm his favorite son. See, after the Americans took the moon, Khrushchev came to Dad and was like, 'Look, Dad, we're fucked. The Yanks are playing baseball and building shopping malls on the moon. What do we do?' And Dad told him his plan."

"Tell me," I pleaded.

"Dad's idea was to build a capsule that could keep a man alive for twenty years. The Americans might kill all life on earth with a nuclear war, but the last living man would be a Soviet citizen, up there, in space. Khrushchev had one of those expansive Russian souls novelists are always writing about. He loved it. But Brezhnev put him in an old folks' home before he could authorize Dad to build the thing. So we've got to do it."

We rushed to the ticket office to tell our father.

"My true heirs," he said. "Born scientists. You'll go far."

When the museum closed for cleaning that Sunday, my father towed the rusted skeleton of a lorry cabin onto the warehouse floor. "The capsule!" he declared. I examined it from various vantage points. It didn't resemble a lorry cabin, much less a capsule. More like a decapitated whale's head that had spent several years on the ocean floor first as food, then as shelter, for an extended family of eels. "It needs a little work," my father admitted, but his cheeks remained red with excitement and dermatitis.

We transformed the lorry cabin into a capsule with tinfoil. Kolya taped one end of foil to the hood, slid the roll onto a broomstick, and circled the lorry as the silvery scroll unfurled behind him. It took sixteen rolls and hundreds of revolutions. Kolya orbited, until the cabin became a fully bannered capsule. With black shoe polish, we carefully drew *USSR* across the bow. A maroon dentist's chair became the pilot's seat. We used a fishbowl for the portal window, a rusted desk fan for an air filter, a busted radio for communications, a cassette-tape deck for last messages.

The summer was a twenty-four-hour afternoon. For three months the river thawed enough for ships to pass, and newly canned goods and sugary cookie-like lumps replenished *produkti* shelves. It warmed enough to walk outside with only a heavy coat, scarf, mittens, and fur hat, so warm that drivers held tar-soaked torches beneath their cars for a scant two minutes before the sludgy gas tanks thawed. Ah, summer!

We played in the museum when there were no visitors, which was nearly always. The sun streamed through sooty windows spaced along the second story.

"Cosmonaut Kolya," I murmured, descending to the basement of my vocal range. "The moment we have feared has arrived. Reagan declared on American television that rather than surrender, he would destroy the entire earth. He was facing the wrong camera. We doubt his sanity."

And Kolya would snap to attention, clucking his tongue as he clicked his silent rubber heels. "Comrade Alexei, I am prepared to venture into the vastness and bring the wisdom of Lenin to all alien life." He marched to the capsule and gave a stern-faced salute to an invisible flag before hunching inside. I secured him to the dentist's chair with straps cut from a rucksack and set a motorcycle helmet on his head.

"One final thing, Cosmonaut," I said, flipping up the helmet visor. I would give him a cassette tape, or a notebook, or a file containing instruction on further adventures to be had in deep space. "Open this only in case of emergency."

I counted down from ten as Kolya hummed the national anthem. Sometimes he'd clasp my hand to his chest and as his pulse throbbed against my palm the act seemed less like make-believe than the rehearsal for a final good-bye.

"You will have the last human thought," I whispered.

"You will be that thought," he said.

"You will have the last word."

"Your name will be the last word."

When the countdown plummeted to zero, the rocket launchers crackled into ignition. Blue heat seared the oxygen from the air. An instant inferno engulfed the surrounding two square kilometers of land, ripping a crater into the tarmac. The blaze incinerated my nerves before they could transmit the agony to my brain. In a millisecond I became the echo of a scream rising through smoke. All around American warheads fell from wispy chutes. The sky bruised with fire. This is it. The end. The thrusters kicked in, lifting the capsule through blossoming mushroom clouds. Cataracts of light carried Kolya from this world. Through the portal window, he watched the decimated horizon become Earth, become nothing.

3

I shared a compartment on the night train back with a father traveling to Petersburg with his daughter for her orthodontia work.

"She's stumped half the dentists in Moscow," the father explained with obvious delight. The spotlight of paternal pride is fickle and faint, but when it shines on you with its full wattage, it's as warm as a near sun. "My little prodigy."

Tree trunks flicked over the cabin window. I wanted to be loved as much as he loved his daughter's bad teeth.

"Go on, show him," he urged.

She gave a great yawn. Her open mouth was a dolomite cavern. Only divine intercession or satanic bargaining could save her. "Just a little bit crooked," I said, then gave a wide *ahh* of my own. "Mine are a little crooked too."

"Mine are in a dental textbook," she declared.

She had me there. Couldn't have been older than twelve and already she'd accomplished more in her life than I had. Rotten little overachiever. I pulled the Polaroid Galina had given me from my wallet.

Pale fold lines graphed over the photographic surface that had lost its luster years earlier. But there we were, Kolya and me, wearing leopard-print bikini bottoms, flanking our mother. None of us had ever worn a swimsuit before. Clouds foamed from the Twelve Apostles in the background. Lake Mercury lapped at our toes. Splashes glinted from our calves in points of molten light. I showed the Polaroid to the girl and her father.

"My brother and mother. And that's me when I was your age," I said. It felt urgent that I share this with them, that they know that even though my teeth weren't so disfigured, I was worthy of inclusion in their family. The girl's lips didn't open when she smiled. Then her father told her to get ready for bed. I carefully folded the Polaroid into my wallet.

In the morning, we'd leave the train together and they'd be so charmed by my small talk they'd ask me to the dentist with them. They'd fix me, starting with my teeth. The girl would think of me as a much older brother. Her father would think of me as a much younger brother. They'd invite me to move in with them in their titanic Moscow mansion. I'd consider the offer. It'd cramp my free-wheeling bohemian lifestyle, but they'd plead and offer me great sums of money. I'd turn down the money. I'm not for sale. But I'd accept the invitation to join their family, for their sakes obviously. I'm a Samaritan. I'd teach the girl all about growing up, and teach the divorced father how to forget his first marriage and find a new one. I'd only stay a few months because I won't be held down. They'd talk about me in reverent tones for years.

The following morning the cabin attendant yanked me by my ear from a restful slumber. This was to be expected, given the only required experience for Russian Railways employment is a history of anger issues. The father and daughter had already gone. Must've forgotten to leave their names and phone number. They'd probably regret it the rest of their lives.

4

In July 1990, when the warmest month in Kirovsk's fifty-three-year history coincided with the collapsing of Soviet authority, the elderly began swimming in

Lake Mercury. In the mornings they gathered on the gravelly banks with their gray hair bunched beneath fur hats and they stripped to their undergarments. When they raised their hands, their triceps sagged from the bone. One man gazing at the waters patted his potbelly tenderly. Maybe he'd spent the last fifty years wondering if it could be deployed as a flotation device, and now, finally, would find the answer. There's nothing quite like the sight of two dozen half-naked octogenarians. We enter the stage of life as dolls and exit as gargoyles.

"Why are you swimming here?" I asked one of the women. She stood beside a rusted sign that warned off swimmers. She was no taller than me—which is not to say I was short, just short for a biped. Her hazel eyes held my fuzzy reflection. Her generation had journeyed through hell so we could grow up in purgatory.

She glanced to the rusted sign. It depicted a grapefruit-headed man made of forty-five-degree angles falling into the open jaws of a shark. Perhaps before she was arrested and condemned to Kirovsk, she had grown up by a lake where her father had taught her to float by keeping his hand beneath her arched spine so she knew she wouldn't sink, that he would be there, until one day she lay on the calm surface, her back parabolic, her arms crucified on the water, her brown hair sieving algae, and she flitted her father a look and he raised his hands as if her glance was a loaded gun, and for a second she floundered, terrified she would sink to the lake bottom without him to hold her, but she stilled her arms, gulped the air, she was doing it, all by herself, she was floating. Perhaps she wanted to tell me that if she had outlived Stalin, the

Berlin Wall, and the Soviet Empire, a little dirty water wouldn't kill her. Instead, she glared at the sign. "I've fried scarier fish with just a sliver of butter."

She joined the other grandmothers. Clad in nothing but discolored undergarments, they hobbled to the gravel bank. All around, smoke blabbered endlessly from the smelter stacks. A woman with a noose of scar tissue carried her wooden cane right into the water. The others followed, and all together, they waded in. After a half-century drought, they remember how to swim.

A husband and wife backstroked across the lake, water glistening toward shoulders, legs splashing in unison. A rope, lashed around their waists, tied them together, in case one began to sink.

A one-legged man paddled with slow thrusts of his arms. Both real and phantom legs were weightless in the water below.

A man with a mustache as wide as his waistline, whom all the world had nicknamed Walrus, took his first tentative strokes, marveling at the cool rush against his skin, the freedom of movement, and began weeping right there in the water for the countless times he had given up hope, the countless times he had prayed for death in the mines, in the prison camp, and now, now gratitude cracked him open, and he thanked God for ignoring his prayers, for letting him live long enough to learn to swim.

And in the middle of the lake the woman I'd spoken with floated on her back, eyes closed, as if nothing in her many years had ever gone wrong.

August grew warmer. Centrally planned weather patterns were in open revolt. To everyone's surprise, the bathing babushkas didn't turn lime color, or grow third ears; if anything, the chemical mélange restored to them a long-ago dissipated vitality. Soon grandparents in their sixties joined the geriatric swimmers, followed by people in their fifties, then forties, and so on until the youngest children of the youngest families dipped their baby-prawn toes into the water. No one believed the state-sponsored propaganda: *The philosophy of Marxism-Leninism predicts the inevitable contours of history, the individual is significant only in his submission to the collective, the chemicals in the water cause cancer.* Our revolution was a Sunday swim.

My mother, as I've said, wanted no more from life than an afternoon at the Black Sea. That August, my father came home with leopard-print bikinis.

"What're we supposed to do with these?" Kolya asked, eyeing the two-piece.

"It's a swimsuit. I'll give you one guess."

"It's a bikini."

My father grabbed the top piece from Kolya's hands and tossed it in the trash. "Now it's a Speedo."

This summer Lake Mercury, the next the Black Sea, my father promised. But contrary to his plans, by the next summer the pain in my mother's chest would have already taken her to the doctor, then the hospital, then the crematorium, and finally the living room bookshelf, where her ashes still rest, and will likely spend eternity, in a pickle jar between a can of spare buttons and two phone books, despite my father's promises to someday scatter them in waters off Sochi.

But before all that, we went as a family to Lake Mercury, my mother in her leopard-print bikini, my brother and I in our leopard-print bikini bottoms, and we splashed in the lake, the water a mouthful of dirty change, my open eyes burning as I watched the flailing limbs of the decapitated swimmers, and at the end of the day, when everyone was sun drunk, or punch drunk, or just drunk, that hour in summer when falling inhibition and rising permissibility intersect, my father chased my mother across the gravel bank. With leaping strides he lunged for her in her leopard-print bikini, claiming he was a leopardopterist, that he would pin and mount her, and my brother and I chased them, two cubs protecting our leopardess. We bared our teeth and snarled, we clawed and growled, we were wild, we didn't care, and all the while my father chased and my mother fled, her laughter held by the stadium of smoke rising from the Twelve Apostles, never had I seen her so happy, never so loved, so wanted, never had I seen her as a sexual being, as desired quarry, as anything but a taciturn and dissatisfied figure at the kitchen sink who occasionally walloped me over the head with a soup ladle; and even though my father had no appreciation for metaphor, or feline biology, or the sunbathers he hurdled over, even though he was my father and she my mother and we were all a few steps from the precipice, I look back at that moment, that afternoon, with flooded longing, and think: *We should all be so lucky to get from life a sunny-day swim in chemical waste.*

That same afternoon, my father borrowed a Polaroid camera and lined us up on the bank of Lake Mercury. I'd never seen a Polaroid before, never seen any camera more advanced than the Zenit E-series. In the sulfurous light, Kolya's chest was as pale as amphibian spawn. We flanked our mother and waited with pinched smiles as my father framed the photograph. Goose bumps pinpricked my mother's bare thighs; they had never before seen direct sunlight. We had ranged far above our natural latitudes.

The camera clicked and the moment disappeared in a flash. For years, I kept that photograph. I gave it to Kolya when he went to war.

It was that very day, surrounded by smokestacks, soon after my father caught my mother and pinned her elbows to the muddy ground and planted a sugary smooch on her lips, that she coughed blood. A galaxy of crimson phlegm unraveled to the gravel. She blushed and stammered, embarrassed to interrupt that moment of unlikely magic. For weeks we pretended it was nothing. My mother insisted it was a summer cold, and we believed her, or pretended to, because chemotherapy, radiation treatment, and thoracotomies were luxuries reserved for the politically connected, and we could afford no more for her than a bottle of bleach-flavored cough syrup. The days shortened as the months slipped away. By winter, when she had shrunk to two-thirds her normal size, the battering ram of reality breached my father's fortress. The doctor confirmed what we already knew: "One in two people in Kirovsk will die of lung cancer."

Until her final day, my mother insisted on doing the dishes. "Of course not. Don't be absurd," my father countered. But she demanded in a voice that fell through the air like a brittle thing we scrambled to catch. The hot water was inconsistent, the soap was chemical burns in bar form; few chores promised more misery than the dishes. Yet my mother, masochist or no, saw standing at the sink before the Black Sea postcard as the most tranquil moment of her day, and she wouldn't let illness take that from her. To make things easier for her, my father, brother, and I shared a single plate, glass, fork, knife, and bowl. We ate in rotation, each of us alone at the kitchen table with a single place setting.

That winter, in the fifteen minutes of daylight, Kolya and I climbed to the roof of the warehouse and snow dived. Five-meter-tall snowdrifts filled the road outside the museum. From the roof of the warehouse, five stories up, they were the swells of a frozen sea. I'd never snow dived before. I was afraid I'd fall straight through the snow and splatter on the tarmac, only to have my blini-thin remains removed by spatula the following spring.

"Ivan broke both legs and a windshield last year," Kolya said. Cinder-block crenellations ringed the roof. We peered over the edge. "The first rule of snow diving is to watch out for cars."

"Then why are we jumping into a road?" I asked. The snowbanks rose high enough to conceal aircraft.

"Have you ever seen a car parked in front of the museum?"

I hadn't, but that didn't make the idea any wiser.

"We'll check if it makes you feel better."

"It would—" I began, but before I could finish the sentence, Kolya's hands planted into my lower back and launched me over the cinder-block lip, and I was flailing, falling, a dust mite pulled in earth's terrible inhalation, the yellow-white dream tumbling around me, and I knew I would die, my heart de-valved, the air rushed up, it was glorious. A soft glove of snow caught me. Water would've hurt more. I opened my eyes and couldn't see. The air had been everywhere. Now it was gone. I butterflied the snow. My arms, frantic. Through a jag of compacted powder, sunlight slanted in. I lunged for it.

I couldn't see Kolya's face clearly enough to make out his expression. In his erupting laughter, I heard his relief.

"Any cars?" he called down.

"See for yourself!"

He crouched and exploded, thrusting aloft, legs straight and arms wide, jackknifing at the waist and falling in a slow, deliberate backflip. I remember Kolya in the space capsule, breaking the heavy grip of gravity, soaring forever, and I remember him arcing, falling, returning in a spray of snow. He swam to the surface, red-faced and wheezy. We raced back to the roof.

Our little flat above the museum shared a ventilation system with the adjacent nickel smelter and everything, even canned trout, stank of sulfur. My father feared nothing on this earth more than a draft, but even he propped open the triple-paned kitchen window to blast in polar night. "To air out the room," he repeated as justification, admonishment, threat. We lived in our greatcoats, scarves, and *ushankas*, while my mother lay immobilized beneath the weight of a dozen blankets. One day I entered the flat and found my father in bed with her. He held her upright and her head lolled on his shoulder as he rocked her back and forth in his arms. He patted her back, helping her burp, and watching it I remembered how playful they had been, how lustful, how unabashedly magnetized to each other's bodies. Glacial winds tore through the room as he rested her against a pyramid of pillows. A centimeter of snow covered the kitchen floor. She drifted in and out of consciousness. One of the pillows slipped and fell across her face and she startled from her haze.

"There's nothing there," he said, trying to calm her.

"I know there's nothing there," she replied, as if this were the source of her distress rather than its assuagement. He went on whispering in her ear, too low for me to hear, and she was in such a state, who knows what she understood then, what any of us understood, one moment she was there with us, the next she was gone, entering without fanfare the flat, dark line we will all one day become part of, and my father didn't notice, he went on whispering to her, pressing his lips to skin as if to summon the cancer, to draw it out like a venom, because if every one of two people is fated to die of lung cancer, he wanted it to be him.

The funeral was on a Tuesday. Afterward our neighbors and friends came over with plates, pans, and platters. My mother had feared being buried alive—a not altogether unreasonable phobia given our city history—and generally disliked graveyards, cellars, and basements, so after she was cremated in Kirovsk's newly built crematorium, the pickle jar containing her ashes went on the bookshelf. Behind it we'd posted her Black Sea postcard. She'd bask in its view for the hereafter. An inebriate third cousin mistook a bowl of potpourri for potato chips and munched the lavender flakes until the bowl bottom held his fissured reflection. Laid-off smelting techs wandered over from a table crowded with open-faced salami sandwiches, fish, beet, and potato salads, to express condolences in careful voices made uncomfortable by my grief. A quick word of sympathy, an awkward pause, and they turned back to the food, having done their duty, perhaps remembering it as the only unfortunate moment of an otherwise wonderful party. Shaking their hands was like clutching squirming herrings, and while I've now forgotten much of that day, I'll never forget their tendrily fingers, moistened with salami grease, as well lubricated as the machines they had manipulated.

The following morning my father stood before dirty dishes towered about the kitchen. The sink hadn't held more than a single place setting since the day my mother reclaimed her after-dinner washing. Now dishes climbed over the lip, stretched along the countertop, rose in narrow stacks on the stove range, descended the staircase of open drawers to the kitchen floor where bowls, plates, and glasses filled the floor. A tumor of crockery had grown on our home. My father reached for a white ceramic serving dish and examined it curiously. Orange grease dripped down the side. He tried to wedge it under the faucet, but the sink was too full. He made a halfhearted swipe with a sponge and dropped his arm. He looked down at the sink. A short, powerful scream erupted from him. He was usually such a quiet man. I didn't know he contained such volumes. Kolya rushed from the bedroom and asked, "What's wrong?"

Our father turned. We stood there in our pajamas. He held up the dish. Oily amoebas dripped to the floor. "I don't know what to do with this."

Our little family might have ended right then as our helplessness, our collective failure, amplified within the uneven triangle we made. But Kolya took the dish from my father and opened the kitchen window. "To air out the room," he said, and he calmly lobbed the dish out the window. My father turned to Kolya, as if to hit him, but when the dish shattered in the alley below, his entire face loosened. "You know, I think that belonged to Boris's wife," he mused. "Your mother always hated her."

"This belongs to her too," Kolya said, and flung a massive platter out the window.

"And this," I chimed in, throwing a glass.

"What about this?" Kolya asked, tossing a soup pot before anyone could answer. A loaded glass pitcher burst with silverware shrapnel. My father lifted a dozen stacked dinner plates and calmly slid them out the windowsill. We pitched sugar jars and salt shakers and saucers and teacups and large plates and small plates and soup bowls and porridge bowls. We threw every dish brought by neighbors, friends, and mourners, and then we ransacked the cupboards, tossing frying pans and cutlery, bread boards and cooking trays. It was an exorcism. We stripped the kitchen of any dish, utensil, and mug until nothing survived that would ever need to be washed. It was the morning after my mother's funeral and there we were, we couldn't stop laughing. We went on until there was nothing left but one plate for each of us. When the last excess plate shattered in the alley below, my father finally closed the window.

5

For several weeks I left the painting suffocated in bubble wrap beneath my divan. Well, I say *divan*. Really, it's a stingily cushioned hunk of aluminum built to last rather than to provide comfort, like something you'd find in a fallout shelter. *I'll sleep when I'm dead*, I tell my friend Yakov. No other choice, really. Sometimes I find condom wrappers between the cushions. They're all mine, definitely. The flat is owned by a widowed she-huckster who'd sell me into slavery in my sleep, if I slept. Her two grown sons live here too. They think they're tough just because they've been to jail, joined a gang, survived stabbings. But I could teach them a thing or two. *It takes less courage to criticize the decisions of others than to stand by your own*, for instance. Good advice. Attila the Hun said it, and he ransacked half of Europe! But to some people ignorance is a sleeping mask they mistake for corrective lenses. They'll quote me on that someday.

The two sons smoke as if desperate to commit suicide but only by emphysema. Their mother only lets them smoke in the bathroom, which they've filled with a black-and-white television, a broken boom box, a dozen ashtrays, and a sawed-in-half sofa. It looks like something between an outdated disco and the office of a pornographer who's seen better days. When I asked on my first morning if they might leave so I could use the facilities, their eyes became death rays. The bathroom was a foreign land whose culture and traditional way of life I was oblivious to. I backed out with my hands raised and eyes lowered. I spent most of my time in St. Petersburg, the most beautiful city on earth, searching for an unoccupied toilet.

One of the finest I came across in my wanderings was in a café three blocks from the Teplov Gallery, where Galina had said there'd been an exhibition on Zakharov a year or two back. Yakov walked with me part of the way. He's an excellent listener. Most cats are. Except Siameses, the chatty little bastards. I have human friends, obviously. But everything's easier with a cat. He wants a little fish soup in a saucer and the occasional scratch on the head. I want the illusion that an animal bred to trade affection for food can understand the inquietudes of my soul.

Yakov had gone to investigate a dumpster by the time I reached the Teplov Gallery. The door handle was a silver bracket. The marble foyer was poorly plagiarized from an imperial summer palace. None of the art would hang above eye level, but the ceiling rose to the lower stratosphere. Even the air tasted imported from a country ranked high on the quality-of-life index.

Behind the ticket counter stood a man as skinny as a soaked poodle. He sported a shirt of swatch-size plaid and a blond ponytail that, unless destined for a chemotherapy patient, should've been immediately chopped off, buried in an unmarked grave, and never spoken of again. Hipsterdom's a tightrope strung across the canyon of douche-baggery. He clung by a finger.

A few ruble coins glinted on the floor before the ticket counter. Were they just coins, or part of an art installation? The modernists ruined reality for laypeople.

I approached the counter. The temperature was set to meat locker. A couple tourists consulted a cinder-block-size *Lonely Planet*. Banter's the doorway into a stranger's good graces and I entered guns blazing. "Rapunzel, Rapunzel, let your hair down!"

"Excuse me?" the ticket cashier asked.

"I need to ask a bit of a favor," I said, slouching

into the counter. “Not long ago there was an exhibit here on a Chechen painter. I’d like the phone number of the exhibit curator. She lives in Grozny.”

“Fuck off.”

“Thank you, but no, just her number would be fine.”

Had I lived a life well watered with affection, I might not have withered under his arid stare. Before I could mount a fuller defense, I met the grim glare of an Orc in a security guard’s suit. Our atoms must’ve been polarized like repulsing magnets, because for every step he took toward me, I involuntarily took one toward the door. As much high culture as a prison weight room, that museum.

The door swung closed behind me. The problem with rejection is that it feels imposed even when it’s earned. I told that to Yakov. He was perched on a yellow Citroën. He hopped down, scampered to me, and rubbed his pebbly nose on my shoes. Life’s little pleasures are the consolation of the paupered. But Yakov’s nose on my shoe, his hot purr up my pant leg, well, you take your triumphs where you can.

I should’ve gone to class, but I hadn’t gone once this term and didn’t want to confuse the professor by showing up. If I’d devoted as much brainpower to finishing school as I had to staying in school, I’d probably have a Nobel by now. I’d become one of those prisoners you read about who’s lived locked up so long that he tries to break in once he’s been let out. Who in their sane mind would ever want to leave?

Yakov followed me across the street and through eight blocks of midday monotony.

A vacant-eyed man studied a tram schedule under

Plexiglas, but it was clear that no map could show him where he was headed.

Elderly women who hadn't smiled since Gorbachev was general secretary queued outside the post office. They wore overcoats in midsummer, distrustful of every source of authority, even the calendar.

Up ahead, a supermodel as lean and pointy as a stiletto stared right at me. She was probably part of a stylish *Ocean's 11*-like con. She'd size me up and see I was perfect for the role of the dumpy clown whom the whole crew rallies around when George Clooney gets distracted by his charity work. We'd rob a Dubai emirate blind. I'd give my cut to starving orphans because I don't do it for the money. I do it for the thrill. She'd leave George Clooney and we'd live forever in the desolate beauty of a Malaysian beach. Drinking mai tais for breakfast would never get old. Roll credits.

"Your zipper's down," she said as she passed me.

Endurance, I reminded myself, is the true measure of existence.

Back home, I disinterred the painting from its bubble wrap for the first time since returning from Moscow. The canvas itself was hardly larger than a sheet of notepaper. This is where Kolya died. I'd known that, obviously, for several weeks, but seeing it there I flinched. I set the canvas on the shelf between the two pickle jars holding my parents' ashes. Rather ghoulish, but family reunions usually are. I was twenty-eight years old, too old to be an orphan, but too young to be the sole survivor of the Kalugin tribe. Good God, I was probably expected to carry on the family name. Never has so much been asked by so many of someone who has so little.

Behind my mother's jar hung the Black Sea postcard. For years I've been telling her I'd scatter her ashes there.

The whole scene freaked me out and I called Galina.

"Yes?" she said.

"It's Alexei."

"Who?"

"Alexei Kalugin. Kolya's brother."

"*Who* gave you this number?"

"You did."

A crestfallen sigh. "I really am my own worst enemy. What do you want?"

Everything, now, without working, waiting, or doing. "Just to talk, I guess," I said. "I'm looking at the Zakharov. I've propped it up next to the jars holding my parents' ashes."

"You should get in touch with my husband. Ex-husband, now. He's always looking to add another psychopath to his staff."

"The divorce went through?"

"It did."

"I'm sorry."

"Oh, it's only a legal formality. In our hearts, we've been living in different time zones for years. I'm moving back to Kirovsk."

"In your heart?"

"No, you dimwit. In an airplane."

"Why?"

"What else can I do?" A slow sigh of resignation leaked from her. "Let's be honest, I haven't been seriously considered for a part in years, and now that I've fallen from political favor, I'd be lucky if *Deceit Web* is still bootlegged. Besides, it'll be nice for Natasya to grow up outside Moscow. Kirovsk isn't that bad, is it?"

It's a poisoned post-apocalyptic hellscape. "It's a wonderful place to raise a family."

"You mean it?"

"I don't lie to anyone"—present company excluded—"You can stay in the museum, if you need to. No one's lived there since Kolya left."

She snorted so loud I worried she'd choked. "You are a dear, but no, thank you. Oleg's lawyers still haven't seized my dignity. Though no doubt it's next on their agenda."

"I went to the Teplov Gallery," I said, tacking into unclear waters. "I tried to get the number of the people in Grozny you bought the painting from."

"What ever for?"

"I was thinking I'd talk to them. About the place where Kolya died."

"A picture's worth what, a thousand words? More than that, if you're to judge by the reams of shoddy copy on Lindsay Lohan's crotch shot. Besides, I *gave* you the painting so that you *could* see where he, well, you know."

"I know, it's just that . . ." The sledgehammer of epiphany swung cranium-ward. "It's just that I was thinking I'd go there."

"Don't be a fool."

Far, far too late.

"I was thinking I'd go there," I went on, "to the hill where Kolya died. It's the last place he was. I'll go there. I'll actually do it. I'll stand where he last stood and see what he last saw."

"What ever for?" she asked again.

I looked to the two pickle jars. I'd never received Kolya's remains. I told her I wanted to go there, to the plot of land where he died, and fill a pickle jar with the dirt.

"Well, maybe you should," she said.

"Really?" I couldn't recall the last time I'd actually acted on my daydreams.

"What do you want?"

"What kind of question is that?"

"I'm serious, Alexei. The life expectancy of a man from Kirovsk is, what, forty or fifty years? You've burned through half of that already. What do you want from the rest?"

"I want to be quotable."

"What?"

My blush was hot enough to soften the receiver. "I'm studying philology and I don't even like reading. At least not books. I mean, why read a book when you can sum up the point in a pithy little line? I like sayings, fortune cookies, single-serving packets of wisdom. But you have to be famous or climb Mount Everest or something for people to take you seriously as an aphorist."

"You want to be a professional aphorist?"

"Well, yes."

"Jesus, Alexei. You were always a sweet kid, but you're not a kid. Go to Chechnya. Go somewhere. Do something."

Turning *I would* to *I did* is the grammar of growing up.

6

Kolya's story collided into Galina's the day he wandered into the school gymnasium/boiler room for an orientation led by the principal, a fleshy man with a neck like a sea lion's. Pig-iron pipes mazed over mattresses, creating an avant-garde gymnastics course of perpendicular bars and unbalanced beams. No one from the men's or women's gymnastics team had ever made it to the Olympics, not for lack of talent, but because they performed like freewheeling jazz soloists in a sport judged by classicists. The principal punctuated his speech with dull jabs of his forefinger. If occupations were assigned by disposition, he'd be the supreme leader of a volcanic island republic devoid of natural resources. On stiff benches that had once populated the gulag canteen, the assembled fourteen-year-olds slouched forward or back, aged by boredom until they resembled, in posture at least, their grandparents who'd once bruised their backsides on those same seats.

When he finished, the principal goose-stepped from the room to a fanfare playing only in his head. Upperclassmen gymnasts had already begun somersaulting on the hot water pipes. The several dozen first-years had begun to stretch and mill about, but Kolya stayed seated. He didn't often feel nervous or bashful, but he was new to this school. He'd been booted from the last one and he knew nobody in this class. The seconds ticked by and Kolya knew he had to do something tough or clever, something that would secure his social standing, because every school must have its outcasts and weirdos, and I know from personal experience that there is no escape from that untouchable caste but suicide or matriculation. Kolya sifted through his frozen insides for a loose leak of the courage and charisma that flowed so freely in my presence. Time was running out. Already his classmates had clumped into bantering clusters soon sealed from outsiders with inside jokes. But right there, several benches away, a lanky, densely lashed girl also sat alone.

His gaze climbed her legs. When he reached her eyes, she'd already seen him.

"I'm Kolya," he managed to say.

"Galina," she replied. Her lips flattened and curved at the ends like something wet that hadn't dried right. It was a smile. His chest unzipped from the inside.

She sat next to Kolya in the dimly lit history classroom. Built during Stalin's purges, our school had originally been a prison, and the bars gridding the history classroom windows cast toothy shadows across the warped floorboards. Galina couldn't sit still. An invisible flame burned beneath her desk chair, too weak to set the wood alight, but strong enough to singe her skin if she sat too long in the same position. She twirled her pencil between her fingers, but her hand–eye coordination was similar to her foot–eye, and it inevitably tumbled to the side of the desk she couldn't reach. Kolya retrieved it.

"Thanks," she whispered.

"It's nothing."

A peculiar intimacy grew from the daily transaction of recovered pencils. It became a game. The pencil somersaulted from Galina's slender fingers, while Kolya watched with a throb building at the base of his throat. The front of the room, where the teacher expatiated on the conquests of dead European empires, was as distant as the medieval battlefields themselves. He overlayed his fingerprints on hers, making himself the willing collaborator to any crime in which the pencil might be used. He held it by the point and she accepted it by the rounded rubber eraser, leaving its yellow length between her fingertips and his. As the pencil shortened with each sharpening, Kolya's fingertips came closer to hers, until one splendid day they touched. On that day, Kolya asked Galina if she wanted to go for a walk.

November winds skewered loose newspaper to bent flagstaffs, imprinted grit on windshields, inscribed the corona of smelters whose furnaces were the sole reason for our life in the Arctic. Clad in heavy layers, Galina looked twice her true width. They sauntered to the center of the Twelve Apostles along the gravel road that lassoed the silvered lapping of Lake Mercury. The gravel had stiffened to a frigid corpse on which Kolya fixed his eyes to avoid the face of the young woman so near he felt her heat signature like a phantom of spring sun.

She told him how much she hated the ballet, how terrible a dancer she was, and Kolya took her mittened hand in his own. He placed his right hand on the small of her back, pressing through the layers until she fell toward him, into him. He made fingerholds of the valleys of her vertebrae.

"*Bum Ba-da-da Dum Bum, Dum Dum Dum*," he trumpeted. It took her a moment to find in his atonal exhilaration the melody from the first march of *The Nutcracker Suite*. By the time she did, she was already cantering, cratering the frost.

"What are you doing?" she asked. Dance was supposed to be choreographed, rehearsed, and sterilized until its most trivial imperfections had been obliterated along with any vestigial joy, and performed to silent, judgmental audiences. It wasn't spontaneous. It was never fun. "This is a march," she stammered. "You don't waltz to a march."

"I don't even know what a waltz is," Kolya breezed, breaking his a cappella rendition long enough to spin Galina in small circles, dipping her until her hair swished against the gravel. She wanted to weep but she laughed. She joined in when he reprised the march. This feeling of rightness, of belonging-to-ness, it wasn't an idea or a word, but an absence of ideas and words, an airiness where blood and bone had been, right out to her weightless fingers, safely fastened within his in case she floated away.

The Twelve Apostles spouted golden pillars. Shadows widened beyond wedges of electric light.

Kolya entered the chorus with an orchestra of punch-drunk madmen living in him, belting the tune to the velvet yellow, to the misting lake, to the carcinogens no song could dislodge from his capillaries, and in this amphitheater of decimated industry, on this stage of ice and steel, he taught the granddaughter of a prima ballerina to dance.

Around the same time, I fell into a different kind of love. It began when our father sent us to a warehouse across town to conduct a little business for him. Yes, it might have been crime but it certainly wasn't organized. Besides, in Kirovsk the line between crime and business is as slender as an orphan's forearm.

My chilled breath grew and vanished like a unicorn's horn continually poached from my face.

We slogged through a twilight town banked with snow so high the first floors of buildings were their third stories. No street signs or addresses marked that side of the city—a ploy, Kolya claimed, to confuse invading Yankee armies—and we walked for what felt like hours before we heard the music: thunderous drums, shimmering melodies, a bass loud enough to put the beat back in a stopped heart. Around the corner, BMWs idled at the curb, languorous Nordic swans stretched their limber necks, lips tightened on fancy cigarettes, lizard-skin shoes, golden chains, men's shirts stitched of siren light, yawning pupils, noses in their glory days between rhinoplasty and cocaine collapse, nymphs dressed in diamonds large enough to fund Third World civil wars, tasteful neon signage hummed over the entranceway: *Dance Party Place!*

A line stretched halfway down the block, but Kolya wrapped his arm around my neck, and we jostled to the front. The bouncer had the flattened, scarred face of a well-loved anvil. He glared at our muddy shoes with little admiration. But Kolya could sweet-talk the deaf, and within moments the bouncer had ushered us inside. How to describe the paradise within? In a word, women. The dance floor awash in steel-tipped heels, leather boots gripping sweat-slick calves, skirts small enough to seal inside an envelope. Fake lashes, nails, and breasts that collectively enlarged reality to normalize their obscene dimensions. Coin-thick cosmetics. Flesh coruscating in strobe light with the depilated iridescence of deep-sea invertebrates. Our flat-faced Virgil led us through the swelling sea of bodies, but I wanted to drown, die, live forever, there is no difference, within the sequined sound.

In a shadow-dampened room behind the DJ booth, Kolya spoke with a ladder of a man whose vermillion suit jacket sat on his shoulders as if still on the hanger.

His greased, blond, butter-cleaved hair stood at attention, and I could tell from the way he held his cigarette that he could commit murder on his way to dinner and still have enough appetite to order dessert.

He handed us a brown attaché case and dismissed us with a quick flick of his cigarette. We duckling-waddled behind the bouncer as he left the room.

"Can you introduce me to a woman?" I asked him.

"Which one?"

Let's be honest: It didn't matter. The heat-seeking desire flowing from my heart via my south-lands was indiscriminate in its aim. A woman needed only acknowledge my existence to become the love of my life. I was twelve years old.

"Her." I pointed vaguely to the crowd.

He buckled with laughter. He had to clasp my shoulder to keep himself from falling. I was no more than a serf allowed to glimpse the Winter Palace ballroom before being shoved into the open arms of the communal night. But beneath it all, the bouncer was a deep and empathetic soul. Before he escorted us to the exit by our elbows, he grabbed a black mixtape from the DJ booth and stuffed it in my sagging coat pocket.

The next morning I woke to the sharp scent of vinegar—my father had long been an amateur pickler—and wondered if the previous night had been a mirage baked in slumber. But there, right beside me, on the rickety nightstand, the mixtape soaked in a pool of honeyed daylight.

Kolya was still asleep. I dove beneath his bed and rooted through his library of sexual congress: peach-flesh magazines for every perversion, lusty paperbacks, bodies clothed only in unmarked VHS cases, stalagmites of used tissue, unsent love letters to Galina, and, floating on that sordid sea, a tiny one-shot-size vodka bottle filled with my mother's ashes, which he'd stolen from the jar-urn right after the funeral to save some small part of her from the Black Sea. I unearthed and flung it all behind me until I found his cassette player.

For waking him at that unholy hour, he walloped me with his boot, the first in a migrating flock of projectiles aimed at me over the course of the next few minutes. I sat in bed, facing the wall with my blanket sprawled tent-like over me, locked in the stereophonic groove, oblivious to the storm breaking over my back.

For the rest of my adolescence, the visions promised by *Dance Party Place!* and other dance party places formed the bank into which I deposited the loose change of dreams. The headphones, volume cranked to ten, formed a cocoon nothing could pierce: not Kolya's bullying, not my father's deepening depression, not even my mother's memory, which could sharpen suddenly at the sight of soapsuds, and leave me impaled on sorrow. As if I could just die for the length of a track, slipping into sweet oblivion as my heart took a rest and the bass circulated my blood. I surrendered to the Dictatorship of Dance, the Supreme Soviet of Sound.

I jury-rigged two ancient gramophones into turntables that flaked green gunk in time with the drums. Mixtapes and LPs from Moscow, Petersburg, and Minsk flooded through the post, and alone in my room, I studied track lists like a techno-loving Tatyana Larina. Due to my lacking status and surplus acne, I couldn't hope to pass the face control of a place like *Dance Party Place!*, so I tried crappy discos, basement raves, summer field sets, bad scenes, worse scenes, scenes where contact highs were unavoidable, where you felt way more liquid than solid, where you'd enter a free soul and leave eight hours later having exchanged your shoelaces and short-term memory for bruises on your knees, elbows, and stomach that no one could properly explain. I waited outside the finer venues, bumming cigarettes from DJs and club kids on break. Cigarettes were all I asked for, but they gave me so much more: spare change (sometimes they thought I was a vagrant), the last spittly sips of shared vodka, the mobile numbers of drug dealers and petty criminals, conversations that conveyed the illusion that I was a peripheral star in their cosmos.

Sometime around then, I started making mixtapes of my own.

7

I said good-bye to Galina, hung up the phone, and re-bubble-wrapped the Zakharov before the urgency knifing into my back lost its point. I packed it in the duffel along with a half-dozen mixtapes, my Walkman, toiletries. On further inspection, I added a pair of socks, lucky blue underwear, and a secondhand Speedo.

The rubles in my pocket couldn't get me three Babaevsky bars, so I crept into the hallway to see what I could steal. The stereo rattled the hinges of the closed WC door. A thin thread of smoke unraveled from its keyhole. I centimetered past. A worn leather wallet was passed out on the nightstand in the bedroom the two brothers shared when they weren't sharing the WC. So much money in there it barely fit in my front pocket. I know it's wrong to steal, but it's also wrong to prohibit your lodger from using your bathroom, and everybody knows that wrongs cancel each other out. That's why it's called moral arithmetic.

Back in my room, I scanned my modest belongings. Bottles filled with dusk light stood in the corner. The long-rotting carcass of my academic career sprawled across the desk. A few flyers for raves long past were crumpled in the corner. The whole scene should've made me properly depressed. All I was leaving behind was a mess someone else would have to clean up. Not much of a legacy. There I was, Napoleon's height and I couldn't even conquer the apartment WC. I slipped the two pickle jars into the duffel, the Polaroid into my pocket, and then slipped myself out the door.

I chose the airport over the train station. Trains have too many stops, too many points to turn around. I took a gypsy cab to Pulkovo and for the first time in my life accepted the fare without protest. My blood felt twice as thin and my heart twice as strong as I stepped up to the counter and bought a ticket for the morning flight to Grozny. I spent the night in the terminal between a husband and wife no longer on speaking terms.

The next morning, I waited beside the gangway as boarding began. The harsh fluorescent lighting made everyone look like they'd just donated a liter of plasma. The men, mainly Chechens, ignored the gate agent's increasingly frustrated instructions and stood to one side until all the women had boarded, before boarding themselves, and only then in order of age. Bunch of maniacs. Who'd ever want to wage war against people so insistent on independence they'd rebel against airline boarding procedure? I was seated between a child who mistook my shirtsleeve for a handkerchief and a man who called me a collaborator for complying with the fasten-seat-belt sign. My duffel was safely stowed overhead.

The engines whirled throaty whispers.

The airport smeared gray in the fogged glass.

The tarmac, then the city, then the earth peeled away.

Liftoff.

8

Kolya and Galina met on weekends and after school, using errands, clubs, sports teams, and youth organizations to excuse their absences. Friends believed them deeply involved with family life and family believed them deeply involved with friends, but they were only involved with one another. They shielded the infatuation between them as a secret that would evaporate if exposed to the ultraviolet scrutiny of their peers. They snuck into alleyways, stole kisses beneath staircases, slowed their courtship to a pace of demure caution last seen when frock coats were in fashion. Each clandestine meeting was a new discovery. The nebula of who they were when they were together shifted and reshaped. When Galina learned she could make Kolya laugh so hard he seized with violent hiccups, cured only by drinking water from the far side of the glass, she felt she had fallen down the barrel of a microscope into an intimacy invisible to the naked eye. He hunched over the glass between his knees and made watery chirps as she patted his back. And when he discovered she prepared for bed as if sleep were a contact sport—hair braided, herb mask applied, ground-down mouth guard inserted, ears plugged—he teased her mercilessly, and she slid the sheet over her face in embarrassment, and he didn't stop, and she laughed so hard the sheet dampened with tears, and then he started hiccuping.

One summer night, when the twilight sunbathed the Arctic in a dull white wonder, they hitched a ride south on a departing river ferry. A biological dead zone, sixty kilometers in diameter, encircled the Twelve Apostles, but once they crossed the sixty-kilometer threshold, the bleached land gave way to dried grasses listing in the breeze. They disembarked to a long wooden dock. They peered through the gaps left by rotted planks and found their river-washed faces fragmented, dispersed, and reassembled in ripples. They crossed the bank and climbed a slope studded with the twiggy skeletons of dead shrubs. On the far side the land plateaued into a field of wildflowers peeking through thawed tundra.

"I love Galina!" Kolya yelled. Without buildings, walls, or topographical rises to echo his call, the words passed over the bulging blue flower heads and disappeared over the horizon.

She reflexively glanced behind her, fearing someone, anyone, might hear Kolya's declaration. She had grown up in a city where history did not exist, where you kept secret what was real to prevent its erasure. But no one stood behind them.

When they entered their last year of secondary school, Galina came up with a list of potential career choices: schoolteacher, cashier, secretary. Beauty queen wasn't on the list. *Beautiful* wasn't an adjective she attached to herself. Okay, she was tall and thin, that she would admit, but she had feet that could fill clown shoes and broad eyebrows sloped into an obtuse angle of cartoon disappointment. Some days she felt her face was the caricature of someone else's. She took self-portraits with a rust-rimmed Zenit rented by the hour from the proprietor of the city's sole darkroom. The camera timer gave Galina ten seconds to cross the room and drape herself liquidly across the divan. The desire to pose in every angle and light arose not from vanity, but from the vacuum where vanity should be. She lay supine and the shutter snapped. She stood high-cheeked, pouty, and the shutter snapped. She seduced the aperture, but when studying the developed photographs, she couldn't seduce herself. The photographs confirmed what she already believed: All that was admirable in her lay between her neck and her ankles.

Kolya tried to convince her otherwise. Every Saturday morning he climbed six flights of ash-stained stairs to her flat. Those few A.M. hours, when her father was at work, were the only hours of the week they spent alone together in a flat with a bed. She left the front door unlocked for him and he pushed it gently. Model battleships crowded the living room bookshelves. He crossed the threadbare carpet scripted in faded flowers. Galina stood at the kitchen sink, her hair aloft in a messy bun, her fingers ten splinters of heat in the frigid air. Window light washed out her skin into a peroxided canvas on which she would later apply her features with eyeliner and lipstick. He stood behind her and felt the whole of himself contract around the shiver of her voice. She was wrist-deep in soapsuds. He ran his hands down her forearms, through the blinking bubbles, finding hers in the gray dishwater. Entire minutes passed in a gentle sway.

Then, later, her bedroom. Old rugs hung from the walls for insulation. The floor was twice carpeted, once with rugs, and again with their scattered clothes. Kolya kissed her wide eyebrows, her neck, every square centimeter of her nose. The parts she mentally amputated were the ones he most adored. Beneath the sheets they were pale and naked and they pouched their hands in the warmth between their stomachs. They pressed together with a need that is never satisfied because we can't trade atoms no matter how hard we thrust. Our hearts may skip but our substance remains fixed. We're not gaseous no matter how we wish to cloud together inseparably. Nothing less would have satisfied Kolya, nothing less than obliterating himself in her was sufficient.

They rarely used prophylactics. Galina was two months pregnant when a white postcard striped with a red, declarative diagonal arrived for Kolya. As far as I know, it was the first piece of mail he'd ever received. It ordered him to report to the Department of Conscripts and New Recruits for his physical within three days.

What followed in the days leading to his deployment: carousels of conversation that never stopped moving forward and never arrived anywhere; professions of fidelity; self-pity shaping to every vessel it filled; the kind of reassurances that promise everything and therefore mean nothing. One afternoon, Kolya proposed to Galina in the vegetable aisle of the *produkti.* He dropped to one knee, pulled a rubber band from his pocket, and wrapped it around her ring finger. She said yes, not because it was something she wanted, but because he was on his knees, begging her.

A half an hour at the civil registration office was all that was necessary; in those days, marriage and divorce didn't take much time or effort. But they postponed it until no time remained. He spent the Saturday morning before his deployment at her flat. The bedsheets nested at their feet. They projected hypotheticals that hardened to reality in Kolya's mind over the coming months: a shared family, a shared future.

"It will only be two years and I'll be back," Kolya said, staring up at the paint-fissured ceiling. "Two years is nothing. And if you have twins, that's an automatic deferment."

"You say that like a grandfather would say it."

"What do you mean?" He rolled over and pulled the sheet over their heads so they lay in semi-darkness with the freckles on their noses nearly touching. If they could just stay like this, sealed from the world beneath a pink cotton bedsheet. If they could just hit pause and cocoon themselves in this moment. They passed back and forth a single breath that grew heavier with each exhalation.

"I mean if we were sixty or seventy years old, two years would be nothing. You're eighteen. Two years is forever. If we get married, have the child, get divorced as soon as it's born, you might get a deferment."

"You might have twins. Then we wouldn't have to get divorced at all."

"Either way, there'd be a child."

"What are you trying to say?"

She sighed. "You hear what I'm saying, even if you're not listening."

"It's just two circles around the sun, then I'll be back," he said, a shaky sweetness to his voice. "The little guy will be a year and a half old by then. We'll find a flat of our own. You and me and the little one. I'll get a job at the smelter and you could give ballet lessons."

She wove her fingers through his. There was such tenderness, such mercy to her lie, that Kolya took it as truth. "Of course. We will," she said.

At the time, I was still making mixtapes. My favorite cassettes were the Assofoto MK-60s because they came in bitching grapefruit pinks and sherbet oranges; plus you'd feel like James Bond because they were so poorly made they'd disintegrate after one listen. Free advice: When purchasing a tape deck or preamp, you *want* a fake, so don't forget to bring a knife with you. You need to pop off the back and scrape the black paint and stenciled Cyrillic from the superconductors. If you see Asian-looking letters beneath, you're golden. Japanese is best, but Korean, even Chinese, will do. If there's no foreign lettering, then it really is genuine Russian-make, and it's more likely to roast your loved ones in an electrical fire than to play Cybertron's *Clear* all the way through.

But my prized possession was a Maxell XLII-S 90-minute cassette, still swathed in golden shrink-wrap. It took me forever to save enough pocket change to afford it—at least five weeks—and I held it like Michelangelo would a hunk of Carrara. For the longest time, I didn't use it, didn't even open it for fear of squandering the potential coiled within that plastic case.

I showed up at Galina's one afternoon. Her father answered the door, his fingers tinny with model battleship paint. Galina emerged from her room a moment later in an oversized sweater and staticky hair, still so unbelievably unaware of the celebrity she'd become. "I want to make a tape for Kolya to take with him. I need your help," I said, and showed her my Maxell. We got to work.

I gave him the mixtape the morning of his departure. We stood across the street from the military commissariat. He and Galina had said their good-byes the night before. He held the mixtape in both hands and read the label. *For Kolya, In Case of Emergency!!! Vol. 1.* A teary glaucoma kept clouding my eyes.

"I don't have a tape player," he said.

"It's okay," I said.

"It's okay," he repeated.

"Come home." I barely got it out.

He pulled me to him. I knotted my fingers at the base of his spine and squeezed him hard enough to imprint a bruised blueprint of his bones on my flesh.

"The world is ending," he said.

"Don't die," I said.

"The imperialist warheads will land soon."

"You will have the last word."

"Your name will be that word." He tapped the mixtape case on my forehead. "And when my time comes, when I'm way out there in space, I'll be listening."

9

I arrived. The Grozny terminal was gray-gloss new. The airport gift shop sold knives. Women who'd left their hair bare in flight donned silky, candy-bright headscarves. The baggage claim was a closet passengers entered one by one. Judging from the well-armed luggage attendant at the door, I wasn't at all convinced they'd reemerge. It was about ten million degrees outside and my underwear had bunched into a sweat-swamped thong. Directly across the asphalt, the midday sun poured across the golden cupolas of a mosque.

The road stretching along the airport was empty. The men lugging suitcases all wore tasseled skullcaps and slack, pajama-y things. Any one of them could've starred as the villain in a grainy hostage video. Maybe the souvenir knives in the airport gift shop were meant for arriving tourists. I fidgeted until a slender, clean-shaven man about my age pushed through the exit doors. His long limbs piped through the sleeves of a tight, 1960s mod-style suit either teetering at the cutting edge of fashion or plunged somewhere far over the cliff. As a general rule, people in suits are more likely to take advantage of you than people in pajamas, but Chechnya requires you to reevaluate deeply held assumptions.

"You going into town?" I asked.

He gave me a *well-what-do-we-have-here* head tilt. His hair was slicked back into a glistening helmet. "Maybe. You're not from around here, are you?"

Didn't know I'd be such a dead giveaway. "Listen, I'm just looking for a lift. I thought there'd be a metro or at least a bus or taxi or something. Can I get a ride with you?"

"Are you FSB?" he asked, then examined my haircut and found his answers. "Of course not. FSB would never payroll someone with his name shaved into his head."

"I'm growing it out. So can I come?"

His shrug said he didn't much care either way. I followed him to his Lada. I went to put on my seat belt. "This is Chechnya," he said, in a tone of bafflement, pity, and maybe even a little wonder. "You don't need seat belts."

"You're coming from Petersburg too?" I asked. I knew I wasn't actually in danger of abduction. I also knew it's important to build a rapport with your captor.

"Just connecting through. I live in London."

"London?"

"Yeah, I'm getting my master's at LSE."

"That's the London airport?"

He smiled. "London School of Economics." Suddenly I was the yak-humping bumpkin from the Republic of Whogivesafuckistan and he was, well, the kind of person I wanted to be.

"I'm Alexei, by the way."

"Akim."

"So in London, have you seen the queen?" I asked.

"Only in my wallet."

The road doglegged, as if the paver billed by the meter and was deeply in debt. Our fellow drivers took the lane markers as well-intended but misguided suggestions they freely ignored. I don't know how we managed to a) stay alive, and b) make such good time, given we were mainly headed into oncoming traffic.

An owlish man walked along the roadside with closed eyes and leathery beak aimed sunward. His jagged grin was a pink miniature of the half-eaten watermelon slice in his hand. Speed-chilled air flooded through the cracked window, wonderful on my face.

We passed a massive billboard with a stern and puffy-chested Vladimir Putin standing beside a younger guy with a cropped beard. The two stood in a misty mantle of white, blue, and red patriotism.

"Didn't think I'd see him down here," I said, pointing to Putin.

"To the victor go the advertisements."

"So it seems. I can't even tell what's being advertised. Steely resolve?"

"You can't go out for an ice cream without passing two dozen posters of Putin." He said it like he'd really kept count. "Even a Magnate Gold sours under a dictator's glassy gaze. Ridiculous, really. Imagine going to Baghdad and finding George Bush's weaselly mug on every street corner?"

The guy next to Putin was Ryan Gosling from a parallel universe where instead of becoming a famous actor, he smoked too much weed, ate potato chips for breakfast, and was dressed by his grandmother. "Who's he?"

"I take it you're not a journalist?" he asked. I couldn't tell if he actually wanted to know. A question mark can turn any innocent sentence into an accusation.

"I'm a university student, technically."

"That's President Kadyrov. Very popular. He received a hundred and two percent of the vote last election."

"I've never been good at math."

"You might have a future as an election overseer."

We swerved out of the broad headlights of an oncoming truck. "You haven't seen his Instagram?"

"That's where I recognize him from! He's the one with all the photos posing with tiger cubs and ducklings and kittens!"

His brows bunched over dirty-copper irises. Never seen such a grim response to baby animals. Maybe petting a duckling's the final taboo down here.

"You're not from around here either, are you?" I asked.

A tractor towing bushels of green-sheathed corn cobs trundled along the shoulder.

"Yes and no." His volume knob in his throat had dialed down to movie-theater whisper. "I was born just outside of Grozny. But in 1994, just a kid, I was sent to Holland as a refugee. A lot of tea glasses had to be sweetened to make it happen. My parents could only afford to send one of us and I was the youngest. Lived there a long while, and even now I speak Dutch much better than Chechen."

"So are you staying in London after you graduate or going back to Holland?"

A low wind peeled a gauze strip from the underbelly of a cloud.

"Of course I'm moving back here."

Fifteen minutes later, he nodded to an empty field. Shards of concrete grew where grass should've been. "I lived there," he said.

"Where?" I asked.

"Exactly," he said.

Another few minutes passed, and he said, "All I'm trying to say is don't trust someone who posts photos of himself playing with puppies and kittens online.

Chances are, they're sociopaths. You know who loved little animals?"

"You want me to name names?"

"Adolf bloody Hitler," he snapped. "He was even a vegetarian. And look at the mess he made."

White-orange flapped atop a flare stack.

A blackbird cursored across the blue screen of sky.

I made a note to more carefully curate my Facebook profile pics.

Grozny was the cleanest city I'd ever seen. Its walls weren't old enough to have seen a hoodlum's paint can. The mortar between bricks was still white. The streets must've been swept hourly. Sapling-shaded promenades unfurled down wide boulevards. A Japanese sushi bar called Mafia advertised a *bizniz* lunch of pho, Thai green curry, and a fortune cookie. In 1995 when Kolya was deployed for the first time, then in 2000 when he returned as a contract soldier, I'd read every newspaper and magazine feature on the war I could find. The Grozny in those photos was a 1944 Dresden look-alike. The Grozny in the windshield was Dubai. In the city center five glass skyscrapers huddled together.

"I didn't think it would look, well, so city-like," I said.

"What did you expect?" Akim asked. Before I could answer, he nodded to a squat gray building of vaguely defined bureaucratic provenance. "First floor's the art museum," he said.

On the ride in, I'd told Akim about my brother and the painting, altering the details just slightly (in my version, Kolya was a human rights worker). Risky move, maybe, but I hadn't thought any of this through and he seemed about as trustworthy a character as I could hope to find. He'd just nodded with the glazed-over indifference of someone subjected to detailed narration of another person's dream. I guess our lives are all dreams—as real to us as they are meaningless to everyone else. He said he'd help, until four o'clock at least.

We parked and entered the museum. It was clogged with paintings and empty of patrons. The docent's face bathed in the glow of her blocky Nokia cell phone. Her narrow brown eyes met ours when we walked in. I remembered those long winter afternoons at the ticket counter of the Kirovsk Cosmonautics Museum when the sudden appearance of a museum visitor was cause for celebration and alarm.

"Yes?" Her voice rose a half octave toward suspicion. She couldn't've been older than eighteen or nineteen. Her hair was covered in an electric-pink headscarf that obeyed the letter of the law while exorcizing its spirit.

"I have something to return," I began and pulled the canvas from the duffel bag. She inhaled sharply. She looked from me to the canvas and then back as if we were two mismatched puzzle pieces she couldn't fit together.

"You've seen this before?" I asked.

Her Nokia buzzed on the table in a universe far from us. She nodded.

I pointed to the dacha in the painting. "Do you know where this plot of land is?"

"The man this belongs to, he lives there now."

While she showed Akim the route on a Yandex map, I circled the museum. The earliest date I found etched into the display placard thingies was 2003. Most were portraits of the family Kadyrov. In several, the president cuddled calico kittens.

The Lada's rear tires ejected dusty rooster tails, but the car wouldn't budge. I checked my phone. Zero bars. Anywhere beyond reach of MegaFon cell service is well beyond the sight of God. The roads had broken, disintegrated, and washed away the farther from Grozny we'd come. Here, somewhere in the southern mountains, what we referred to as "road" was in fact "impending landslide." The wide green bowl of valley stretched down the ridge. Akim floored the accelerator. The motor *vhrooooomed* but gravity pulled harder than the engine pushed.

"I think this is it," Akim said. A clear sheen of perspiration mustached his upper lip. He still hadn't loosened his thickly striped ash and navy necktie.

"I can't believe we made it this far." And I couldn't. Given the state of the car I was surprised it didn't explode into a Michael Bay finale every time Akim punched the accelerator.

"This"—he glanced to the line of white rocks weaving up the ridge—"whatever this is, isn't on the map. But I reckon we're only four or five kilometers away. You start walking now, you'll probably get there in a few hours."

"Thanks," I said. "And thank you for taking me around, particularly when you're just getting home."

"It's nothing. It's been nice, actually. No one's met me at that airport before."

"It's not nothing. I'm sure you're busy and have family to see and everything."

He looked away from me. His voice was flat and inflectionless. "That field we passed where I said I'd grown up? That's the last place I saw any of them."

He slid his Ray-Bans up the cliff of his nose. I should've asked for his phone number or email, or even just his last name to look him up on Facebook or VK. I should've told him that my family was gone too. But I was afraid. Even though Kolya had been killed, he wasn't a victim, and neither was I, not really. There was a pause, five seconds when I felt him looking at me as Kolya had in those rare moments when we'd worn through our deceptions. I could've described the loneliness of living far from home, among people you don't know. I could've shown him the jars containing my parents' ashes and he would've understood me entirely. Maybe we would've become lifelong friends. Maybe he was the person I came to Chechnya to meet. I won't know. I just thanked him again, stepped out of the car, and watched him navigate the long, broken road in reverse.

10

In his first tour, from '95 to '97, Kolya was stationed in a remote outpost near the Chechen–Dagestani border where even in peacetime telephone lines and mail routes didn't exist. For the duration of his tour, not a single letter Galina or I wrote reached him. The world he'd left in Kirovsk froze over in his mind. In the absence of news, he imagined our lives, invented daily dramas, small triumphs, conferring on us a peace that didn't exist for him. He couldn't have known about the Miss Siberia Beauty Pageant or Oleg Voronov. He couldn't have known that she made the difficult but prudent decision to end her pregnancy.

In the sigh between battle and resupply, between hitting the ground and falling asleep, he imagined Galina making a crib from an empty dresser drawer. He imagined the bizarre foods pregnancy would give her the taste for. He built and populated an alternate universe that was part memory and part the projected future that day by day he came closer to joining. The child in Kolya's imagined realm was a boy, born on September 3, 1995, seven months to the day after Galina announced she was two months pregnant, weighing a robust three and one quarter kilograms, and named Arkady. He announced it to his platoon, and even though they knew better, they congratulated him with handshakes and backslaps. A year later, he celebrated his son's first birthday by wedging an upside-down matchstick into a stale biscuit.

Galina and I had repeatedly submitted written requests to the conscription center, but a clerk with no more empathy than the aluminum stool he roosted on filed our requests in the trash. No one knew when, or even if, Kolya would return, and so no one met him at the dock when he did, finally, come home.

The slushy river port was shadowless beneath a noon sun. Passengers heavy of heart, head, and suitcase disembarked, Kolya among them. He scanned the crowd for a familiar face and at last he found one: Galina's, high in the air, on a billboard advertising *Deceit Web*. What was she doing up there? There must be another Galina who looked just like his Galina but couldn't be his Galina because his Galina was at home with their son. His mind had so firmly wrapped around this one single idea of what awaited him that no space remained for what was actually there. He shouldered his duffel bag and kept his eyes fixed on the mud-spattered pavement, refusing to acknowledge the face he'd waited two years to see again.

But Galina was everywhere. On billboards, bus stops, and tabloid covers, advertising everything from facial cream to mineral water. The face he had searched for in Caucasian cloud formations was pixilated across kiosks. The lips that had only made sense when pressed against his own now pouted at the entire city. The nightmare of finding a missing face everywhere is no less horrifying than the nightmare of finding it nowhere, and Kolya trudged through a hometown no less surreal or foreign than the Chechen hamlet he had left.

Most cinemas had gone bankrupt, yet the ticket line for *Deceit Web* wrapped around the block. He stopped to ask a man in a pair of slacks creased every way but the right way the name of the starring actress. The man gave a perplexed frown, and then said, "Galina Ivanova, of course."

"Do you know if she's seeing anyone?"

"Oleg Voronov. They're engaged."

Kolya nodded as if it were only natural to return home after two years to find his fiancée engaged not only to another man, but to the fourteenth richest man in Russia, the boss of Kirovsk, a man who could have any woman in the world, and so of course took the only one Kolya loved. He wanted to melt into the puddle of gray water that was slowly seeping into his boots.

"Does she have a child?" he asked quietly, but by now he knew the answer.

The man shook his head, less at the question than at the idea that anyone alive was still ignorant of the intimate details of Galina's private life. He pulled an oil-stained bandanna from his back pocket and gave a foghorn blow of his nose. "Not yet, though what a baby those two will make. I can't believe you haven't heard of our Galina. Everyone knows her."

When he arrived at the museum, I wanted to shout, leap, proclaim, but with one look at Kolya's expression I knew we wouldn't celebrate. He was a shaving of the person he'd been. I'd always been afraid of him—of his strength, of his disapproval—but seeing his stooped, slender figure in a doorway that had suddenly grown much wider, I realized I'd never before felt afraid of hurting him. At the kitchen table he interrogated me about Galina and I tried to deliver the news as gently as I could, but you can't really shatter someone's life gently.

"It wasn't intentional," I said. Weak consolation. "She tried to write you. We all did. Dad practically bankrupted himself buying postage, just hoping one letter would reach you. We didn't even know if you were alive, Kolya."

He played with a pale little coat button that might've been all that fastened him to the world.

"Where's Dad?" he asked. It was all I could do to nod to the bookshelf, where a second pickle jar had sat for more than six months.

The next day Kolya visited Pavel Petrukhin, who was to the city drug trade what Oleg Voronov was to its nickel economy. The army had well prepared Kolya for a career as a professional mercenary, and Pavel eagerly hired him. I only learned about it later, when Kolya informed me that I'd be going to university in Petersburg when I graduated from high school. A bribe to a university admissions official meant I was accepted before I even applied. By the time I'd heard about Lydia, Kolya had already disappeared back into Chechnya, this time as a contract soldier. I'd been in Petersburg for less than a year then. He didn't even call to say good-bye.

"Make something of yourself," he'd told me the last time I saw him, when he sent me off to Petersburg. My half-empty duffel bag slouched against my shin. Oily dock water sludged against the piers. The school year would start in ten days. I'd never been below the Arctic Circle. He put me in a loose headlock and kissed my right ear. "Make something of yourself," he repeated.

11

My legs have become rubber. Bass drum pedals thud-a-thud my temples with every heartbeat. It's like summiting Everest, but without sherpas to carry you. The ridge falls only to rise again, up and down, a bad joke Mother Nature insists on retelling over and over. The air's cooled and dried out at this unholy height. The stony trail's a split scar through the short grass. I'd forswear my immortal soul for a chairlift. But I persist. The rises shorten, the drops deepen, and soon I'm in a valley of green foothills and farmland. A few unsheared sheep laze in the grasses. I wave to them. They don't wave back.

I use the Zakharov canvas as my map, holding it to the horizon to match the topographical contours. A few times I think I'm nearly there, but no, not quite. This is a titanic waste of time. I'll get lost and rebel bandits will chop off my head and donate my vital organs to Saudi charities.

I should probably turn around.

I really should.

But there, up ahead. An apricot tree. A boarded well. A white stone fence. An herb garden. A home. I look back and forth between the real and painted landscapes. The two shouldn't so perfectly correspond, not after two centuries, but they do.

On the hill an adult and child are shadowed within a dissolving orange sunset. Just like the apricot tree, the stone fence, and the herb garden, the two figures silhouetted on the hill match those of the painting.

I wave to them.

I wave again.

I wave a third time.

They wave back.

Side B

Wolf of White Forest

Kirovsk, 1999

NO ONE COULD EXPLAIN WHY THE WOLVES returned in the early years of the newly formed Russian Federation. Biologists arrived with honorifics and plastic binders, departed with unpaid hotel bills and findings so disparate it was a wonder they could agree a wolf had four legs, two eyes, and one nose. Some blamed an irregular cycle of population growth and decline. Some blamed global warming and intense logging of woodlands to the distant southwest. Most blamed their mothers, for one thing or another. Vera had her own theory, but no one thought to ask her.

The wolves howled in White Forest just across the colorless meadow from Vera's house. She stood at the stove boiling water in a saucepan dented sixteen years earlier, when she'd thrown it at a telephone that kept on ringing long after she'd hung up. The kettle had been a gift from her mother-in-law, a direct descendant of Genghis Khan, and Vera had sold it with a set of dull knives and what remained of her daughter's clothes. But the saucepan boiled water as well as the kettle, the knives weren't sharp enough to slice a slab of cold butter, and her daughter's clothes, well, Lydia had moved to the right side of the world and these were difficult times. She strained the *Ivan-chai* into teacups.

"I didn't know you drank such a weak brew," Yelena commented, in the living room, with a thin smile of insincerity stitched between her plump cheeks. Her eyebrows were plucked brown sickles. Every two months she flew business class to Moscow—always bringing a stack of airline napkins as "souvenirs" for Vera—to have her hair recolored, her skin reapplied, and the toxins leached from her body by a Tibetan healer. Not a very good Tibetan healer, Vera would think to herself. If he properly leached all the toxicity from Yelena, there would be no Yelena left.

"I prefer a subtle brew in the evenings," Vera said. It was two in the afternoon. Any more subtle and they'd be drinking straight water. "Otherwise I'd be up all night."

Yelena slinked her arms into her coat sleeves with a slight shiver, which she realized wasn't even theatrical. But there was nowhere she'd rather be. How many times, as a young woman, had she come to Vera cold, hungry, impoverished? How many times had Vera subjected her to audiences no less humiliating than this? Grand Inquisitors had treated heretics with more clemency than Vera had treated her closest friend. So yes, Yelena had every right to enjoy this. She would've conjured more empathy for Vera's present difficulties had they not been her own so often in the past.

The furnace glowered at Vera from her late husband's favorite corner of the living room. Even broken it wasn't quite as useless as he had been—if nothing else, she could hang wet stockings over it—but for two weeks now, it had produced no more than a stray cat's body heat.

"You know it's been hard recently," Vera began. She steepled her fingers to catch and shelter some vestige of fleeing dignity. "If prices keep going up at this rate they'll look like postal codes soon. What once bought bread for a month, now buys half a loaf. My pension stays the same and even that they don't bother paying half the time."

"The economic shock treatment has hurt the weakest members of society," Yelena pointed out. "Not just you. Also the enfeebled and alcoholic."

The shadow of her collected Gorky was dust-etched into the empty bookshelf. The leather-bound set had gone for less than the kettle. "Please, Yelena. Can your son help me?"

"Pavel?" She only had one son. "I wouldn't want to bother him with something like this. You know how busy he gets."

They both knew that in the end she would help Vera. In the end, they always helped each other. Yelena relented. "I'm going to Pavel's for dinner this Sunday. If the subject comes up, I'll ask if he has work."

"Thank you." Vera said it as nicely as she could, but the cold condensed her gratitude into a curse. After Yelena left, she washed up. She'd been born in this house sixty-three years earlier and intended to die here: It was one of her few life goals that she still had time to achieve. There was coherence in exiting by the same door through which you entered, bookending with order this senselessly churning existence.

In bed, she prayed for that mercy. One night as a girl, huddled in that same bed with her parents for warmth, she'd seen them bow their heads and speak a formal language whose wide vowels yawned with wanting. They had thought she was asleep. A half-century had passed—and with it the Soviet Union, Marxism-Leninism, the infallible tenets of communism that had undergirded her faith—and now she found herself the citizen of a nation politically enfeebled and spiritually desolated enough to permit prayer to an authority more omnipotent than its government. But how do you trade your gods so late in life? Six decades of Soviet-speak had left her vocabulary crowded with slogans. She had little practice articulating the complexities of individual desire.

Now Vera closed her eyes and imagined the sound of wolves carrying her to sleep. Before there had been a gulag, a mine, a city, there had been wolves. An early scientific expedition had reported multiple encounters with a roving pack that had never before encountered prey as portly and pusillanimous as academics. Ten of the thirty-two geologists who had discovered the first nickel vein had been killed by wolves in 1928. In the late 1930s, when engineers had hastily assembled a gulag around the nickel mine, the Red Army had hunted the wolves nearly to extinction. It became well established in university biology departments that wolves were the capitalist imperialists of the animal kingdom, and so the army went to great lengths to be rid of them. But the wolves had returned during the Great Patriotic War, when all Red Army units had been sent southwest to face encroaching panzer divisions. Wages had been paid in hunks of bread measured to the grain and gram. Vera had watched her parents and neighbors scavenge to survive. After the war, people had resumed killing wolves and Kirovsk had returned to silence.

Now, curled beneath heavy blankets, Vera remembered when the howling of wolves had signaled a coming hunger.

The year of the German invasion had been the high point of Vera's life. That year she was extolled in schools, newspapers, and radio broadcasts from Minsk to Vladivostok. In the official version, Vera had witnessed her mother break into the commissariat canteen, pledge loyalty to Trotsky, and abscond with a hundred kilos of flour and a dozen live chickens stuffed in a sack. *Pravda* praised Vera for immediately reporting her mother's treason to a commissar. "My mother is an enemy of the state and an enemy of the people," she said, to which the commissar replied, "Though the state and the people are one and the same, you are the hero of both."

In reality, the hoard was no more than a pouch of powdered eggs, a palmful of flour, and a cube of butter. The collaboration was not with the fascist enemy, but with Vera herself, who had dwindled to a bony thing made of stool legs and billiard cues. Despite swearing secrecy, Vera had boasted to Yelena about the small pie her mother had baked for Vera's birthday. There had been no sugar in it, but nothing in her young life had ever tasted sweeter. Yelena had whispered it to another girl and soon the story had swept through the class, then the school, then the city, a rumor that grew more virulent with each host it infected. Kirovsk had only one mailbox for postal mail, but several hundred mailboxes for denunciations. To send a letter, you'd have to walk to the central post office and wait in line for the better part of a morning; to send a denunciation, you wouldn't need to leave your factory, school, or apartment block.

By the time the tale had reached the town commissar, it seemed perfectly plausible for a starving woman to carry off a hundred kilos of flour and a dozen live chickens that never existed, all while reciting Trotsky speeches verbatim. The commissar, of course, knew such a story was sheer lunacy, but he'd ascended to the rank of commissar by welcoming the lunacy the world so graciously handed him.

"You really believe I used a hundred kilos of flour for a single pie?" Vera's mother asked in her defense at the trial.

"Profligacy," the commissar replied, "is characteristic of the fascist." Five years later, when the commissar was stripped of his rank and sentenced to the mines, he learned for himself that a malnourished body is incapable of carrying a hundred kilograms of anything, including the nourishment it needs. A certain amount of flour had in fact gone missing from the gulag reserves over the course of several months; had Vera investigated the town archives during glasnost, she would have learned that it had all gone to the commissar's wife. The archives give no evidence of chickens, alive or dead, in Kirovsk in the summer of 1941.

Vera's mother sent letters from her cell that eventually became a history classroom where the curiosity and childish wonder of several generations of Kirovsk schoolchildren would asphyxiate in the leaden air. The letters, which went by way of the commissar's office, took more than a week to cross the three hundred meters to Vera's home. Each was folded into a triangle and let in the cold air as it fell through the mail slot. A censor's marker striped her mother's crimped handwriting. Piecing together meaning from the few uncensored words became an exacting lesson in how little she knew her mother.

On October 21, 1941, soldiers young enough to still check their cheeks each morning for pimples marched her mother into the wilderness, where she received her sentence from the barrel of a gun.

Vera's father, a prison guard demoted to custodian after his wife's arrest, led Vera into what would become White Forest. He wasn't a cruel or vindictive man—he would later be eulogized by former inmates as a prison guard whose kindnesses had saved dozens of lives—but he felt he had the responsibility as a father and bereaved widower to show Vera the repercussions of her careless words. They wandered for two hours without speaking. He'd nearly given up, nearly turned for home, when his hands dropped to his sides. There she was, his wife, his dear. Cigarette ends lay among snowy paw prints. Wolves had already found the body. Vera hid before the scene in a bony crouch as her father buried the remains. When he finished, he collected the cigarette ends. Those ends would haunt him more forcefully than the bits of viscera he had gathered from as far as fifty meters from the execution site and buried in an unmarked grave. He would never smoke again.

The mail slot clattered a week later and Vera found a letter. For a brief, spectacular moment, she was able to believe that her mother was still in jail, that the sentence hadn't been carried out yet, that the corpse ringed by paw prints belonged to someone else's mother. The letter was dated ten days prior. In it, her mother wrote: *I have been given—years without—to correspondence———the last——receive———. Ten years——————and when———you will—old, a woman——children and——————.*

Various journalists approached Vera over the years and she parroted lines about duty, sacrifice, and patriotism. She accepted honors from the Young Pioneers, the Komsomol, the electricians' and ironworkers' trade union, despising all, refusing none. "The world will give you pig shit," her mother had once told her. "The secret to a happy life is learning to accept it as pork sausage." On account of her heroism in defense of the people, Vera was upgraded to a commissar's rations and her father was reinstated to his former position. She didn't have to worry about hunger for many years.

Yelena's son found work for Vera. Once a week Pavel's men arrived with two duffel bags and Vera left for the day. That was it, just leave for the day and don't ask questions. She'd expected jewel-festooned thugs, but Pavel's wiry underlings looked like boys adrift in the seas of their fathers' rumpled shirts. Between them they had a combined spoken vocabulary of perhaps two dozen non-scatological words. Vera used the time for errands: the town pharmacy for arthritis medicine, the post office to send letters to her daughter in America, the Leninsky Prospekt kiosk for chocolate bars so aerated they could be used as packing material. As winter neared, she felt herself drawn across the meadow stretching from her house to White Forest.

Sheaves of plastic foliage drooped from metal branches, giving the impression that, despite the chill, she stood at the threshold of a melting realm. She followed the tree line for a kilometer. When her knees ached, she spread a shawl on the ground and sat to draft a letter to Lydia. She spoke the sentences aloud to see in her frozen breath their dissipating shapes. If each was perfect she could live in her daughter's imagination more prosperously than she ever could in the new Russia. There are so many paths to contentment if you're open to self-delusion. To that end, she invented stories, built town rumors into fortresses of truth. She wrote that her pension increased each month to keep pace with the hyperinflation, leaving enough in her budget to afford a Korean television. She wrote of compensation, reparations to the victims of state-sponsored terror, that she would finally be compensated for the loss she had, however inadvertently, inflicted upon herself. Justice would prevail in the fertile fantasyland of her Americanized daughter's mind. Daylight had flattened into burgundies across the horizon.

White flour packed the nicks and divots of the kitchen table where the envelope of money lay waiting for Vera when she returned. Pavel's men must be bakers, making good use of her spacious kitchen. A few days later she found powdered infant formula and quinine beneath the sink. Yes, she had an idea of what went on in her absence, but better to not think about those things. One evening she returned to find a man still sitting at the table.

"I'm sorry," she said, rankled by having to apologize for entering her own home unannounced. "Am I early?"

"No, I'll be going," the man replied. A boy, really, though these days anyone who hadn't lived through Stalin was a child to her. Early twenties, the same age as her daughter, the thin gray work shirt and unevenly barbered hair of someone recently released from a grim state institution. The musk of extinguished cigarettes percolated in the heavy air. He sat in a weary slump.

"Stay for a cup of tea," Vera suggested. He looked as surprised to receive the invitation as she felt offering it. Associating with characters of ill repute, at her age! But there was a forlornness about the young man she recognized, a heavy-lidded exhaustion to his expression mirrored in her own.

"I should go." He stood, stretched his limber arms.

"Stay. Have some tea. I have cake."

The man glanced to the front door as if hoping a momentary variance in air pressure might suck him out into the night, then sat down. He'd never know why this woman with eyes too wide for her head and pens sticking from her pockets had shown him insistent, if self-serving, kindness that cool autumn evening. And Vera would never know that eleven hours earlier, the man had watched *Deceit Web* for the one hundred and fifty-eighth time. He'd long ago memorized the dialogue and camera cuts, could replicate the film beat by beat in his mind, was less an audience than a second screen for the film to keep on playing after the final credits rolled. He missed his brother more than he'd ever thought he could miss someone he hadn't exchanged bodily fluids with. He'd bribed a university official, secured his brother a seat at Saint Petersburg State University, saved him from mandatory military service and the unrest in Chechnya. But as he'd waded through snow soup that morning, he had considered his brother, parents, ex-fiancée. Each had taken different exits from his life for which he couldn't reasonably be blamed. Yet he couldn't shake the sense that he was the architect of a city made entirely of off-ramps, all leading away from him.

Vera climbed the stool her father had climbed, and had then stepped from, some thirty-seven years earlier, with a noose around his neck. She rooted through the cupboard, a largely symbolic performance since the cake sat in plain view on the otherwise empty shelf, but she wanted the man to think her pantry was so prosperous a cake could get lost in it. The cake was a thin pedestal on which a monument of pink-striped chocolate frosting towered.

She cut two slices with a spoon. He accepted the pink parade warily.

"Good, isn't it? Would you like some more?" She still took orders from the sweet tooth—an actual tooth, she imagined, her right canine, the only one of her thirty-two natural teeth without a cavity—she'd developed even before she was upgraded to a commissar's rations.

He thanked her as she plopped another massive wedge on his plate. She wanted to ask his name. To have a man for tea and cake without knowing his name was indecorous. Then again, so was renting her house to drug dealers, but she had long ago learned to ignore her largest moral failures by attending to the smallest social proprieties.

"Do you have any children?"

"No."

"Pets?"

"A brother."

"What's his story?"

"His story, well, it's all beginnings," the man said, glancing down. "Still finding his way. Do you have pets?"

"I have a daughter. She lives in America. Married to a man named Gilbert. He is Glendale, California's preeminent *pi-an*—" and here, after the second syllable, the word would normally veer away from reality, but talking to a petty criminal, she felt liberated from the need to lie "—piano tuner."

The man whistled enviously—and the envy of others was the closest she came to feeling proud of Lydia. When asked about her daughter, Vera added rooms to Gilbert's modest condo, added zeros to his salary. She recounted her daughter's life in America just as she wrote of her own in the carefully constructed letters she mailed each month at the city post office—with aggrandized half-truths, little lies that had grown beyond her control. But she didn't fear the judgment of this man sitting before her, licking pink frosting from the back of his spoon.

"She was a mail-order bride," Vera said.

"In a catalog?"

"A catalog. Several websites. She had to pose for pictures in a bikini. A shameful thing."

"Does she eat cheeseburgers and watch basketball?"

"I don't know," Vera admitted. Lonely American men reading Lydia's marriage website profile had had greater access to her daughter's inner life. "She's not particularly forthcoming with me. She's sent six letters in the last year. Mainly to tell me about the weather. Do you know how many types of clouds there are in Glendale? Three. She's described them all."

"America's far away and the only mailman I've ever known would need a map to find his own feet. Many letters must get lost along the way."

"I've told myself that."

"Tell me about this husband. What sort of man is he?"

Vera shook her head. "What sort of man finds his wife in an Internet catalog and still calls himself a man?"

"A trailblazer. In a few years, we'll all be embarrassing ourselves on the Internet."

"You must be around her age. Did you know her?"

"In passing," the man admitted. "I dated one of her friends. Galina Ivanova."

Vera had, like everyone, watched Galina's ascent into stardom. She might've been the only soul in Kirovsk to pity Galina's good fortune. "And do you have a wife?"

"Only a brother."

When the man left the house that evening, he lit a cigarette. He'd wanted one for hours. A few days earlier he'd beaten the gold teeth from an unlucky but persistent gambler who possessed no other form of payment, yet he found himself too sheepish to ask Vera for an ashtray. Snowdrifts darkened in the shadows. The end of his cigarette was the closest thing to a working streetlamp for eight blocks. Behind Vera's house, White Forest loomed. A decade had passed since he'd last walked through it. He'd been a child then, but when he'd shielded his brother's eyes from the execution they had stumbled upon, he'd felt like a father for the first but not the final time in his brief life. His name was Kolya and not long ago he'd returned from Chechnya. In less than a year, he would be back there, where he would spend his final moments planting dill seeds on a mined hill.

Each week Kolya slunk into Vera's house as wordless and grim-faced as his associates. But when she returned eight hours later, she found her new kettle humming with steam, two teacups on the kitchen table, Kolya singing quietly to himself as he cut thick cake slices at the counter. He told her about his brother, the games they had played, rooftop leaps into snowdrifts, the outer-space museum their father had run, which Vera admitted she'd visited several times over the years. He described the heroin trade like a market analyst, cloaking the brutal business in the hazy virtues of laissez-faire capitalism. The cultivation of poppy fields in Afghanistan, the refinement into opium and overland transport through Tajikistan, the whole greased chute of corruption on which heroin simply slid northward, from Kandahar to the Arctic. The Ecuadorian birds Yelena's son collected in his private aviary. The money paid for police protection. When Vera asked, cautiously, why such a big-brained and convivial young person had gotten into this business, he smiled, and said he could ask the same of her. Regardless of what penthouse politicians might say, there was nothing reckless in his logic: Schools had only taught him how to cheat; the military had trained him in ballistics, subordination, and intimidation; he had returned to a mining town where the jobs had become automated and the narcotics business was the only prosperous industry that would benefit from his skill set. For someone in his boots, the drug trade was the only path for economic advancement. She asked if there was a woman in his life since Galina, and he said no, not to speak of, then looked away.

She told him of her husband, who had died, a heart attack, ten years earlier, just after he'd finished brushing his teeth. He had had broad cheeks and a nose that had healed crookedly after a beekeeper's escaped colony chased him, face-first, into a concrete wall. He'd thought they were demons. It was the only time in his life he would see a winged insect fly through Kirovsk. She admitted she had wanted to join Lydia in America, but that Gilbert objected. She admitted writing misleading letters to her daughter in an effort to lure her home. The unfairness of growing old, watching her body lose shape like a snowman in the sun, without relatives to blame, or to provide support, or to bear grievance—it just wasn't right. Now and then, when she thought of her own mother, she felt herself at the edge of a darker injustice, but this she did not confide in Kolya.

"I've heard stories of you as a child," he said one afternoon.

"Everyone has stories from childhood," she said. "You tell me a dozen a day." The first heavy snow had come late that year, and across the field ice encased the corroded branches of White Forest. Kolya sat at the kitchen table and tapped his cigarette into a plastic ashtray.

"None of mine made the front page of *Pravda*."

"I don't want to discuss it," she said. Kolya went to the living room and flipped the channels of the Japanese television he'd brought over the previous week. Of late, he'd spent more and more time with Vera, refilling the kettle far into the evening and coming for dinner on his days off. The few friendships he had all revolved around alcohol, flatulence, and the gleeful inflicting of violence, so in that sense Vera wasn't a friend. She was too warm and caring for him to think of her as a maternal figure. She was simply Vera, a vague but benevolent presence whose approval and affection he wanted to receive as much as she wanted to bestow it.

Vera stood at the stove, frying chicken in a pan still greasy from the morning's eggs, when the mail arrived. A maze of black cancellation marks caged the price of international postage. The envelope edges were worn, but the seal was unbroken. A dozen years earlier, a letter from America would have never reached her without having been read and noted by invisible men in distant offices.

"What is it?" Kolya asked, sensing her disquiet. The letter, sent by land, bore no markings of urgency, but it lay on the coffee table like the gravitational center around which the rest of the room slowly spun. The whole universe of Vera's fear, heartache, and regret was thin enough to fold inside that envelope. With the blunt side of her house key, she opened it and held the letter close to her face. The piano tuner in Glendale had divorced Lydia for a woman in Minsk and Lydia's petition for conditional residence had been denied. She would be back within the month.

Before slipping into bed that night, Vera pulled a shoebox from beneath her bed. It held the money Kolya left her each week, the newspaper clippings praising her denunciation, both letters her daughter had sent from America and the ones her mother had sent from her cell. She flipped through the brittle newsprint because even in their celebration of her betrayal, they were a reminder that she had been young and beloved, that she had not spent her entire life old, alone, and ignored. Five decades had whittled her remorse to pieces of manageable neglect—she had been a child, had been manipulated, innocent in any eyes but her own—and as she flipped through the clippings, she couldn't shake off the disappointment for how ordinary the rest of her life had turned out. She had peaked before her eighth birthday.

The shoebox lay open on the floor beside her as she repeated her mother's prayers. She no longer prayed for life-changing miracles (wealth, forgiveness, new knees), and instead pinned her hopes on day-size miracles (an unbroken sleep, a bakery sale, a rash of adolescent acne blooming on Yelena's cheeks). When she finished, she ran her finger across the broken seal of her daughter's new letter and placed it in the shoebox along with the others. Everything large enough to love eventually disappoints you, then betrays you, and finally, forgets you. But the things small enough to fit into a shoebox, these stay as they were.

Lydia arrived after five days of travel, flights from Los Angeles to New York to London to Petersburg to Novosibirsk, then north by rail, barge, and bus to Kirovsk. She returned with the same suitcase and pleather handbag she'd left with. She had lost two sweaters, a framed photograph of her parents, all faith in online relationships, regular contact with her friends, and replaced that sum with a thorough knowledge of drive-through menus, a few luggage tags, and a bit of a drinking problem. Her mother met her at the station, a little shorter and wider than Lydia remembered. Snow fell on them.

Vera hugged Lydia in the blue kiosk light of a vendor selling Sylvester Stallone VHS tapes, Ukrainian cigarettes, Gosloto tickets. A lighter tied by string to the kiosk crossbar swung in the breeze. Even through the padded overcoat, she felt the narrowness of her daughter's figure.

"You're crushing me," Lydia groaned.

"I know."

The city slid across the soot-mottled bus window. Say what you will about Southern California, but the place had color. Cacti of army-grade green alongside irrigated lawns. The incandescent signage of bodegas and check-cash swindlers. From the air above LAX, bungalow blocks formed interlocking periodic tables of pastels. In New York, she'd said good-bye to green. In London, red. By the time she'd reached Kirovsk, the palette had been scraped of all but the grays and yellows that painted the clouds, streets, snow, and even the vitamin-deficient pallor peeking from her mother's coat collar.

Lydia undressed in her bedroom. A knit hat, outlet-mall scarf, and wool mittens. A winter coat with a detachable hood clinging from half of its buttons. A bright pink sweatshirt with the flared image of a screen-printed elm. Her underwear, to Vera's mind, was far too narrow in back and far too translucent in front. Vera had held this body when it was moments old, had washed, fed, clothed it, and on her best days she couldn't look at her daughter without swelling with self-regard for having given birth to someone so worthy of love. Now that body had grown beyond the jurisdiction of her protection. Though it was rarely deployed in Vera's emotional vocabulary, she could think of no better word than *wonder* to describe the startling closeness of just standing here beside her child. Forget Lydia's poor choices. Forget the demons Vera could only guess at. The very fact Lydia was alive gave her mother the faith to believe she had done this one thing right.

"Where are my clothes?"

"In your suitcase, I imagine," Vera said.

"No, the ones I left."

Vera had been worried both for this conversation and for the possibility that they would never have to have it. The open closet held nothing but bent wire hangers. "I didn't think you'd be back."

Lydia retrieved the elm tree sweatshirt and skinny jeans from the floor and put them back on with a despondency she knew would wound her mother more than anything she said. She had worn these clothes for five days and some seventeen thousand kilometers, she could wear them a little longer.

"Brush your hair," Vera said. "We're having company after dinner."

Kolya knocked on the front door four times, the first two of which sounded timid and hollow, the kind of knock to announce a bellboy rather than a rising gangster, and so he battered the door twice more for good measure. In his other hand he held a bright bouquet of artificial roses tightly wrapped in green tinfoil.

After introductions, Kolya presented Lydia with the plastic flowers. He recognized her as one of the six or seven girls who had had an unhealthy fixation on Galina in school. Galina had never really liked them, and the idea of sleeping with one from their ranks felt like the kind of potent but ultimately meaningless act of self-assertion that appealed to him. She wore a sweatshirt, blue jeans, and no makeup. She didn't even realize this was a date.

"What are these?" she asked, as if she'd never before seen a rose.

"They are made of plastic," Kolya said proudly. "Much safer than real roses. And they will never die."

Still, Vera put them in a vase with water and set it on the living room coffee table. She told them to sit where they wanted, then made sure Kolya sat next to Lydia. She had high hopes for the night. Sure, Kolya was involved with some unsavory business, but it showed ambition, didn't it? Besides, Lydia would only benefit from spending time with a young man who was fond of Vera.

"How do you like being back in Kirovsk?" Kolya asked after they toasted to their health.

"It's exactly as I imagined it would be," Lydia said. She looked to Vera. "You wrote in one of your letters that they were distributing compensation money."

Vera nodded. The mail worked one way, at least. She tried to remember what she had written. Whatever it was, it hadn't been an outright lie, but rather a statement made from the distant borderlands of truth. She had seen some sort of televised documentary program on reparations. Maybe it was about the Great Patriotic War. Maybe Germany was paying Belgium, rather than Russia paying its citizens. Who could even remember now. She shrugged. "From Moscow to Kirovsk is thousands of kilometers," Vera said. "Every kilometer along the way someone puts their hand into the pot so by the time it gets here: nothing left."

Kolya padded his tender neck with a napkin. It looked like he'd shaven with a guillotine. "Speaking of letters, your mother has not received many from you. I told her overseas mail is often lost."

"Yes, I wrote every two weeks."

"I never doubted that," Vera said. Let the two believe they had fooled her. Meanwhile she'd fool them into falling in love.

But as the evening progressed, Lydia grew intoxicated. She had two shots for every one of Kolya's, and grew angry when Vera tried to take the bottle from her.

When Kolya was leaving, Lydia stumbled to the door to kiss him good-bye. She spilled her drink on him as she leaned forward. Kolya placed his hands on her shoulders and firmly pushed her away. One look at his face was enough for Vera to know he'd never be her son-in-law, they would never be a family together, and she ached.

Later, Vera woke to splashing water. In the bathroom, she found her daughter on her knees before the toilet, holding her hair in a loose fist behind her head.

"You stupid child," Vera said, dropping to a knee beside her.

Lydia's head bobbed over the toilet seat.

"You stupid child. What have you done?"

"I don't know," Lydia mumbled, letting the fistful of hair go slack. Vera had an urge to shout, but she laid her daughter on the floor and made a pillow from the bath towel. A mother comforts, a mother cleans. A mother gives when any reasonable person would deny. Life might affix any number of labels to Vera—Russian, pensioner, widow, daughter—but when she looked to her washed-out reflection in the bathroom mirror, she saw only Lydia's mother.

December approached, and the days shrank. Each Wednesday, hungover or not, Lydia left the house with her mother when the men arrived. Kolya nodded curtly. This peasant of a man must've been too intimidated by her worldliness to speak to her. And those ridiculous plastic flowers—he'd probably never smelled a real one in his life, whereas she'd once lived in a city where roses were so plentiful a stadium was named after them.

On the day Vera came upon her daughter at the forest edge, Lydia had been thinking of Gilbert's piano-tuning kit. The brown leather case contained a gooseneck tuning hammer, nickel lever heads, and rubber mutes. Tuning forks that gave warm, round rings when she flicked them. A manual that Gilbert had ceased referring to years earlier, filled with terms like *equal temperament*, *fundamental frequency*, and *coincident harmonics*. When she first arrived at LAX, she wasn't sure if she should kiss her fiancé or shake his hand. His flesh was the color and texture of an overcooked potato, and he wore Hawaiian shirts to counter the otherwise overpowering blandness that emanated from him. When she joined him on calls to factory-size suburban houses, she read through the manual. She couldn't find the technical terms in her Russian–English pocket dictionary, and Gilbert had done his best to explain them in simple language. He would have made a better elementary school teacher than a husband. A friend of Gilbert's found Lydia a job as a minimum-wage caregiver at the Glendale Sunrise Rest Home. She couldn't understand why so many of its residents viewed nursing homes as elderly storage where sons and daughters imprison parents to recompense unresolved childhood traumas. Compared to elder care in Russia, it was a beacon of warmth and compassion. When she saw her first wheelchair ramp in LAX, she had mistaken it for some kind of weird public sculpture. When she learned what a wheelchair ramp was, when she learned that they were mandated by law, she felt a pure rush of patriotism for a country she'd only been living in for a few hours. Of the century's magnificent and terrible inventions, what was more humane, more elegant, more generous than the wheelchair ramp? The happiest day of her life was many decades away, she believed: when she was an elderly widow wheeled up the wheelchair ramp of Glendale

Sunrise and into their care. She was only twenty years old and she knew where she wanted to die. One Friday afternoon, Gilbert emerged from a rare autumn rain shower, set his tuning kit on the floor, and told her he had met a Belarusian woman online.

Lydia continued trudging along the edge of the rusted forest. Wolves—or was it the wind?—howled deep among the steel branches. But she'd stopped caring a long while ago. A figure appeared ahead, stenciled against the dim sun. Her mother.

"December is cold," Vera said. Her daughter's presence leeched her powers of observation, and she couldn't sustain a conversation with Lydia that extended beyond statements of obvious fact.

Lydia gave an unexpected smile. "You've grown wise in your old age."

"I'm growing senile."

"At the nursing home I worked exclusively with the bewildered and mentally deranged."

"How far along am I?"

"We both crossed that border a ways back."

"Will you take care of me when I'm old?" she asked Lydia, more seriously than she'd intended.

"Mama, you are old."

Vera glanced down the field to the small squares of lamplight encased behind the triple-paned glass of her kitchen window. "We can go back soon."

"You do know what they're doing in there, don't you?"

Vera looked away. A ballpoint pen was clipped to a folded sheet of paper in her pocket. She had been writing a letter to Lydia as if she still lived in America. In it she had described Kolya, how handsome and polite he was, how he and Lydia would make the most gorgeous couple, the most beautiful grandchildren. How everything in her life was on its way to being made right, and how, at the age of sixty-three, she had never felt more blessed.

"We have food on the table and money in the jar. Isn't that enough? Why does it matter where it comes from? We're not doing anything wrong. We're not doing anything at all."

"You're from another world, Mama. Criminals are packaging drugs on our kitchen table and you act like this is something to be proud of."

"Be quiet," Vera commanded. She wouldn't be lectured on self-respect by a mail-order bride. "You must be quiet."

Vera turned toward the house. Lydia fell in line behind her and they hiked the half kilometer in silence. At home, the men packed bundled vials into a duffel bag. Vera looked away.

"We're on our way out," Kolya announced. He didn't look at Lydia. He no longer stayed after work. The kitchen table had only two chairs.

The men left. Lydia unfurled her long legs on the divan, kept drinking, then left too. What accounted for her daughter's unhappiness? Lydia had grown up in the party, had spent her childhood in the placid years of Brezhnev, her adolescence in Gorbachev's glow. She'd never known hunger. It had been the best upbringing Vera could provide. In a kinder world, her best would've been enough.

Lydia returned a few hours later, so drunk she couldn't fit the key in the keyhole. She had gone to a party thrown by one of her childhood friends. The girls, now women, with girls of their own, had gossiped about Galina and the oligarch until Lydia had let slip that Galina's ex-boyfriend worked at her house. A hush had fallen over the five women. They had cajoled, promised not to tell a soul. They'd never been so interested, so concerned for Vera's well-being. But by then, Lydia had been too drunk to care. She'd described Kolya, his associates, the drugs, her mother's complicity. Her friends had given hushed assurances of confidentiality that hadn't fooled anyone. They'd spent their lives narrating Galina's story and this tragic coda to the plot line of her first love was the best news they'd heard in ages.

Vera found her at the door, trying to unlock the mail slot with the house key. She mumbled about peasants, drug criminals, and piano tuners. "Be quiet. You can't say these things," Vera warned, but Lydia wasn't listening.

The men didn't show up the next week. Vera waited an hour before going to see Yelena. At two in the afternoon, the sun had already set.

Yelena opened the door with a nod. She'd been expecting Vera. The samovar was still warm in the kitchen.

Vera sat hunched at the edge of the leather sofa, which Yelena never failed to mention had been imported from Italy. She tapped her foot, folded and unfolded her hands. All her nervous energy drained to her extremities. A pack of Benson and Hedges lay open beside a silver ashtray.

"Sugar?" Yelena offered, sliding the teacup to Vera.

"They haven't come today."

Yelena stirred three scoops of sugar into both teas. She took her time. It was a strong brew. She had a child any mother would be proud of.

"It's over," she said.

"But why?" Vera asked.

"Your daughter. She talks."

Without asking, Vera slid one of the scrawny cigarettes from the pack. Was this why the wolves had returned? For her own daughter's denunciation? For her? A ridiculous idea, she knew, but in a world so topsy-turvy, superstition was the only rational system of belief. She drew on the cigarette, her first in twenty-three years, and held the tickle in her throat.

"What will happen to me?" Prison, she imagined, was the best possible outcome. She expected something far worse. "Will I be arrested?"

You're living in the wrong decade, Yelena thought. *The police have nothing to do with it.* Yelena watched her old friend's hands tremble ash to the carpet. No, *friend* wasn't the right word. What bound them was more enduring than friendship. In school their teacher had applauded Vera for her courage, for her self-sacrifice in the name of the people; and even during the famine of 1947, when Yelena had shrunk to a malnourished sliver and buried her two brothers, Vera had always had enough to eat. And now Yelena wore shoes whose price, even on sale, exceeded Vera's net worth. In the end the world is just and righteous. One is always compensated for what one has earned.

"What will happen to me?" Vera asked.

"You?" Yelena shook her head. "Nothing will happen to you."

Vera returned home to find the front door unlocked. An uncapped bottle stood beside the divan, three fingers from full. A trail of footprints began at the back door and ran in a perforated line across the snowy field to White Forest. Her knees ached as she followed the trail toward the trees. She didn't stop to count the sets of footprints. She recognized the smallest of them.

A crescent of moonlight dissolved in cloud wisps. Snow soaked her boot linings. Decades had passed since she'd last run, but she did, now, adding her footprints to those that entered the forest. In the darkness she lost the trail. She found blown-out tires, mulching waste paper, yellow plastic leaves everywhere, but no footprints. She spun around, sifted through refuse, searched for a sign, a voice, a clue, an answer, a reason. She'd never know that fifty-two minutes earlier and a hundred and sixteen meters away, her daughter had looked toward that same sky. Even through her terror and bewilderment, the trees of White Forest had reminded Lydia of the redwood forest Gilbert had taken her to a week after she'd arrived in America, when she still could speak no more than a dozen words of English, when she still couldn't believe her luck.

Two men walk in front of her, two beside. She has no shoes on and her feet are wooden blocks fixed to her ankles. Raw copper wiring binds her wrists behind her back in rings of pain. She focuses on her wrists, on the copper infinity wound around them, her skin a frozen lake into which a skater carves figure eights. Beside her the man's leather jacket squeaks. He pulls a small bottle of motor oil from his pocket, splashes a bit under his arm, and his jacket silences. Ahead, a hole. An oval missing from the ground. Every particle inside Lydia rises. She has something to say. She must articulate the monstrousness of that hole, the impossibility of her ever going in. If they could only feel what she feels, if she could just position the right words in the right order, they would understand. A whimper is all she summons as she's pushed to her knees. The moon is a distant and indifferent witness. Mute clouds collide. Kolya's stricken face appears beside hers. He doesn't want to do this. No one could ever want to do this. This is her life. This is what she has. There's so much she has to fix. There's so much she still has to do. She can't die now, not when she has so little to lose. She tries to explain this but Kolya frowns at her as if she speaks a language he briefly studied but no longer remembers. She bargains. She'll leave Kirovsk forever, she'll quit drinking, she'll go to university, she'll get a job, she'll have kids and they'll have kids, she'll live a long, happy, useful existence, she'll turn her entire life around, she's never felt more powerful, more capable, more aware of what her life might become if they will just give it back to her. Kolya reaches behind her and gently holds her hands. "Close your eyes now," he says. "When you open them, you'll be home." He releases her hands but his voice still holds her. "I'm right here. You're nearly there." This is a good thing, she tells herself. This will change me. I'll be a better person. I'll be the person I want to be. Everything will be different. This is what I've been searching for.

In the flash there's no final thought, no final reflection, just the breath carried from her body on the back of the bullet.

That night Kolya returned to his flat above the space museum that had been shuttered since his father had passed the previous year. His porridge was still on the table from the morning. He set it in the sink and reached his hand out to press his fingertips against the faint square of less faded wallpaper where his mother's postcard had hung.

To say he felt guilty would ascribe to him ethical borders that were lines on a map of a country that no longer existed. At least, that's what he told himself. Better to deny the existence of objective morality than to live in its shadow. Better to tell yourself that the world of right and wrong is not the world you belong to. In the bathroom mirror he saw the face of a man his seventeen-year-old self would have disdained with the vanity of someone yet unaware of the many means the world has to break him.

He turned on the VCR. *Deceit Web* played. Galina hopped on her motorcycle, paved a narrow corridor of speed down a wide avenue, dodged kiosks and *pirozhki* stands, the bike steered by her flared hips. Her hazy whisper sounded like Galina's, but it conveyed no sentiment that could ever come from her natural heart. On the bookshelf lay the Polaroid of his family in leopard-print swimsuits, and on top of it the mixtape his brother and Galina had made for him. It struck him that this mixtape, whatever it contained, was the only question he had to which he could ever hope to receive an answer. Everything else was an afterlife he shared with the child whose first birthday he'd celebrated with an upside-down matchstick wedged into a biscuit.

He tucked the mixtape in his shirt pocket, along with the Polaroid, and stayed awake in the blue television glow until the army recruitment office opened the next morning.

There was no funeral, no body found to wash and consecrate. Vera still went to church. She didn't believe in

God because there was no evidence that God existed, and now there was no evidence that Lydia had either. Vera stood at the front of the church before an icon of the Virgin and child. The great golden god was helpless in his mother's arms. Though she held him across her chest, she looked outward rather than at her son.

On her way home, Vera passed a young woman holding a clipboard. She'd seen the woman before, milling about on street corners to ambush innocent pedestrians with solicitations for signatures. The young woman was still naive enough to believe in whatever big ideas she had on that clipboard.

"Would you sign this?" the young woman asked, thrusting the clipboard into Vera's hands. "We're petitioning the mayor to turn White Forest into a nature preserve."

Vera couldn't believe it. "You're not from around here, are you? Have you ever been into the forest?"

The woman blushed.

"The trees are made of metal. The leaves are plastic. It was installed forty years ago to make people forget that we're living where humans don't belong."

The young woman was unperturbed. "Whatever its origin, a rich and vibrant ecosystem has emerged. Feral dogs and cats, yes, but also arctic rabbits, foxes, and even wolves. This biodiversity, unlikely as it may be, deserves state protection."

"Protection," Vera slowly repeated, recalling Kolya at her kitchen table, a fat slice of cake on a saucer, explaining why his boss didn't fear the police. The clipboard clattered on the sidewalk. The strip of concrete, scabbed in gray frost, stretched to the intersection where it linked with another sidewalk, which in turn intersected with another and another, circumscribing the limits of her life. How often had she walked down them silently? How often had she censored her thoughts, her judgments, her beliefs, her desires, consigning them to some region of her soul where they couldn't betray her?

"Protection," she mumbled, low enough that the young woman leaned forward to hear her. She had received honors from the Young Pioneers, Komsomol, the iron-workers' trade union, had been anointed the future of socialism by *Pravda*, and only now, at this late date, had she discovered a denunciation that had been building in her for all her sixty-three years. She would denounce Kolya, Yelena, Yelena's son, the gangsters and bandits that governed the city no less brutally than had the prison guards. The commissar, whose hand she'd shaken and whose congratulations she'd accepted days after he sentenced her mother. Her primary teacher, so afraid of Vera she'd never marked a single quiz less than one hundred percent correct, even when the girl left half the questions blank. Her husband, who had claimed cunnilingus was antirevolutionary and had lived so distantly from her that he'd closed the door to the bathroom as he had a heart attack inside. No one was innocent, no one was unconnected, no one was not complicit. The strongest, most damning adjectives she'd reserve for her own silences, if she could only now raise her voice. But it never went louder than a whisper. She didn't know where to begin. "Protection," she said over and over as the girl bent over to pick up her clipboard.

Vera's reaction didn't surprise the young woman, who had recently watched her own grandmother descend into dementia. The young woman's grandmother had cursed the clouds, the factories, the loved ones whose faces she no longer recognized. And here, this babushka cursed a nature preserve. One must have patience and compassion for the elderly, the young woman thought, as she took hold of Vera's hand and shushed soothingly. They are from a different time. "Just breathe. Everything's okay, grandmother. Everything is fine."

Vera clutched the smooth hands that had appeared in hers. She'd have fallen without the young woman's shoulder for support. Until that moment, she hadn't realized she would never be a grandmother.

A week later, a knock at the door. Vera approached. In the peephole Kolya was a beaky gargoyle. She held her chin in her hands.

"I know you're there," he said. "I can see your shadow at the glass."

She pressed against the peeling paint, willing herself to slide through the wood atom by atom and dissolve.

"I've reenlisted in the army," he said. "As a contract soldier. I'll be back in Chechnya. You don't need to worry about seeing me again."

The mail slot lifted, then fell shut as a manila envelope dropped to the floor. Vera's insides tightened. She knew what the envelope contained. It had to be true. It had happened before. A final letter from Lydia, her last words transcribed by Kolya under frozen branches. She swelled with a cardiac rush of hope so entire she could've forgiven Kolya, right then, for murdering her daughter, if he had delivered a last message for her to save inside the shoebox, beside the final letter from her mother, a last message in which Lydia said the one lie Vera would've sold her soul to make true: that she had died knowing she was loved. Vera fumbled with the envelope.

It was far too large, too thick, too heavy for a letter. Inside were ten stacks of banded thousand-ruble bills: compensation money.

Vera opened the door, ready to fling the bills at Kolya because this time her silence would not be bought. But he had already receded halfway down the block. She gripped the envelope tighter, afraid she might drop it. The winter still had months of life left. The gas bill was due. The cupboard was nearly empty. It was late in the day, late in the century. Too late to become someone else.

In her bedroom she pulled the shoebox from beneath the bed. The manila envelope wouldn't fit inside, not with the other envelopes. She withdrew the various letters and newspaper clippings, laid them on the bed, and began stacking the banded bills in the shoebox. When she finished, she knelt beside the bed and prayed for her daughter, for her mother, and finally, for herself.

Palace of the People

St. Petersburg, 2001

"IS THERE MORE, SERGEI VLADIMIROVICH?" my father demanded the day I received my conscription notice. His stomach filled half the doorway. In the slip of paper pinched between mustard-rimmed nails, he held a half-gram of heroin. My shoulder blades *snap-snap-snapped* spirals of peeling paint as I slouched down the wall to the bedroom floor and gazed up with the all-iris innocence of a cartoon kitten.

"Is there more?"

The phantoms of two hundred thousand cigarettes and a street *pirozhki* haunted his breath.

"Is there more?"

He steadied his wheezy frame against the doorway. He was already an old fart when I was a little boy. Now he qualified as antique. I still hadn't answered his question.

Strength regained, my father lumbered into my bedroom and pulled the drawers from the dresser, plunged shoulder-deep into the hamper, scattered CDs, crunched videocassette cases underfoot, left the mattress listing drunkenly against the wall, the sheets dangling from the bedposts, employing all his considerable bulk to rip and toss, throw and stomp, until it became clear that whatever he searched for was more elusive than the half-gram stashed in receipt paper at his feet. Once everything shelved, hung, or standing was strewn across the floor, he slumped into the rocking chair and finished the final drag of the cigarette I'd left smoldering in the ashtray.

"Is there more?" he asked.

The year before he went to prison, when I was eight years old, he'd taught me to keep silent in an interrogation. He planted one of my mother's earrings in my coat pocket, kept me home from school, and grilled me in the kitchen with the windows closed, the oven on, the lamps unshaded. Cold cottony clouds ruffled the skies, but in that kitchen I sweltered like flesh skewered on a grease-brown rotisserie. In the end I would've confessed to killing Kirov. I opened my mouth, ready to admit anything and everything, but before I muttered a single syllable I felt the wrath of God in my father's backhand.

"Is there more?" His voice surrendered to my silence. He knew I'd never confess. He knew he'd taught me well.

"More of what?" I finally said, when his repeated question had softened to whispers.

My father just looked at me as if I'd invited in the national billiards team to practice break shots on his nuts. "You talk? A rat as well as an addict. More of this." He unfolded the paper. A winter wonderland lay in its creases.

"It's just sugar. For tea."

"Sugar, right. And do you put it in your tea with a hypodermic needle?"

When you can no longer deny logic, begin denying everything else.

"Do you have the virus?" he asked. His anger had burned away. Only the sad residue of paternal concern remained.

"Of course not." I'd only shared needles with my three closest friends.

My father stood and trundled to the door. "Seryozha," he said, without turning back, "until the army takes you, you will spend your days working."

"Or what?"

"Or I'll shoot you."

"That would violate your parole."

"I'll claim self-defense. 'May it please the court, I was only trying to *save* my son from the lunatic drug addict who's moved into his room and begun wearing his clothes.' No judge in heaven, hell, or the national judiciary would convict me."

Next morning's light was unwelcome proof that the world hadn't ended overnight. I followed my father to the top floor of the apartment block. A dark gash leaked hall light into the metal door of the last flat on the left.

"Do you see this?" he asked, pointing to the door with a fully cocked frown of indignation. What my father lacked in education, he made up for in opinions. I silently prepared to hibernate through the long winter of his lecture. "They make new doors from recycled fish tins and burglars need only a can opener to break in. Bullshit for brains, these—"

The tin door swung open, thank the merciful heavens. On the other side sat the legless man. Late twenties, clean-shaven, hair the greased silver of a ball bearing, smelling of cheap Ukrainian tobacco and burnt vegetable shortening. He sat in a wheelchair. Two strips of pig leather and canvas sagged between rubber wheels—probably the most advanced mode of transport owned by anyone in the building.

"This is my son, Sergei Vladimirovich, but you may call him 'asshole,'" my father announced, then gestured at the legless man. "And this is Kirill Andreyevich."

"Junior Sergeant Kirill Andreyevich," the legless man corrected. Only his unimpressed gaze met my outstretched hand.

I poked around the flat while my father spoke with Kirill in the kitchen. I expected chaos, disarray, but only chair and table legs touched the living room floor. A dish rack sat beside the bathtub. A bit of that morning's oats ringed the drain. Large glass water jars stood along the bathroom baseboard with red rust clouding their bottom centimeter. Did Kirill know something we didn't? My throat was dry and my mouth tasted like a compost bin, but it's never a good idea to drink from jars found in a stranger's bathroom.

Party-approved volumes lined the bookshelves: Red Army field manuals, censored editions of nineteenth-century novels, flinty odes to heavy industries—the sort of kitsch sold to Western tourists outside the Winter Palace or down the Embankment. I picked up a copy of *How the Steel Was Tempered.* Had I been born a few decades earlier, I'd have been assigned a novel like this in my final year of school, and I'd have known exactly what the book was about without reading it, and I'd have aced whatever literature exam they gave before the UGEs. But I was born in 1983, assigned *The Master and Margarita*—a long canal to nowhere, that, no wonder Stalin was a Bulgakov fan—and scored a two on the exam. No university wanted me. The army did.

A black pistol lay on the coffee table. I picked it up and rubbed my thumb across its dark luster. Heavier than they look in movies. Holding that gun made me feel taller up top and longer down below. Somewhere in Chechnya was an eighteen-year-old Muslim holding a pistol for the first time and feeling this same surge of power?

"Put it down."

Kirill wheeled through the doorway, my father behind him.

"You know what Chekhov had to say about loaded guns," I said. Kirill didn't smile. Probably hadn't passed the UGE either. I rubbed my prints from the metal—another childhood lesson from my father—and set it on the table.

"Now you're employed," my father said. He was radiant.

"By whom?"

"By Kirill Andreyevich."

"Junior Sergeant Kirill Andreyevich," the legless man corrected.

"Yes, you'll be working for the junior sergeant."

The future looked darker than a mortician's closet. "You must be joking," I said. My father never joked.

"Tomorrow morning you'll begin," my father said, quite pleased with himself. "It's the early rising rooster who sticks it to the fattest hen."

His smirk left little question as to which bird I was.

"And Seryozha," my father said. "Remember, I'm not afraid of breaking my parole."

Deferments went to university students, fathers, and prisoners, only the last of which me and my friends had any hope of becoming in the near future. Prison would be our trade school, the only one to admit us, the only one to provide the skill set that would expand our futures. We should've gone into a PTU after our ninth year, but our class boasted a bumper crop of underperforming students, making the one dumpy neighborhood vocational school harder to crack than Cambridge. No matter; if your business is crime, there's no better business school than prison.

During our final spring of our last year as high schoolers, when we were well on our way to becoming the people we'd be for the rest of our lives, we skipped class to drink Baltika 7s and whistle at women in the Tauride Gardens. Black eyes of frozen muck peered through the snow. A pair of ten-thousand-year-old hermits played bullet chess at an icy table. We stood in a small shivering huddle.

"My grandpa fought his way all the way from Stalingrad to Hitler's bunker and you know what they did to him when he got back? Popped his patriotic ass in a gulag," Valeriy declared. He picked white grains from his scalp. Lint or dandruff, couldn't tell. "I'm ashamed to be related to such a sucker."

"Two hundred got beat to death last year before even making it to Chechnya. And if they're reporting two hundred, the real figure's got to be as long as an international phone number. *Dedovshchina*, no joke."

"Two years with nothing but your canteen to fuck, *that's* no joke."

"That's why I'm saying jail time's soft time."

"Where's Tony with those beers?" Our names—Aleksandr Kharlmov, Valeriy Lebedev, Ivan Vladim, and Sergei Markin—fit who we were, not who we wanted to be, so we'd rechristened ourselves: Tony Montana, Joe Pesci, Don Corleone, and Tupac. Our spirit animals were all of the genus American Kingpin Tragically Slain in His Prime. Our parents learned English from the Beatles, but we learned from Biggie.

Different afternoon, different park, same conversation.

"The trick's to jail just till the insurgency's over."

"And how you gonna do that?"

"Easy," I boasted. Never forget the first three letters of *confidence*. "You forecast how long the war will last, how long you'll need to jail, then find a felony that fits the sentence."

Crime and Punishment. We knew nothing of history—decent odds that three of the four of us couldn't tell you what year Jesus was born—but we staked our futures by predicting it. We took bets: The war would finish in a year, two, five. Browsing old newspapers and Yandexing court reports, we found sentences to fit each prediction. A year for assaulting an ethnic minority. Two to five for armed robbery. Three to seven for narcotics smuggling.

We wanted to become gangsters, but who could we look up to? Where were our heroes? Our fathers drove gypsy cabs, washed dishes, and pumped gas, their blood so timid a guillotine couldn't make them bleed. They longed for the old days, not because their lives had been better, but because there had been an equality of misery back then. We were their sons and we wanted more.

Conscription season began in spring. The steady sluice of burgs had dissolved down the Neva. A bask of geriatric crocodiles sunbathed at the beachfront wall of Peter and Paul Fortress. Daytime drunks extended their working hours. The arctic winter unraveled into pastel peach, lavender, plum. We received postcards from the military commissariat the same day and carried them with us to the park. Mine was the first correspondence I'd received since the letters my father had sent from prison.

I compared my red-bannered postcard with my friends'. They were identical but for our names. By law, the commissariat could send us to a military base for testing the day after graduation, but for whatever reason, they'd given us until August. If we all died in Chechnya, would our families receive form postcards, identical but for our names, or would the army honor our sacrifice with a form letter?

"I'll knock off an electronics store," Aleksandr announced, killing his cigarette in five colossal puffs. He had the lungs of a blue whale. "Three years, that should cover it."

"Too long, Tony," Ivan said. "Any day now Putin's going to tear off his shirt, jump on a brown bear, ride that bitch bareback to Grozny, and finish those beards by himself. Six months tops. I'll mug a tourist."

"Four years," Valeriy said, still picking the rice-white flakes that had turned out to be lice. "I'm going to steal a police car."

We exploded into laughter.

"Laugh it up," Valeriy said, "but you know no policeman's going to worry himself about a robbed electronics store or tourist. Shit, robbing tourists is *their* job. Take a policeman's ride, though. Four years, easy."

They turned to me. "I haven't decided how many years," I said, a beat too slowly. "But don't worry. I'm in. I'm all in."

We pounded fists, then swaggered toward Ploshchad Lenina to pick up a thousand-ruble check, so named because the heroin comes folded in receipt paper. Oily rainbows arced the swollen sparkle of the Neva. Tourists clambered from pontoons, all *oohs* and *aahs*, jumping for their cameras as though the imperial mansions lining the banks were a flock of rare birds. I didn't see the rush. Those pink powder puffs weren't flying anywhere. We turned onto Arsenalnaya, then onto Komsomola. In the distance, brick-walled, spired, and domed, a tourist would be forgiven for mistaking Kresty Prison for a palace. In history class, we learned about the red herrings caught, descaled, and fried up in the 1937 show trials. In literature class, we read an Akhmatova poem about the prison. Her son was detained for seventeen months. With hundreds of other women she waited outside those great brick walls for news of the accusation, verdict, sentence. "Can you describe this?" a woman with blue lips whispered. And Akhmatova answered, "Yes, I can."

Now, outside the brick walls, their granddaughters waited, a few lost in oversized overcoats, the wives, girlfriends, mothers, and daughters of pretrial prisoners. We catcalled. We hooted. We asked if they wanted to party. Had they stood there seventy years earlier, their sorrows would've been worth a great poet's words. But who reads poetry anymore?

"I'm not scared," I stated, and Valeriy, Ivan, and Aleksandr all agreed they too were unafraid. I didn't know if we meant Kresty or Chechnya. Up ahead a Lenin statue toupeed in pigeon shit silently perorated to masses. I gathered the sweat-softened bills from my friends and climbed to the third-floor flat of a crumbling communal housing complex to pick up the thousand-ruble check.

The job was like nothing found in the classifieds of regional papers and blog forums, where postings sought multilingual men with business degrees and attractive single women to work as dancers in European strip clubs. No glamour, no glitz, no status to propel me past the face control at Jakata or Decadence nightclubs, whose bouncers are harder to bribe than Peter at the Pearly Gates. That first day I dragged my ass out of bed at four in the morning to help Kirill dress. His shirt, trousers, and bedsheets were cut from the same square of bureaucratically blue canvas.

"How the hell do you normally get dressed?" I asked.

He sat at the end of his bed with a ten-thousand-watt smile. He was actually *enjoying* this! Happiness is zero sum, and the lower my stock in it fell, the higher his rose. Any moment it'd burst right through the ceiling.

"I can do it myself," he said. His smile revealed teeth the color of cooking oil. "It just takes longer."

"We've got all day."

"You're mouthy," he said, "for a virgin."

Devil! Who'd told him? And more importantly, had he told anyone else? I'd never live it down. Maybe I could sell my kidneys for the identity of a reindeer herder on the Yamal Peninsula? A place that means "End of the World" in the local tongue just might be far enough. In my mind, I'd already built an igloo and married a muskox when Kirill cut in.

"Look at you, I've eaten borscht with less color than your cheeks." He closed his eyes with the serenity of a man whose desires are modest enough to be met. "I remember when I popped my cork for the first time. It was my thirteenth birthday."

At eighteen I wasn't just a virgin. I was an elderly virgin.

"My father took me to his favorite prostitute to celebrate my becoming a man," Kirill went on. "He stood just beside the bed while I went at it. Not close enough to make it weird, mind you. He just wanted to make sure I did my part. I finished about five seconds after I began and he burst into applause. Never made the old man prouder.

"But you." His eyes zeroed on mine. "You think you're too much of a man to pull trousers on an amputee and you haven't even popped your cork. Shameful."

I hoisted his trousers up his knobby hips. Hemmed mid-thigh, they looked more like volleyball shorts. He pointed to a roll of duct tape encircled by gummy rings on the floor. "You need to tape the stumps."

"Hell no."

"You need to learn how," he stressed.

"You're missing your legs, not your hands. Tape them yourself."

"Virgin," he commanded.

After I ran a few rings of tape around the stumps, Kirill greased his hair with vegetable shortening, combing it through a dozen times before satisfied with the part. "They can scoop this crap into a jar with a French label and charge ten times the price," he explained. "But they can't fool me."

The last touch was a squirt of embalming fluid–scented cologne. I heaved Kirill into his wheelchair and pushed him into the hall.

"I'll go down myself," he said when we reached the stairs. With a sheet of cardboard beneath him and his gloved hands clasped to the rail, he tobogganed down the steps. Seven flights of stairs, not a problem, and yet his trousers had been a peak only I could carry him over. Cheeky little shit.

"Wait," he said. The apartment buildings's front door

clunked closed behind us. A medieval siege engine couldn't break down that thing. "I want to catch my breath."

"You're in a wheelchair. Breathing is about all you can do."

He shook his head, lit a cigarette, and spoke as if I were the unreasonable one. "In such a rush, this one, to do anything but lose his virginity."

Following his lead, I lit up too. The White Nights always dead-ended into Gray Mornings. The clouds just dozed in the sky without a care in the world. Lazy bastards. Across the Neva, the odd smokestack stood taller than any imperial obelisk. If eras are remembered by their greatest monuments, ours will be remembered by billboards advertising Beeline mobile phone plans. Across the street, a pack of feral dogs chased a homeless man through a vacant lot. Our school textbooks said as many as a thousand serfs died building Petersburg. Our teacher put the number closer to a hundred thousand. But he'd say anything to sleep with you. The lead dog lunged for the vagrant's ass, and as he stumbled a bison of a Rottweiler charged into his back. Three brutal steps later, he toppled over. I'm not sure the city would be worth even him.

"I thought you wanted to get going."

"Breakfast is the most important meal of the day," Kirill replied, holding up his cigarette. "It's important we take time to savor it."

The white onion domes of Smolny Convent disappeared behind us as I pushed Kirill along Shpalernaya Street. We took a left at Prospekt Chernyshevskogo. A casino's colors glowed like lollipops held to lamplight. Sushi restaurants and Irish pubs everywhere. Tinted town car windows the same obsidian black as their drivers' sunglasses. Fires twitched through the grates of rusted ash cans. Weird how fires shiver as if they're the ones cold. We waited for a break in traffic.

"You need to carry me over the gate," Kirill said when we reached the entrance of the Chernyshevskaya metro station. I plunked two tokens in the turnstile and hoisted him by the armpits. Heavy, for half a man.

Newspaper vendors flashed headlines as I broke down the wheelchair. *Sochi Mega Resort to Open Next Year. Sydney Prepares for Summer Olympics. Kresty Prison to Be Turned into Hotel-Entertainment Complex.*

"The Chernyshevskaya metro escalator is one hundred and thirty-seven meters long. Do you know what that makes it?" Kirill asked.

"Enough of a ruler to measure my member of the party," I said.

"We'll have to take your word on that, virgin," he replied. "A hundred and thirty-seven meters makes this very escalator the longest escalator in the world. A world record, right here in our own neighborhood, and ninety-nine out of a hundred people who ride these stairs don't even know it."

"Why'd they build the tunnels so deep?"

"So they could be used as shelters if the Americans nuked us. You're too young to remember, but when I was coming up in the eighties we were still afraid Americans would drop a nuclear warhead on us."

"Do people hit by nuclear warheads ever lose just their legs?" I asked.

"I don't know." He frowned at his stumps. "I've never been hit by one."

The marbled metro platform was chessboard checkered.

Kirill strapped on his leather gloves, planted his palms on the marble, and swung his body between his arms. For Kirill, the world was made of parallel bars. I pushed the empty wheelchair behind him.

"How do I look?" he asked. Dressed in full military uniform, from his peaked cap to his hemmed trousers, he looked too solemn for me to take seriously.

"Short," I said.

A tube of muggy air as long and swift as the train it preceded gushed into the station. Kirill gave instructions. The act was nothing new. You couldn't go more than three metro stops without seeing a crippled vet from the war in Chechnya. They sang folk songs, sat on wooden pallets, recited Pushkin, pretzeled lifeless limbs, held cardboard signs advertising their suffering. Others just got drunk and murmured stories so depraved they could never be true.

The train exhaled a congested breath of passengers. Kirill knuckle-walked through the shuffling legs and I followed behind with his wheelchair. Young men offered their seats to women and the elderly with a decorum you'd rarely find above ground. Doors closed, wheels hummed on rails, and Kirill began. He didn't sing the national anthem, didn't produce a tray of ten-ruble trinkets from his wheelchair satchel or a horror story from his past. He simply crawled through the parting crowd on clenched fists, head raised, eyes meeting every glance. I just pushed the wheelchair behind him and watched the rubles tumble into the wicker basket.

"Give him a few rubles, Masha," a babushka shrink-wrapped in a kerchief whispered to her friend. "Pity the poor soul."

"You're a hero," an elderly man in tortoise-rimmed glasses observed. "Better to lose your legs than your honor."

For the length of the train ride, Kirill didn't speak. He neither solicited nor acknowledged the alms that just kept falling from the wallets and purses of morning commuters. He put one fist in front of the other, his peaked cap tilting, his limp stumps dragging behind him, not a caricature, not a freak show, but a brave man crawling across a battlefield that raged in his head. I nearly opened my own wallet.

He made two hundred and forty rubles in the two minutes to Ploshchad Vosstaniya. I couldn't believe how many coins and crumpled bills lay in the basket. It was more than my father made in three hours.

"You don't want them to think you're making money," he whispered as he pocketed the change. At Ploshchad Vosstaniya, we moved to the next car.

We rode the one and two lines until early afternoon. Twelve hundred rubles by ten o'clock. Twenty-three hundred by noon. Who knew my fellow citizens possessed such patriotic generosity? For lunch we surfaced at Baltiyskaya and bought shawarma and kvass from an elderly street vendor with dyed purple hair. I watched short skirts pass through the long afternoon light. "My assistant here is stricken with an incurable case of virginity," Kirill called to a really cute young woman whose dark brown bangs awninged the open pages of *Harry Potter*. "Will you take pity on him?"

I wanted to punch Kirill right then. I'd read the Harry Potter book three times through and it was a secret I'd carry to my grave. I might've told her. She'd already taken her book and walked away.

"Forty-one new stations are scheduled to be built in the next ten years," Kirill announced between dainty bites of charred lamb. I wished I'd chased after the brown-haired girl, but then I'd be the Stalkerish Virgin Who Hangs Out With a Legless Guy. Presently, I was just the Virgin Who Hangs Out With a Legless Guy. Some dignities are earned only by comparison.

"Forty-one new stations, you know what that means?" Kirill asked.

"That only three will be built."

"It means more people will ride the metro every day. More people means more money."

"You make too much already. Beggars shouldn't make more than the people they beg from."

"We work harder, I assure you." Kirill smiled at a flock of schoolchildren flying to catch the crosswalk light. You'd think a man without legs would be a tragic sort. But Kirill seemed to live as if always staring into a field of sunflowers. "I'm saving for a dacha. Wheelchair accessible. I'll be able to wash dishes in the sink."

It was hard to take him seriously. Only crooks, oligarchs, and politicians—often the same person—could afford dachas. Men who could walk, who had never gone to Chechnya, whose sons would never go to Chechnya. And here was Kirill, thinking he could be one of them. Whatever parts he'd lost, he still had two billiard balls in his corner pocket.

"What a racket," I said.

"It's an art."

"Taking people's money?"

He squinted at me. "No one's giving me anything. I'm a businessman."

"What're you selling?"

"All these people who opened their purses on the metro, when they see a legless vet, they feel ashamed and maybe a little pity. But when they see me crawling across the metro car, they see someone defiant, silent, not *begging* for anything, and they feel pride. They're paying me for the privilege of feeling proud when they should feel disgraced."

When I returned home that night, my father was sprawled on the divan in his underpants. He ate tinned fish from the can and let the cat clean the oil from his fingers between bites.

"Come here," he commanded, and examined my pupils by television light. The cat wrapped its tail around my father's forearm and purred lovingly. A devil in fur, that cat.

"Tell me what you learned today," my father asked.

"The Chernyshevskaya escalator is a hundred and thirty-seven meters long."

"Anything else?"

"I learned Kirill makes more money than you."

"And how much of that money did he let you keep?"

"None," I admitted. "But he bought me a shawarma."

"Then we both make more money than you." Satisfied with my silence, he turned back to the TV. All the parts, including that of the voluptuous femme fatale, were dubbed in the gruff monotone of a lobotomized Vladivostokian chain smoker. A strong-jawed actor survived a bomb blast by climbing into a refrigerator. I hoped refrigeration technology had reached Chechnya.

"Kresty's going to become a hotel," I said.

"Again? When?"

"The newspaper said as soon as a new prison's built outside the city."

"They were saying that even before I was arrested. Wish it had been a hotel. It wasn't."

I turned, but couldn't escape him—around fifty

portraits of my father hung in thin black frames from the living room walls. One for every year of his life, from the age of five to sixty-nine, except his prison years. His mother had taken him to the photographer once a year, a precaution in case the police arrested her and sent him to a state orphanage. His father had been an enemy of the people, so she had to think about things like that. He'd still dress in his best suit and go to a photographer's studio on his birthday and come home with a new portrait to hang on the wall. Bit mad, really. Even if somewhere in the world there was a girl who wanted to come home with me, I couldn't bring her here.

I crossed the living room and stared at my father's portrait from 1983. Like all of them, it looked like a blown-up passport photo. That was the year I was born. He looked rather grim.

"You know, I never wanted a wife or child," my father offered. "I was fifty years old, I thought I'd won. Then I met your mother. Then she got pregnant. Couldn't very well leave her then, could I?"

"Some crimes are best left unsolved, Papa."

"Nonsense. If you don't know where you began you won't know where you'll finish. Everyone needs an origin story."

I closed my eyes and did my best to humor him. "Then please, enlighten me."

"You, my dear boy, began with a broken condom."

Patricide really should be decriminalized. I turned toward the hall when I noticed a new portrait hanging above the tea-stained armchair. "When was your birthday?" I asked.

"Few weeks back," he said. "Don't give me that look. These photos, they're all for you."

"You realize how insane you sound, right? You've got more than fifty photos of yourself on the wall. Not photos of me or Mom, just of you. It's like you saw a photo spread of Kim Jongil's living room and really liked his style."

He scratched the bridge between the cat's ears. We'd had this conversation about a billion times.

"There are no photos of my father. There used to be, but my mother had to destroy them. She would show me the photos when I was a little kid, but now they're gone, and I can't remember his face. I don't know who he was. I don't know where I began, Seryozha." He looked up from the cat, to the portraits, and then to me. "They are for you. So you will know. So you won't forget who I was."

Before the cancer took her, my mother worked the cash register at a *produkti* that from its depleted inventory looked more like a shelving emporium than a market. Fifteen minutes after she left the house, my father began his day. He had a mobile phone the size of a boot and he took calls like a man in the trenches, receiving and providing orders in clipped jargon. He wore rubber gloves and a surgical mask when he bagged white powder on the kitchen table. For the longest time, I thought he was a doctor.

"This is very bad for you," he told me, when he let me watch him work after school. He used my mother's measuring spoons to divide the powder into folded paper pouches. "You must never eat it."

"What are you making?"

"A living," he replied.

In the summer, he'd send me on daytime deliveries.

Nothing major, just a few envelopes to university students and prostitutes, infractions so slight they're illegal only by technicality. Before I left, he gave me a series of directions.

"You need to count the money before you give them the product."

"You need never look a policeman in the eye."

"You need to obey all laws but the one you're breaking."

"You need not stop to speak with anyone."

"You need to pretend you're a man and then you will become one."

I bought metro tokens rather than hopping the turnstile, and I waited for every crosswalk signal. I was shorter than the peepholes and had to knock forever before anyone opened up. The prostitutes sometimes invited me in for tea and an Alenka chocolate bar. A few years after, I began to feel like Tsar Dipshit II when I realized I'd entered the flats of some of the most beautiful, least virtuous women in Petersburg and been only tempted by sweets. Now I just feel sad for whatever happened in those rooms that they needed drugs to endure.

Heroin on the kitchen table and snow on the windowsill; the tattoo of a lone wolf running up his forearm; the surgical mask halving his face; gloved hands performing a delicate operation: That had been my father. He was a capitalist, a man built for the New Russia, someone I thought I would forever look up to.

My mother knew, of course, but pretended otherwise. It came to an end when she discovered that I was my father's errand boy.

"Where were you?" she asked when I strolled through the front door one August afternoon, fingers still sticky with ice cream melt. She'd come home from work early.

"Delivering a living," I said proudly. She slapped me with her right hand and embraced me with her left.

"Criminals, everywhere," she said. "On the TV. In the street. In the Kremlin. Now in my home. I won't live with two of them."

She called the police. That afternoon my father was arrested outside our apartment block.

Now that I was wheeling Kirill around, I had to avoid my friends. I didn't return their phone calls and kept away from the parks, school yards, and apartment block basements we'd pass out in. Our paths only intersected once, in late June, on the Gostiny Dvor metro platform, as Kirill rambled on and on and on and on and on about the history of rail ties. Valeriy's zombie eyes latched onto mine. He was scratching his crotch. The head lice must've migrated to his southern tropics.

"Tupac, where you been at?" he asked. Behind him Ivan stood in baggy jeans and a T-shirt XXXL enough for a family of four.

I nodded to Kirill. "Just working."

Valeriy smirked. "New friend?"

"My dad's making me." I tried to speak soft enough that Kirill wouldn't hear.

"You get word about Tony? Knocked off a computer store last week," Ivan said. "He left his internal passport right on the counter and still couldn't get himself arrested. Had to walk to the police station and insist that he was a criminal. Embarrassing, really."

"He's in Kresty?" I asked.

Valeriy nodded. "Till the trial at least. It's not bad, by

the sound of it. No water shortages. Free electricity. Bet he's making all *kinds* of connects. We'll join him this weekend."

"On what charge?"

"We're gonna steal a police car," Ivan said, grabbing his jeans as they slunk toward his knees. Kirill pretended he wasn't listening by looking away. "You want in?"

"I promised my dad I'd help him move some furniture this weekend," I said. "But I'll see you there."

"You promise?" Ivan asked.

"Yeah, no doubt."

"It's your neck," Valeriy said, before walking off. "In prison, your head might stay attached to it."

Kirill didn't speak until Ivan and Valeriy had disappeared into the white-tiled pedestrian tunnel toward the Nevsky Prospekt station. A gypsy vendor passed by with a tray of single items usually only sold in packs: disposable razors, condoms, Twix bars.

"Will you go through with it?" Kirill asked. There was no disdain in his voice, nothing even approaching disapproval.

"I don't know," I admitted.

"In my time, mental illness deferments were the most popular way to dodge conscription, besides university. You'd bribe a psychiatrist into saying you were certifiably cuckoo. The problem was that so many of the new rich received mental illness deferments, none were left for the actually mentally ill. My unit had two schizophrenics, a handful of manic depressives, and a guy who received regular visitations from angels. The insanity of war, eh?"

"How much did the deferments go for?"

"More than you can afford," he said. The breeze of an approaching train whipped through my hair, but

Kirill's, slick with vegetable shortening, remained unmoved.

The weeks passed. I hadn't touched heroin since the night my father found what remained of the five-hundred-ruble check. I kept waiting for withdrawal to kick in—they can't send me to Chechnya if I'm bouncing around a padded room—but I guess you don't get withdrawal after using it four times in five months. Can't even get addicted to drugs properly. Each morning I woke at four thirty and helped Kirill dress. We breakfasted on Java Gold cigarettes and worked the train cars until noon. One day we bought lunch from an elderly Georgian whose osteoporosis lived in him like a black hole slowly sucking his whole body stomach-ward. Kirill was going on about the metro system again.

"It's the thirteenth busiest in the world," he said between small bites of sausage. It was a holy day, the Feast of Peter and Paul, and humidity leached from the city's pores. "Yet Petersburg is only the world's forty-fifth biggest city. What does this tell you?"

"That we're too poor to afford cars?"

"Idiot. It tells you we have a metro to be proud of. New York, London, you think their metros have crystal chandeliers and marble floors and bronze statues?"

"Of course they do."

"They do not," he insisted. "They have graffiti and crumbling walls and hoodlums who push decent commuters into oncoming trains. They do not have beauty. They do not have a Palace of the People."

"That's a TV show, right?" I said. Finally, a shared interest.

"I'm not talking about a TV show! I'm talking about

the metro. The Palace of the People, that's what Lenin, Stalin, and Khrushchev called it. A palace not for tsars or princes, but for you and me."

"Off to your palace then, Comrade," I suggested, and wheeled him to the Pushkinskaya station entrance.

"You shouldn't work on April twentieth," he said as I lifted him over the turnstile. "The skinhead gangs are always the worst on Hitler's birthday."

It was still summer. I didn't see how his advice applied to me.

"What would you do if, you know," I said, nodding to his stumps when we reached the platform.

"If I still had legs?"

"Yeah."

"I'd start an autoerotic asphyxiation service," he said without hesitation.

"What?"

"Autoerotic asphyxiation. Don't tell me you haven't heard of it?"

"Is that a new TV show?"

His jaw slackened with disbelief. "It's a hobby. You should try it. It's great fun."

"What is it?"

"It's when you tie a belt around your neck and get off."

"That doesn't sound like much fun," I said. "It sounds pretty awful, in fact."

"A virgin and a puritan. You'll grow up to be a nun!"

What he'd lost in limbs, he'd gained in lip. "So what's the service?" I asked. "It sounds like a private affair."

"There will always be a risk when you wrap a belt around your neck and bring yourself to the point of strangulation. It can be a life-changing or life-ending experience. Like skydiving. My service would provide the proverbial parachute. Say you wanted to autoerotically asphyxiate yourself. You'd call me up ahead of time. I'd already have the spare keys to your flat. If you didn't call back in, say, one hour, I'd come over to check on you. By then you'd probably be dead. So I'd hitch up your trousers so your loved ones would have the comfort of thinking you'd died by ordinary suicide."

"And if they didn't die, you'd have the keys to their flat, so you could rob them blind."

"There's hope for you yet, *molokosos*."

We waited at the platform edge and I don't know why it came out then but it did. I asked Kirill why he never recounted how he had lost his legs, why he was silent and defiant when seeking charity.

He frowned, displeased that the conversation had taken a precipitous turn into seriousness. A train arriving on the opposite track nearly whooshed away his words. "You can live off others' guilt," he said. "But if you want a dacha, you must also make them proud."

Air surged from the tunnel with the catcall of train breaks. "But how *did* you lose them?" Saying the question aloud, hearing the tremor of my voice, I recognized what I'd long suspected: I was a coward.

"It wasn't what you think." He shook his head and smiled to himself. The wall of air broke over us. "I'm only telling you this since you'll be going south into the Zone. It wasn't a land mine. It wasn't even in Chechnya. I was shit-drunk one night a few years back and passed out on a tram track right here in Peter."

That evening a threadbare military uniform lay on the living room coffee table. It was the blue-gray of rain clouds. I unfolded the trousers, held them to my waist. The legs reached past my ankles and flapped at the floor.

"Your grandfather was a tall man," my father said from the doorway. Hell-cat watched from between his legs. "A pair with hemmed legs, you'll look so grown up."

Hearing him say it killed me.

"I don't want to go," I told the cat. The little sadist tilted its head, then snapped its tail and strode from the room.

My father hooked my chin with his finger and raised my face to his. "If we had a choice, none of us would ever put on trousers." His half-smoked cigarette made my eyes all watery. He dropped the stub in a teacup and thumbed the tears from my cheeks.

"Oh, Seryozha, sometimes I wish you could see what I see when I see you." His face was a big bright sun. I had to look away. I tried to find a neutral space to rest my gaze, but his framed portraits filled the walls. I couldn't escape him. He was everywhere, watching over me.

"What do you see?" My voice cracked for the first time in two years. I'd have traded the rest of my life for a Cloak of Invisibility. I'd apparate to Chechnya, Kresty, anywhere beyond sight of my father's eyes.

"I see a clever young man, too clever for his own good maybe. I see someone kind and sweet-hearted in a world that encourages and rewards neither. I see a son who is unlike me in every way I've hoped he would be unlike me."

"I don't believe you."

"You'll have a happy life. You'll see."

I wished then, more than I'd ever wished before, that I trusted my father.

"Look at you," he said, and leaned in to plant a kiss on my forehead. "My Seryozha. My holy little fool. You've spent these last few years working so hard to become an asshole. Despite your best efforts, you're becoming a man instead. And I know you want to become so great an asshole that centuries from now people will speak of wiping their Sergeis. But you're not an asshole. You're my son. So when you want to disgrace yourself, remember, little one, that you are all of your father's pride."

The next morning, both head and heavens had clouded over. I ignored Kirill's history lessons as I pushed him to Chernyshevskaya. In four days, I was to report for duty.

For hours, I barely talked. Kirill fist-marched across train cars and I pushed the wheelchair behind him. Rubles dropped into the wicker basket, and he collected them at every stop.

"Let's take a break," I said when we reached Ploshchad Lenina.

"It's only eleven."

"I want some air."

Kirill sighed, but agreed. On the escalator he counted the morning's earnings, pleased with the sum. "You need to keep your money in your front pocket," he said. "Thieves will be too wary of your stumps to go anywhere near them."

"You keep saying 'you,'" I whispered. It was a quiet realization.

"I'm talking to you. How else should I address you?"

"You keep giving me instructions. Like you're training me. 'You need to do this, you need to do that to be a good beggar.'"

"I'm speaking in generalizations," he began, but I'd already stopped listening. The whole summer long I hadn't realized it. I wasn't Kirill's assistant. I was his apprentice.

I can't remember the faces of bystanders, what was shouted by whom when I let the collapsed wheelchair crash down the escalator, what Kirill said, or if he said anything at all. I remember grabbing Kirill's pressed blue collar and pushing him against the slow slide of the escalator wall. If he wanted, he could've stopped me. Those arms of his walked three kilometers of train cars every day and still had enough oomph left to lift weights by night. But he didn't resist, didn't fight, surrendered before I threw that first punch, and when I had him by the neck, when his hat toppled and the escalator wall unmade his impeccable part, I swear a grin crossed his lips, and beneath his knotted brows his face held no fear. He had bet with his dead-eyed doubt that I was too craven to commit even this act of cowardice. I punched him once to prove that I could, and then kept punching him because I was too afraid to stop. My knuckles were four burst berries by the time I grabbed his greased hair and slammed his face into the escalator step. Finally, Kirill went limp. I reached into his front pocket, palmed the bills and loose change, and sprinted up the remaining steps. From a half block away, I saw the escalator deposit Kirill at street level. He lay lifelessly while the ascending steps snapped against his stumps. Hurried commuters stepped over him.

The realization of what I'd done cannonballed into my guts. *I killed a man.* And not just any man, but a crippled war hero. I'd never go to Chechnya because I'd spend the rest of my life locked up. I was on my knees, dry-heaving, when I heard his shouts.

He was still sloped across the escalator exit. His nose pointed the wrong way around, his face throbbed with blood, he spread his arms, he closed his fists. "I am alive!" he screamed. "I am alive! I will not die!"

I fled to a shooting gallery in an outer suburb where I rented a needle for two rubles a blast. Even in a narcotic slumber, I couldn't escape Kirill's proclamation of immortality.

Kresty Prison was originally the imperial wine warehouse and stored enough booze to keep the royal family and their courtiers pickled through the long winters. After the emancipation of the serfs, when the state assumed from landlords the responsibility of locking up the newly freed, Kresty became a jail. For a century, according to my Russian civ teacher, it was the largest in Europe. After the Revolution, it's where NKVD men beat confessions from communists and traitors. After the Collapse, it's where drug offenders awaited trial. It was only designed to hold around a thousand inmates, but when my father went through the Komsomola Street gate, its population was ten times that.

I visited him just once, bribing a guard with a few hundred rubles I had lifted from my mom. Later, when I recounted the story to my friends, I made it sound like the prison scene in *Goodfellas*, my father the capo of the entire place, no worry greater than the tomato sauce recipe. But the only garlic wafting down those halls came on the guard's breath. I followed that guard's clicking footsteps down a long corridor into the cell blocks. Men with twigs for arms and caverns for eyes leaned against the bars. The cell my father shared with nineteen others had originally been designed for solitary confinement. It had rained earlier that morning.

The air around my father tasted of sweat, ammonia, and chlorine. He looked like a man born on a planet without vegetables or direct sunlight. "You got a smoke?" he asked me. I was nine years old.

He was released four years later. My mother had died just before his first parole hearing and state orphanages were more overcrowded than Kresty. But the parole judge was disconcertingly law-abiding and humane, perhaps the only judge in the entire Justice Ministry whose heart hadn't been surgically removed and replaced with a charcoal briquette. He let my father off, having served only a third of his sentence. After his release he went civilian. Working as a gypsy cab driver, he stopped for every yellow light. I'd like to believe he began living honestly for my sake, but it was for his own. He feared Kresty more than the disappointments of a lawful life.

A few months after his release, I got my ass beat by a couple older kids. I came home with black eyes and a gashed-up forehead. My father looked me over.

"Who did this to you?" he asked.

"It was—" I began, but his hand shot out before I could finish, and he stabbed his finger into the cut on my forehead.

"My son, a snitch?" he asked.

I began to scream, but he clamped his palm over my mouth and watched me with these hollowed, betrayed eyes.

"All these photos of myself on the walls, you think I'm some sort of narcissist, I know," he said. I'd fallen back against the kitchen table. The cut on my temple wasn't deep, but my skull felt impaled on his pressing finger.

"I can't remember my father's face because my uncle made my mother scratch it from every photo with a coin."

I thrashed my legs. I slapped my hands across the tabletop for a knife to slice him, a fork to skewer him. My lips squashed in his grip. His finger hadn't left the open cut.

"A few years later, I asked my mother what had happened to my father, and she said that man who had come to our flat, who had told me this lovely fairy tale about a tsar and his court painters, that man, my uncle, had been involved. Maybe he informed on my father, she didn't know, but she knew he wouldn't have come to our flat to warn us if he hadn't been guilty of something. The next day in school I went to my teacher and made up a story that my uncle was a subversive, that I had seen him conducting business with foreigners. I wanted revenge. Somebody had to pay. I didn't know the man I snitched on. I'd only met him for a few minutes one early morning."

His face was broken with tenderness.

"You can hate me, so long as you don't become me. Do you understand?"

I could barely breathe.

"I'm trying to teach you to be a better man."

He let me go. He wiped the blood from my face with his shirtsleeves. He didn't wipe his cheeks. He opened the window, picked three icicles, and broke them with the back of a butcher's knife. He slid them into a plastic shopping bag and pressed it to my face. I shook as he washed the dirt from my bruises. "Be brave," he demanded, holding my mangled face in his palms. He gave me a tall glass of vodka before going back in with the washcloth. "A man who walks with fear only crawls. He deserves all the suffering of the world."

"I won't deserve it," I promised. Even though my face was pasted in mucus and tears, my father beamed at me with pride.

I lost two nights, my virginity, and all of Kirill's money. In my head an industrious blacksmith pounded away. In my stomach hurricanes brewed. Somewhere a diva belted. Couldn't tell her vibrato from the hum in my veins. In the corner a shadeless lamp was connected to an outlet in the next building over by an extension cord laundry-lined across the alley. From nowhere came a man with crutches. He feet were the size and shade of black bread loaves. No human shoes would ever fit them. He pulled a bag of white powder from his pocket, scattered it on a cooking sheet, and mixed in a different white powder with a razor. In the corner a boy drew ferocious breasts on the wall. The man asked him for a marker and started drawing on my arms. He kept telling me the Latin names for veins and arteries, unreal the study he'd put into the science of self-destruction. The next morning I woke next to a woman with spiderwebs of gray hair. She had deeply burrowed brown eyes that barely reflected light. "First morning you're a man," she said. I didn't know what she was talking about. "Three hundred rubles," she said. Then I understood. "You want a toothbrush?" she asked. I told her I didn't need one, and she said, "But you do, young man. You need to keep those teeth clean. With a healthy set of teeth there's no telling what you'll make of yourself." I bought the toothbrush and shot up again, piercing the little red boat someone had drawn on a blue tributary of vein. I couldn't make sense of my fingers. What lunatic god would trust me with so many of them? White paint chips shook from the ceiling. I waited for it all to collapse. How many years would I get for nearly killing Kirill, and would they be any worse than serving in Chechnya?

When I returned home, I expected police cars, but nothing waited for me but the same rusted bike frames locked to a lamppost and stripped of their hardware. The same dust lay on the same stairs and I climbed to the top floor. Not to apologize, I just didn't know where else to go. I couldn't see my father.

Kirill's door was unlocked. He sat in the wheelchair, an ice pack pressed to his cheek, the pistol on the table beside him. His face made his stumps look like the least of his mutilations. He didn't grab for the phone or call for help. Just reached for the gun and set it between his duct-taped thighs.

He looked at me with the expression I reserved for people like him.

"You need to go downstairs," he calmly said.

"Am I going to jail? Have you told the police?"

He was offended by the questions and answered simply, "I was a junior sergeant."

His chin dipped in and out of a shadow. His remaining teeth were spare pins in the bowling lane of his mouth. He wasn't at all afraid of me. I hated him for it.

"Go downstairs, Seryozha. You aren't going to prison."

But I stepped forward. Raised my hands. One step became a second and a third. One click released the safety, a second cocked the hammer. He held the gun between his stumps. My knee was two meters from the barrel when he realized what I was asking. He nodded with a slow ache of understanding and it was all I could do not to weep with relief. I began to thank him but the gunshot swallowed my gratitude. The floor fell from under me. The bullet passed through my knee. I don't know how long I lay there before I crawled to him, and he lifted me into his arms, and whispered, "You are alive. You are alive. You are alive."

A Temporary Exhibition

St. Petersburg, 2011–2013

VLADIMIR

"HELLO, IS THIS MRS. JONANNE MCGLINCHY OF 1898 Calvert Road, Ohio? Yes, and your birthday is October 12, 1942? My name is John Smith from IRS. Yes, madam. To my displeasure, your taxes will to be audited unless you provide certain informations. First, you must tell to me your Social Security and bank account numbers. Also, your mother's maiden name. To verify your identity, yes. At IRS, we take the identity theft most seriously."

Look at him go! An incredible thing, really. To sit in the gloom of the Chernyshevskaya Cybercafé and watch his boy work. Some kind of prodigy, Vladimir's boy. In the case of nature versus nurture, Vladimir threw his support behind the plaintiff. The stuff of eugenicists' dreams runs through Sergei's veins.

Don't get cocky, Vladimir. Fatherhood points aren't doled for time served. Should look up at the library the fathers of other wunderkinds: Mozart, Pushkin, et cetera. They too absent in children's formative years? Father's absence forces child to grow up sooner, accelerating child's emotional, creative, artistic maturity?

"Ha! Very witty," Sergei continued, two chairs down, broadcasting broken English into a wiry headset, the café bustle tuned out. "I assure you, KGB and IRS do not have exchange program."

Too much life in his voice to pull off convincing bureaucratese. Too much love in his labor. Only trust a government worker whose personality is as thin and stamped upon as a time card. But who's Vladimir to question the maestro?

"Take your time, Mrs. McGlinchy," Sergei said. "Pocketbooks can be most difficult to find."

Vladimir had missed graduation ceremonies and chess tournaments on account of incarceration. He had never seen his son perform for him. Had this beaming pride been building in him all along, concentrating in his system like a magnificent mercury poisoning?

Mustn't let Sergei forget these last few years when he's fabulously wealthy. Mustn't let him forget that first day home from the hospital. White plaster and bandages had braced Sergei's leg. Poor kid had looked at the knee-high bathtub lip as if it were Everest. "I don't want to take a shower. I'm not dirty," he had said.

"It's okay, it's okay," Vladimir had said, but it wasn't okay. Not at all. He'd never given his son a bath before. Where to begin? Take off Sergei's socks? His shirt? Run the water first? Does he get in with Sergei? Does he look away?

"I don't want to. I'm not dirty."

One whiff would wake a coma patient.

Vladimir had swaddled the bandaged leg in plastic bags and rubber bands. Set a stool in the tub. Changed into his bathing suit. He had lifted his son into the tub and set him on the stool. Spat out the rusty aftertaste of shower hose water. Too hot. Lathered up his son's hair and shoulders. Too cold. The armpit, the hip bone, the belly button. Strange parts he'd last seen unclothed when his son was still too young to spell his own name. This grown man still fit in his father's arms. Just right.

"Are you okay?" Vladimir had asked.

Sergei had replied in a garbled sob, the compact heat of his breath like a hand dryer on Vladimir's skin. If you could trade, but you couldn't. If there was a way to make it okay, but there wasn't. If you can, but you can't. Why are children doomed to remain beautiful to their parents, even when they become so ugly to themselves?

"It's not fair," his son had said.

"It isn't," Vladimir had agreed.

He had gone on soaping Sergei's fingers and underarms. Who can you be but the chest your child shouts into. The shoulder he balances on. The hands washing him clean. The shower drizzled steamy gray stripes. A towel lolled on the closed bathroom door. There was so much Vladimir wanted to make right.

Six months later, he had signed Sergei up for language classes taught by an Australian man with English teeth. Al Pacino quotes and Tupac lyrics qualified as rudimentary English and Sergei placed out of the intro course. Within two years, he spoke well enough to take Business English I and II, which used Donald Trump's autobiography for a textbook. In such richly manured soil, a seed hardly needs sunlight to grow.

"Very good, Mrs. McGlinchy. Last four digits are two nine two one? I will correct the error into the system and we will avert the audit. Indeed, I am originally coming from Russia. Now a resident of Florida. Drinking the orange juice and sitting on the beach most often."

The world's greatest bullshit harvester ties himself to the crop's most insatiable market with no more than a phone line. If this is capitalism, no small wonder communism failed.

Sergei wished Mrs. McGlinchy a fine day and rang off. "Well, what did you think?"

What did Vladimir think? His son was slaying giants, that's what he thought. "I don't know what you said, but you said it wonderfully."

Sergei gave a bashful smile.

Vladimir wanted to pull his boy into his arms and say, *Do you see? I told you you'd have a happy life. Now do you see?*

Instead, he asked, "Why do these foolish Americans believe you?"

"When I first started, they didn't," Sergei admitted. "I was calling numbers at random from online telephone directories, saying to them, 'Hello, you have won the sweepstakes, please give me your bank account number.'"

"And no one believed you?"

Sergei shook his head. "Took a long time to understand the American mind-set. The fear of their cruel and capricious government weighs heavily on their psyches. They're more inclined to believe they'll lose what they have than receive what they want.

"Better to be the tax man than the sweepstakes, I decided," Sergei went on. "But it wasn't good enough. Too many skeptics, still. Then I remembered something you told me."

Vladimir leaned in.

"About the list that you and your mother were on. Because your dad was an enemy of the people. I figured that somewhere online, there must be a list of Americans who will believe anything, no matter how implausible or insulting to their intelligence."

"Is there such a list?"

Sergei spun white froth in his glass. "Tom Hanks's Facebook fan page."

Vladimir had no idea what his son was talking about.

"You remember how Mom had that embroidered pillow? When she got upset, she'd shout into it and no one would hear her. That's Facebook. And *Forrest Gump*, you must have seen *Forrest Gump.*"

"It is a nature film?"

"No, no. Classic cinema. About how every achievement in American society over the last fifty years was really just the dumb luck of a mentally challenged man."

"This was a Soviet propaganda film?"

"No, it's a big Hollywood movie. They play it for children in history class there." Sergei took a final sudsy sip of his Baltika 7. "So I cross-reference the names and birthdays pulled from Tom Hanks's Facebook fans with WhitePages. Why, you might ask, would they put their birthday right there on the Internet when it's one of the three pieces of information necessary to steal their identity? So that strangers will wish them a happy birthday! It's incredible, I know. When I called up Mrs. McGlinchy, I had her name, address, and birthday, told her I was from the IRS, and asked that she provide the necessary information to prove her identity. The trick is to make the American feel he must convince you of his identity, rather than the other way around. Tom Hanks's fans are maybe ten times more likely to fall for this than the average American."

"Because there's something wrong with them?"

"I wouldn't go that far," Sergei cautioned. "I'd just

say that those who enjoy his acting are unfamiliar with human nature."

Wasn't this what every parent hopes for? To equip your child with the confidence and support to seize opportunity, to succeed where you failed? His boy, an entrepreneur. He felt a strange surge of patriotism, a gratitude for the vision of his leaders. Here in the New Russia, you weren't bound by the past. The grandson of an enemy of the people, the son of a convict, his boy, a successful businessman.

Sergei explained that even though he had Mrs. McGlinchy's bank numbers, he wouldn't touch a penny. Of course he wouldn't. Vladimir's boy was honest and sensitive to the feelings of others, his primary school teachers had always said so. Instead, Sergei would sign her up for a few dozen credit cards, link them to phony PayPal accounts, and transfer thousands of dollars into his personal account at Sberbank.

"Even if she's got bad credit, we should still get three or four thousand dollars. And it's not like we're taking anything from Mrs. McGlinchy personally. Just the credit card companies."

A beautiful word, *we*. To be taken into the intimacy of a personal pronoun. Go forth, my child, but take me with you.

"I don't even think what I'm doing is illegal. MMM and those other pyramid schemes? They didn't go to jail. The bankers in the West who cratered the world economy? They didn't go to jail. It's just the free market at work."

"Only terrorists go to jail for what they say on the telephone," Vladimir said. Water this seed of ambition with much love and encouragement. "Don't apologize for your success. The layperson cannot possibly understand the complexities of high finance."

"I'm trying to do good."

"My Seryozha, my little oligarch. You're doing so well."

Sergei limped toward the WC, enough cheer to his gait that he nearly walked right.

Vladimir moved to Sergei's seat. The computer stared him down. No more than a television lashed to a typewriter by wiggly telephone cords, as far as he was concerned. He tried the headset. Nothing.

A halved egg of plastic sat on a square of blue foam. The receiver? He put it to his ear. "Are you there, Gogol? I'm searching for someone."

The monitor didn't blink. "Hello? Gogol?"

The waitress tapped his shoulder. A long grin was pressed between her wide lips. Her eyelashes were thicker than a fountain pen's line. "It's a mouse. You don't speak into it."

He assessed the plastic egg thing. "I know mice," he said. "This is not one."

"It's only *called* a mouse," she explained. "Set it on the mousepad and move it around."

A little white arrow drifted across the bluebird sky.

"Do you see this?" he declared, dashing his palm against the table. "The machine has surrendered without a fight. It may have beaten Kasparov but it knows better than to test me."

The waitress laughed, her thin fingers just touching his shoulder, and ah, what a day this was. She opened Internet Explorer before returning to the register. "It's Google, not Gogol. You type what you're searching for and hit enter."

He studied the keyboard. No sense to its arrangement. Not even the alphabet would submit to alphabetical order. Everyone had to be an individualist, everyone thinking they're precious little snowflakes when really they're just boring drops of water.

Best to start simple, let this Google warm its engine.

is the earth flat, he typed.

Images of globes, biographies of Columbus, circumferences and curvatures crowded across the monitor with dizzying suddenness. Vladimir had expected Google to come back with a simple *da* or *nyet*, but this, this was something else.

He typed *japan*: chopsticks, Tokyo high-rises, Wikipedia articles, travel guides, mushroom clouds.

He typed *knee* and a thousand different knees popped up along with exhaustive accountings of its every bone, muscle, and tendon, diagnoses and treatments for every injury from arthritis to gunshot wounds.

How was a universe of information compressed into this little metal box? He couldn't fit a whole chicken into his toaster oven and this thing fit the entire world. It felt tinged with sacrilege, even for an atheist. No one should know this much. It must be illegal. He glanced behind, certain that dark-suited security forces would storm the room, confiscate the computer, lead him away in handcuffs. Nothing but jittery teenagers blasting each other in blood-splattered squares of light.

If this machine knew everything, would it know his father?

vasily osipovich markin. He didn't hit the enter key, not yet, because he'd never written his father's name before, never seen it written. The cursor blinked impatiently. What good could come from this? You had to keep your eyes forward. Don't turn your head. Don't mind what lies in the periphery. Behind you is only ruin.

He deleted *vasily osipovich markin* and typed *roman osipovich markin.*

He wanted to hit enter but he was already standing, out of the chair, backing away. He was . . . devil, was he crying?

You've ripened into a pungent piece of cheese, Vladimir.

Yes, fine, okay. Just get me out of here.

"What's wrong?" the waitress asked, when he reached the door.

"I have a lump in my throat," he admitted.

"Oh my god," she said. She was young enough to be his daughter-in-law but she looked at him like his mother. "Is it malignant?"

"Tell Sergei I'm not feeling well. Tell him I've gone home."

When Sergei emerged from the bathroom, his father had already left. He sat down at his computer. The cursor blipped behind *roman osipovich markin* in the search bar. His father's uncle. Curious, Sergei hit return.

NADYA

On a July morning in 2004, a surgeon in Moscow unwound the bandages from Nadya's head.

"Everything will be blurry," the doctor said. Nadya opened her right eyelid and three years of darkness peeled away.

The surgeon's office was a 1970s Gerhard Richter, a quarter turn of the focus away from clarity. When she extended her arms, she couldn't count the fingers on her hands but she could see they were there. Ruslan was too. Her fingers slipped into his.

Three nurses ran into the surgeon's office when they heard Ruslan shout. They stood at the door, hesitant, because the cries of the ill, the suffering, the dying, and the bereaved had become well known to the three nurses. They had heard every iteration of pain. They were less familiar with the howling awe of rejoicing.

On her second day of sight, he gave her a paint sampler. It contained eighteen hundred named colors. Coral Fuchsia. Cream of Amethyst. Golden Evening. Siberian Russet. She read and reread until she could identify by name every shade in an ice cream freezer, in Journalists' Park, in the morning sky. As poets went, Aleksandr Pushkin had nothing on the paint sampler copywriter.

They married eight months after she left the hospital. As a teenager, she'd imagined love to be a flare sparkling upward, unzipping the night sky. What she had with Ruslan gave off a warmth nearer to friendship than romance. That was fine with her. Better the dim heat of a hand in yours than all the fire in the sky. He massaged vaseline into her scars and she sat through endless American slapstick comedies. They were building a life of small kindnesses together. Some days it was extraordinary.

She gave birth to a daughter, Makka, at Hospital Number Six in Volchansk. A green-eyed girl, daughter of the head of surgery, mascot of the maternity ward, demanded a souvenir from her with the stubbornness of a bridge troll. Ruslan gave her one of the tourist brochures he still carried in his coat pocket.

The end of Ruslan's career as a tour guide was the

beginning of his career as a ministerial figure. The oligarch who had bought the Zakharov had taken a shine to Ruslan and had him installed as a temporary deputy minister. His predecessor had moved to a place in America called Muskegon and, to Nadya's knowledge, still lived in the basement of his son's pharmacy. As a deputy minister, Ruslan's daily responsibilities largely consisted of accepting bribes. His subordinates nicknamed him The Natural. Someone always had to be paid off and the world seemed to think it was Ruslan's turn. Nadya wasn't one to argue.

To prove he understood that private enrichment was the first commandment of public service, Ruslan's first official act was to de-mine the highlands of his ancestral village, beginning with Zakharov's field. Nadya had never been there herself, had only seen it in the painting. She'd heard stories that Ruslan's former father-in-law, a pumpkin of a man with links to the insurgency, had used the property as a rebel safe house. Some said he'd even kept Russian soldiers prisoner there. Ruslan told her that the property had fallen into disrepair long ago and that they shouldn't be surprised if it was all ruins now.

It was to Nadya's surprise, then, that when they returned for the first time after the mine removal Ruslan pulled her to him. She felt his weight drape over her shoulder. The meadow was mottled Cézanne green. At a dozen meters before her, the land melted in spring light. It would be another year before she could see all the way to the crest of the hill.

"What's wrong?" she asked.

"It's all there," he said in a voice touched with wonder. Nadya knew the sensation, the eeriness of discovering a corresponding point between past and present, of realizing that not all memory is mirage.

She tried to coax him forward, but he leaned deeper into her arms.

"The shed and stone wall are rebuilt. Behind them the herb garden is replanted." He built the image for her in short, declarative sentences, a habit he'd never fully surrender, even after sight was fully restored to her right eye. "It's all here."

"What wrong, then?" she asked.

"Where to begin?"

"What's right, then?" she asked.

"That's a trick question."

She stroked the back of his neck, felt the downy hairs lift onto her finger pads. A gray bird in the sky twisted its shadow on the ground. The sunshine glowed off her cheeks. They rarely kissed in daylight.

In the afternoon, they went to the meadow with a shovel. Ruslan insisted he walk a dozen paces ahead, just in case. The minesweeping team had cleared twenty-three mines from the hill. The repacked hollows were no wider than manhole lids. Sunken among them were two explosion craters, one at the end of the herb garden, the other farther up the hill.

"I don't know which is theirs," he said. "I didn't think there would be two." He frowned and his hands shook slightly. He looked awed and frightened by what he didn't know, how the scope of what he didn't know widened by the day.

He climbed into each hole, sifted through the dirt for remains. He reached over the lip of the crater, deposited what he'd found on the grass, then went back under like a kid diving for coins. Patches of pink silk. A marbled brown button. The melted treads of a sandal. A shattered cassette tape. She fit the fractured plastic face to read its half-erased message: *F r o l a In Case   gency!!! Vol. 1.*

With Ruslan's trousers rolled to his knees, his hands and feet tanned with dirt, Nadya could so easily imagine him as the kind of boy whose mother was forever following with a broom. With nothing else to inter, he divided the artifacts into two piles and set one at the bottom of each crater. For the rest of the afternoon and into evening, he shoveled burgundy dirt into each. He had no bodies to bury, only holes to fill.

Over the following years, they spent spring and summer weekends at the dacha, the rest of the time in Grozny. With funds diverted from a dozen more-needed infrastructure projects, the Museum of Regional Art was rebuilt. Nadya returned as head of conservation. She completed her dissertation on the censor, Roman Markin, and created a website to catalog his falsified images.

One summer day a visitor arrived at the dacha. Young man. Shorn hair and jeans baggy enough to clothe six legs. Ruslan and Makka had been playing on the hill. Nadya watched the stranger approach with a map stretched between his hands. The map didn't bend in the breeze. It was wrapped in a gold-leafed frame.

She tied her headscarf and waited for Ruslan before approaching.

"You look lost," Ruslan said.

The young man glanced to the lush green steps ridging the far slope. The grasses of the empty pasture swayed with the light touch of wind on their tips. "It's a peaceful place," the young man said, now holding the framed map away from them. "Can you tell me if anyone died by a land mine here?"

Ruslan stepped to the young man and grabbed him by the back of the neck. The suddenness stunned Nadya.

"Time to explain yourself," he said.

The young man lifted the map upright and only when its contours matched those of the hill did they recognize what it was.

In the living room, the young man explained himself over tea. He had been told his brother had died on the hill depicted in the painting and wanted to see the place for himself. When Ruslan asked how he'd come across the painting, he shook his head and smiled, as if to say life is well suited for nearly everything but explanation. "Have you ever seen *Deceit Web*?" he asked.

Ruslan ran his fingers over the gilded frame, inhaled the musty coarseness of the canvas. Nadya observed him. Two manneristic figures, painted in black, ran toward the crest of the hill. Ruslan held his fingertips over them, as if testing them for warmth.

Nadya stayed inside with Makka while the two men climbed the hill.

"I was told two Russian soldiers were kept here during the war," Ruslan said. "They rebuilt the place. Did a decent job, actually." He broke off a sprig of mint leaf and passed it. The young man slid the leaf between his lips and tongued it across the roof of his mouth. They climbed to the two grave markers. "I found two mine craters when I returned here. One might be your brother's."

The young man dropped to one knee and unzipped his duffel bag. Nestled among underwear and balled socks lay three pickle jars, two filled with ashes, the third empty. He scooped a palmful of dirt into the empty one. "When we were kids, we'd pretend that the world was ending and he'd climb into a rocket ship and blast off into space."

Ruslan squinted into the liquid shimmer of sunlight at the horizon. There was an explosion. His world had ended. He was still here.

"I guess I'll go now," the young man said.

Ruslan wasn't finished. "Without the Zakharov."

"Excuse me?"

"The painting. It stays."

"But it's mine."

"This is where it belongs."

The young man's soft face hardened like a dollop of melted wax. "I'm going to leave now."

Ruslan stepped near enough to smell the mint leaf wilting on the young man's tongue. "As I see it, you have two options. You can sell it to me and I'll give you a ride to the airport. Or I'll take it from you and you can find your own way. You're a long way from home in a land you don't understand. Choose wisely."

"Memory is the only true real estate," the young man said. "Nabokov wrote that."

"Good for him. What will it be?"

The young man studied the painting for another moment. "I'm sure I can get a poster of it," he said. They looked back at the hill before returning inside. There wasn't a shadow on it.

With three pickle jars and ten thousand U.S. dollars in his suitcase, the young man flew to a resort town on the Black Sea. For three days he ambled along the beaches, his feet sinking in brown sand, his pale cheeks baked to a permanent blush. That beach was nearer to the sun than any strip of land he'd ever known. On his fourth day, he shouldered his duffel bag and walked to the sand. He held a worn postcard and followed the shore until he stood on the spot the card depicted. No one would force him to sell the postcard. The heavily oiled, lightly clad swimmers might have wondered why the skinny young man in a leopard-print Speedo had gone into the water with three pickle jars. More likely, they didn't notice him at all.

A wave tumbled him into a dusky green tunnel. Ropes of seawater uncoiled down his neck. The next wave broke gently over his torso. He backstroked with one arm. The other clasped the three jars to his chest. Silver schools darted at his side. There he was. He could barely believe it. When he'd swum far past the breakwater, so far he had the whole sea, from here to the horizon, all to himself, he unscrewed the jars and let them sink into the dark blue.

SERGEI

He bought his father a smartphone for his birthday.

"I already have a telephone," his father said. "It's connected by cords to the wall so it can't be lost or stolen. You tell me whose phone is smarter."

"I got it for the camera. Look," Sergei said. He pressed the power button and the phone chirped to life. "There's two camera lenses. One pointing out, one back at you."

"We live in troubling times."

"It's for selfies. So . . ."

His father scowled. "Don't be vulgar."

Sergei crossed the room to the wall of his father's portraits. Whenever he wanted to discuss a difficult subject, he addressed it to one of the more sympathetic photographs of his father. "Bit optimistic, leaving all this extra space, no?" he asked, nodding to the bare wall that stretched beyond the last framed photograph.

"It's your inheritance. When you become a father, you can put photos of yourself on the wall and your son will think you're a deluded narcissist."

"Let's hope you live a long time yet," Sergei said. He coughed into his fist. "A couple years ago, I found the website of an art historian in Grozny. She wrote her doctoral dissertation on your uncle. The censor."

His father said nothing.

"She's putting on some sort of museum exhibition on him next month, here in Petersburg."

"Last I checked, digging up graves and horsing around with the skeletons is still against the law," his father said.

"I'm not sure old photographs on a wall are the same thing."

"Just because something's not illegal doesn't make it right."

"Says the man with old photographs on his walls."

His father responded by making a farting sound with his lips. Sergei flopped into the tea-stained armchair. He knew, of course, that his father had typed the name *roman osipovich markin* into the search engine, had left it there for Sergei to find. Neither of them could risk the vulnerability of a direct request; instead each had become sensitized to the intimations of the other. Sergei would make a suggestion and his father would refuse. The more adamant his father's resistance, the closer Sergei felt to the raw nerve anchored so deeply in his father it may have been his soul.

"Go with me, Papa."

"Never."

VLADIMIR

A thick paste of July humidity plugged the spaces between Nevsky Prospekt traffic on the evening the temporary exhibition opened. Vladimir's watch read half past seven. The sun, bright in the sky, warm on his face, said early afternoon. Too early, too late—Vladimir couldn't tell anymore.

"Let's go in," Sergei said. They'd been circling the block for an hour. "It's nearly over."

At the corner, a spindly ice-cream vendor knelt and stuck his head in the freezer.

"You think a freezer does the job as well as an oven?" Vladimir asked.

"I think he's just trying to stay cool."

Vladimir scanned the street for another potential instrument of self-harm. It shouldn't have been so hard. The most inconceivable deaths fell within the municipal borders of any major metropolis. Standing on a street corner in Petersburg should place one in mortal jeopardy.

Let me die before I pass the ice cream stand.

He passed the ice cream stand.

Let me die before I reach the blind man selling sunglasses.

He passed the sunglass stand.

Just ahead the gallery loomed. The polished door handle glinted. If he passed right now—a heart attack, a bolt of lightning—he would, in his last moment, consider himself spared from whatever awaited him inside.

Let me die before I open it.

He opened it.

A few attendees meandered through the exhibit. Vladimir would remember none of them. He would remember opening the door for his son, stepping into the cool gallery air, looking up to see the mug shot of his uncle, blown up two meters tall, staring directly at him. *Roman Markin: 1902–1937*.

"Are you okay?" his son asked.

He hadn't realized he was leaning on Sergei. "I'm sorry. Your leg."

"My leg's fine. What's wrong?"

"Nineteen thirty-seven. That's when, that's when I told my teacher that my uncle was a spy."

"It's not your fault."

"I thought maybe he'd go to jail for a few weeks, until he was found innocent. How could he be shot for something he didn't do?"

"It was the middle of the purges. He was just unlucky, that's all. You were just a boy, Papa."

A woman wearing a long skirt and too much makeup approached. Raised relief scar tissue was mapped over her left cheek.

"I was just a snitch," Vladimir said, and turned back to the mug shot. "A snitch."

The name tag on the woman's blouse read *Nadya Dokurova, Exhibition Curator*.

"Thank you for coming," the curator said.

Uncle, he thought.

"We appreciate your interest," she said.

Uncle, he thought.

"The museum is closing now," she said.

Uncle, he thought.

"Is he okay?"

I don't want to die.

"Sir?"

Not yet.

"Do you need a doctor, Papa?"

Not yet, son.

Sergei wrapped his arm around Vladimir's waist to steady him. "I've got you," he said. Vladimir let Sergei lead him to a wooden chair beside a tray of untouched cheese cut into damp cubes. The woman fanned his face with an exhibition catalog.

"Are you all right?" she asked.

Sergei gave his hand a reassuring squeeze. "Ask her what you need to," he said. "You need to."

What has happened to my asshole boy? Who is this wise man he has become?

"This censor, this Roman Markin—" Vladimir nodded to the enlarged mug shot taken in Kresty the night the censor was arrested "—tell me about him. Please."

The curator peered at her watch and pursed her lips to a pale, uncertain point, but it was clear from the stack of unread catalogs, the untouched cubes of damp cheese, that attendance for the exhibition opening had been lackluster. Here, perhaps, were interested visitors.

"He was arguably the USSR's most talented and productive censor," she said. "His technical mastery was unrivaled. If he'd put his efforts into painting, rather than censoring, this wouldn't be the first exhibit of his work."

"Why was he arrested?" Vladimir asked.

The woman steepled her index fingers. "It's unclear. In nineteen thirty-seven he was convicted on trumped-up charges that he'd been involved with a dancer in connection with a supposed Polish spy ring. A scripted confession appears in the court records, but witnesses to the trial have said that he refused to testify or confess."

"But why? Who informed on him?"

She shrugged. "He worked for the state in nineteen thirty-seven. There's no why about it. Work in a barbershop long enough and someday you'll be the one getting your hair cut."

He could have turned toward the door now. Sergei would have understood. Their silhouettes lay across the empty museum floor. The curator glanced at her watch, down to him, hesitated, then asked, "Feel like taking a tour?"

She took them along one side of the gallery, explaining the security apparatus's awe for the power of images, the history of alteration and censorship, the India-ink masks, the early application and refinement of that postmodern tool of photographic manipulation: the airbrush. He leaned on Sergei. They passed a wall of men and women with inked-out faces.

In a side gallery, a painting of Rousseau's jungle cat hung in a glass stand. He circled it: Stalin on one side, the leopard on the other. Beside it hung a nineteenth-century pastoral flushed with soft greens and yellows.

The curator was speaking and Sergei was nodding, but Vladimir didn't hear them. A jungle cat parted wide fronds. Leaves as wide as dinner plates flopped overhead. A red sun shimmered.

"This is where it all began for me," the curator said as she led them back to the main gallery. "This is the image the prosecution used in Markin's trial. But it also contains one of Markin's mysteries. Take a look. See if you notice anything odd."

In the first photograph a hand floated over a stage. The original, unaltered image hung beside it, printed from a stray negative strip that had outlived the Soviet Union in a mislabeled file cabinet. Vladimir studied the dancer: dark locks flecked with spotlight; gray irises beneath the double arch of thin eyebrows; a laurel of dark feathers; ears rather average.

Irina Portnova was prima ballerina of the Kirov Ballet (today the Mariinsky) from 1932 to 1937, the information card read. *Her career ended when she was charged with espionage, sabotage, and wrecking, as part of a Polish spy ring. If you look at Markin's falsified version, you will notice that Portnova's hand has been left floating above the stage. Is it an error? A warning to the viewer? An act of dissent? It's difficult to say. Take a look at the background of both images. If you study them closely, you might detect the addition of a figure in the censored version where—*

He turned to the altered photograph.

"Roman Markin did one remarkable thing," the curator was saying. "Beginning in the mid-nineteen thirties, nearly every time he expunged a face from a photograph or painting, he inserted one."

Your father is there, his uncle had told him, *in the background, where no one can see him*—where, Uncle, where is he? Within the somber suit? Beneath the general's epaulettes? No, no, no, no, no, until, finally, my god, yes, there he is, in the audience, gray-eyed, cowlicked, peaceful, alive. You thought you had forgotten his face. That he was lost. Expunged. Gone. But there. In the third row. He stares out. Not at the dancer. At you. To be here, at this late hour in your life, and to recognize your father, to find him, it makes the whole world you've wandered through feel as narrow as a blade of grass.

"If you walk along this wall, you'll notice that this person appears in every censored image," the curator continued. "The object labels will tell you exactly where.

Sometimes as a boy, sometimes as a man, other times in old age. Often he is inserted in the space where the censored figure has been removed."

"Who is he?" Vladimir barely got it out.

"I've been trying to answer that for years," she said.

He moved along the wall at processional pace, leaning on Sergei's arm. The photographs and paintings had been arranged chronologically—not by the date of their composition or alteration, but by the age of Markin's inserted figure.

His father as a youngster, climbing aboard a tractor.

His father as a teenage revolutionary in a baggy brown jacket, sprinting through the October streets with a pitchfork raised.

His father dressed in a dark suit and navy cap, one arm around a woman who was, on closer study, Vladimir's mother.

His father holding the hand of a five-year-old Vladimir.

His father as a scientist.

A politician.

A cook.

A peasant.

A farmer.

A builder.

A factory foreman.

A night guard.

A violinist.

A grandfather.

He watched his father age in the background of each image. His hair grayed and thinned to gossamer brushstrokes. His wrinkles drawn, then etched, then engraved in his sinking features. In the final painting, his father stood with a cane, apart from a crowd of cheerful factory workers, staring outward with a bemused smile. The man his father might have become resembled Vladimir.

Am I worthy? he silently asked the figure. *It's been such a long life—what have I done to deserve it?*

He leaned into Sergei and for the second time that day Vladimir felt himself righted in the arms of a son who had, somehow, forgiven him, who now, somehow, sustained him.

"I know this is difficult," Sergei said. "You're doing so well. I am proud of you."

Thank you.

The curator followed them to the last image. "It's remarkable, isn't it? If there was any goodness in Roman Markin," she said, "it's this man, whoever he is."

The long century of his life converged upon this one vanishing point. He closed his eyes. He kept them closed. He opened them. "You have no guess who he might be?"

"A childhood friend?" she asked.

My father, he thought.

"A brother?" she asked.

My father, he thought.

"A son?" she asked.

His heart can hardly hold the moment.

"My father," he answered.

NADYA

The dacha appeared ahead, the hill behind it. She declined her driver's offer to carry her suitcase inside.

"Hello?" she called, but no one answered. She slid the suitcase into the hall closet without unpacking. She went to the kitchen, poured herself a glass of water, frowned at the stack of dirty dishes. Through the window, she watched her daughter spin down the hill, her arms windmilling until she rolled to a gasping halt. At the bottom of the incline, Ruslan glanced up from his open briefcase. He stood, stretched, and climbed up the hill with the girl. The late afternoon sun burned before them, inking them into silhouettes, framed in the pinewood of the kitchen window, the unknowing subject of a work of art only she could see.

She admired the scene for a moment, then walked out the back door to become part of it.

The End

Outer Space, Year Unknown

THE EXPLOSION: A CATARACT OF GOLDEN HEAT, a sudden, rising weightlessness. The dacha, stone fence, the well I lived in, the carefully tended garden, they all fall away as I am peeled from the surface of the planet. Little dill seeds scatter from my palm, constellating the sky.

I wake.

Through the capsule's stern portal, the sun is a coppery wink. But it is no longer the sun, only one star dissolving by degree into the gauzy sweep of the Milky Way, for the moment still polished brighter than the others.

A half billion kilometers past Neptune's orbit, the vaporizer died and the cabin turned into a desert. Dryness unlike anything I've ever felt: a low acrid burn that makes my joints groan, makes my skin hold the shape of a pinch long after my fingers let go.

I sift through the dust for my forehead and press my finger to the skin. The pain is iridescent. I imagine the bruises in lush purples and crimsons, and wish for a mirror, if only to see those colors again. Turning toward the portal window, metal crinkles. Beneath my uniform, sheets of tinfoil hold my heat to my body.

To reach the end of the solar system I must have

journeyed for years, but it feels as if I have only just arrived, just woken here.

The coughing resumes, more spirited than before. It is a point forever pressed against my trachea. The balaclava brings little relief. Goggles fashioned from spectacles, foam, and duct tape shield my eyes. A postage stamp of skin unseals from my wrist and drifts into the air. I am turning to dust. Soon I will suffocate me.

Wiping again the glass, I peer through the observation portal but every point of starlight is small enough to snuff with a thimble. Beyond the titanium and thermal lining of the capsule hull, the temperature treads over absolute zero. Solar panels are winged on either side of the entry hatch. An emergency fuel cell stores enough energy to filter the air and eject the dregs once more, twice more, before reaching the Kuiper Belt.

Consider that last horizon line: the outer limits of the solar system, an elliptical orbit of frozen methane, ammonia, and rock. Even with an operational navigation system, the capsule couldn't pass through. And if it could, what then? Consider the emergency fuel cell, the taste of filtered air. Consider how the last gasp of electricity might otherwise be used. I can breathe clean air again, for a bit longer, or I can power the onboard computer and play the mixtape.

The cosmos began with the poster of the periodic table Father hung on the bedroom wall. Warm sunshine of halogens, deep indigo of transition metals: more color in those elements than the rest of the room. It stretched a pixilated rainbow between my bed and yours.

With his deep shaking bass, a ball bearing rattling in his voice box, Father described the bonded weight of protons, the unmappable orbits of electrons. You sat next to me on the floor in a legless chair and we listened to him explain that hydrogen, with one proton, and helium, with two, were the only elements naturally present after the Big Bang. They gathered into gaseous clouds that then turned into stars fusing protons at tremendous temperatures. Every element heavier than helium was forged in the nuclear reactions fueling stars, then launched across space in the flash of a supernova.

"Hotter than inside the smelters?" you asked.

"Millions of times hotter," Father said. He pointed his cigarette to the twenty-eighth element and held it long enough for the atomic number to disappear within an ash-ringed hole. "The nickel smelted inside the furnaces was first smelted in stars."

The list went on, Father enumerated: the lead in factory paint, the iron in barbed wire, the gold in the party boss's teeth, the aluminum coins of counterfeiters, the sulfur in the air, the radon leaking beneath the police holding cells, they all came from supernovas.

That was the same summer we swam in Lake Mercury, and its mercury also came from supernovas, as did all its exotic chemicals, as did the magnesium in the Polaroid flash that froze you and me in our leopard-print bikini bottoms, our arms hooped around Mother's colorless hips. Father had dropped the camera before it had spit out the photo and he lunged for Mother, roaring, and she screamed with a hysterical laughter on that sunny day below big burgundy clouds. What an improbable thing it was to be alive on Earth.

I float toward this forever night, this starlit amnesia. The nightmares ceased not long after the capsule passed the rings of Saturn. I no longer see visions. Perhaps I have become one. Through the observation portal, I watch the darkness that has dreamed me.

Alexei. The oblivion casts the name. I whisper it. I bring you back.

How long have I been dying? One hundred and twenty kilometers go by in the instant needed to articulate the thought. The watch on my wrist died long ago. And if I wanted, if I tried, what is time quantified by the revolutions of a dead planet around a receding star, what measurement of reality remains to me?

Take the blue pocketknife. Outline my left hand above the observation portal. Trace my fingers, the callused knuckles and tips, my hand the stencil. Thousands of other traced left hands cover the floor, ceiling, and walls of the capsule. I remember photographs of hands painted on cave walls and I sweep my palms across the scored surface. The carvings evidence a past outside the capsule of memory, the only proof that I do not belong to an eternal present tense.

When the dust grows dense enough to suffocate me, visibility will have dimmed to zero. The blindness through which the capsule drifts will have finally entered, will have finally won. Buried beneath the cabin floor rests the emergency fuel cell, coupled by red veins of wire to a circular button the shade of a robin's egg nested on the instrument panel. Coiled in copper is enough energy to refilter the cabin air or power the cassette deck for a short while.

When I lived on Earth I would watch you sleep from my bed. You would listen to your headphones, propped on a pyramid of cushions. When you fell asleep, you would slump to the mattress and the cushions towered overhead. Once, I woke to your cries, a cushion fallen on your face. I turned on the lights and lifted the cushion. Your cheeks were wet plum flesh, a dampness war-painted in the hollows of your eyes.

"There's nothing there, Alexei," I said.

"There isn't?" you asked.

Consider the beliefs of the ancients who hand-printed cave walls. Consider the stars as apertures in a spherical firmament, pinpricks in a veil through which the light of an outer existence shines. And are those pinpricks points of entry or departure? And what darkness does this plane cast onto the next?

Our father entrusted us with the mission. Ostensibly, the operation aimed to put a man in orbit, able to radio the ground with firsthand reports on the global fallout of nuclear war. But we had greater ambitions. We knew what nuclear war meant. We were patriots. Victory was simple: The last living member of the species would be a Soviet citizen.

Father's office was so thick with cigarettes that the divan exhaled smoke when he sat down to instruct us to build the spacecraft. We had everything we needed. A rusted lorry cabin for the capsule. A used dentist's chair for the pilot's seat. A dirty fishbowl for the portal. An old handheld radio that only played static. A decrepit battery with just enough juice to power either the metal desk fan that doubled as the air filter or the cassette player. The Americans might have had superior science, but we had superior imagination. We slid rolls of tinfoil onto broom handles and ran them in circles around the lorry. We inscribed *USSR* on the face of the capsule with shoe polish. We pushed the bounds of technology, breakthroughs never recorded in academic journals. The elements labored to meet our productivity requirements. We only had one pilot's seat and I was the oldest.

There were days when Earth's small glories were luminous enough to dim church icons to duller golds. Diving from the roof into fresh snow. Throwing dishes from the window the morning after Mother's funeral. I have been blessed.

When the capsule passed Saturn, the fragmented rings of ice and rock burned with the light of ten thousand crushed skylines. The surface of the gas giant wheeled with the lazy stirs of buttermilk in a saucer. I thought of Saturn, the father of the gods who consumed his progeny, and I mourned the vanished future as only parents and penitents can.

On the far side of the observation portal spreads a vastness that exceeds conviction. There is doubt. I am gifted with doubt, treasure it as I would a final revelation, as if I have made the call and heard the response and cannot know if the voice in my throat is my own or the echo of the answer I seek.

I turn on the radio.

Transmissions from Earth ceased three weeks after leaving its orbit. Static reigns, my only companion. Cosmic microwave background radiation: the residual electromagnetism of the Big Bang. For 13.7 billion years, this same static has reverberated across the frequencies. The act of creation endures, even after the created ends. This I cannot doubt.

The dust sandpapers my throat. Don't cough. Don't stir the air. Swallow the itch and turn the radio volume clockwise until it fills the cabin. It may be the voice of God.

* * *

You woke me the last day. Anxious and breathless, an apocalypse no longer theoretical. "This is it," you kept repeating. "This is it." You strapped me into the dentist's chair, slid the motorcycle helmet on my head, visor up. Our mother's voice, somewhere, called our names, called us upstairs for breakfast. The distant sweetness of blini frying. How do I say good-bye to this?

You knelt next to the pilot's seat, pulling levers and spinning dials.

"Where am I going, Alexei?"

"Into the stupendous unknown to bring news of Marxism-Leninism to alien proletariats!"

"Where am I going?"

"Beyond the final frontier of time and space! You will be the last living human!"

"Where am I going?"

Together we counted down from ten. My head snapped back three seconds after ignition and the capsule rose on pillars of smoked light. The rocket tore into the stratosphere; I turned to the observation portal. Lines of missile exhaust striped the sky; open, empty atomic missile silos studded the land. What divine imagination could conjure something so imperfect as life?

Consider the face of Earth. The United States and the Soviet Union possessed enough nuclear warheads to destroy all life many times over. Dust filled the skies and the air became blindness, suffocating those not already incinerated—a fate, it seems, that has followed me to the solar system's end. The radiation would mutate every living thing. Galina was pregnant when I left for war.

A cassette deck is rigged within the instrument panel to play important Brezhnev speeches to boost both the morale of the cosmonaut and the revolutionary fervor of extraterrestrial proletariats. The morning the capsule launched, you slid a cassette into my uniform pocket. *For Kolya. In Case of Emergency!!! Vol. 1.*

"Further instructions, final messages, last good-byes," you explained.

Halfway to the moon, I decided not to listen to the tape until the end. First I was afraid the tape would hold a parcel of unbearable loveliness that I could never reciprocate, then I was afraid the tape contained a confession, a confrontation, a long-held secret that would make me remember humanity with the crimson vision of a vengeful deity. But now that I am in a position to make final judgments, none are necessary.

The tape, whatever it contains, is the last song of an extinct world, the answer to the question I have become. I wait with it, weigh it against the taste of filtered air.

The dust thickens as I disintegrate. The upper layers of skin have dried and flaked into the air and all that I am is pink, tender, raw. Is this it? Is this how we end? In blindness? In despair?

I press my goggled eyes to the observation portal. Wipe the window and look out, repeat ad infinitum. Then, one of ten thousand strokes reveals the rim of Pluto. The moon Charon beside it. Beyond, the points of starlight overwhelm.

Unimaginable to see it, with bare eyes, right there. Beige-encrusted rock. Ridges rising beside ravines. Could you have considered this while calculating the ascent? No, this is something else. The intersection of great improbabilities; miraculous, what could be more so? At the edge of the solar system, so far from home, I see a familiar planet.

A moment and it's gone. Crane my neck, push against the glass, but the planet is now far behind. The capsule drifts past the reach of the gods. Pluto and Charon usher me on. I turn from the window with a dance in my chest where my soul has at last risen from its gravity. A sphere of dust fills the observation portal. I can't see my hand reach out, flip the button's safeguard. I can't see the robin's-egg blue of the fuel-cell release. A gentle whirr, something like a fan in oscillation, cuts through the dark.

Slide the cassette from its case. *For Kolya. In Case of Emergency!!! Vol. 1.* Insert the cassette, twist dials, click switches, and then, through the wiring of the cabin speakers, her voice.

Bum Ba-da-da Dum Bum, Dum Dum Dum.

It's her, it is. She mangles the march from Act One of *The Nutcracker Suite* in the feral scat of the deaf or deranged, a voice so bursting and boisterous it's a wonder her slender frame can summon it. Then you come in, beat-boxing at first, then adding your own atonal accompaniment. You belt wildly, off pitch and on tempo, you can't hit a single right note, and clattering dishware provides percussion; you are in Galina's kitchen, I see you, I see. "You can't waltz to a march," she had said as curtains of steam coasted over Lake Mercury, but I taught her how.

Each time the tape reaches the end, I rewind to the beginning, my lips murmuring the melody along with you. I rewind over and over until the energy failure light inflates a rusted orb into the dust and I hit play and in the warped slowness of your voice I know that this is it, the last time, we have nothing left, I am dying.

You have waited for me past the orbits of Mars and Jupiter, past each of Saturn's rings. It's ridiculous, so stupid, I know, to cross the entire solar system just to hear you and Galina butcher Tchaikovsky. If ever there was an utterance of perfection, it is this. If God has a voice, it is ours.

The calcium in the collarbones I have kissed. The iron in the blood flushing those cheeks. We imprint our intimacies upon atoms born from an explosion so great it still marks the emptiness of space. A shimmer of photons bears the memory across the long, dark amnesia. We will be carried too, mysterious particles that we are.

In what dream does the empty edge of the universe hold this echo of vitality? In what prayer does the last human not die alone? Who would have imagined you would be with me, here, so far from life on Earth, so filled with its grace?

One more time through.

From the beginning.

Just give me that.

Please.

Acknowledgments

The following works of nonfiction were invaluable while researching the stories in this book, and I'd urge anyone interested in the region to pick them up: *Gulag: A History* by Anne Applebaum; *The Great Terror: A Reassessment* by Robert Conquest; *The Unquiet Ghost: Russians Remember Stalin* by Adam Hochschild; *The Commissar Vanishes: The Falsification of Photographs and Art in Stalin's Russia* by David King; *Black Earth: A Journey Through Russia After the Fall* by Andrew Meier; *Stalin: The Court of the Red Tsar* by Simon Sebag Montefiore; *It Was a Long Time Ago, and It Never Happened Anyway: Russia and the Communist Past* and *Darkness at Dawn: The Rise of the Russian Criminal State* by David Satter; *Allah's Mountains: The Battle for Chechnya* by Sebastian Smith.

I'd like to thank the following people and organizations: the Whiting Foundation and the Creative Writing Program at Stanford University, particularly Eavan Boland, Adam Johnson, Elizabeth Tallent, and Tobias Wolff, for their support. C. Michael Curtis at *The Atlantic* and Tom Jenks and Carol Edgarian at *Narrative* gave first homes and first edits to several of these stories.

Steven Volynets and Olga Zilberbourg shared their stories from the former USSR and gave generous readings and remedies to mine. Alexander Maksik and Amanda Nadelberg have provided wise counsel, on the page and off. Ali Tepsurkaev, thank you. Ching-chun Shih, Ulrich Blumenbach, Stefanie Jacobs, Achilleas Kyriakidis, Diana Markosian, Vincent Piazza, and Cassidy Horn, for their friendship and creative collaborations. Without Gina and Kevin Correnti, California would be much less sunny, and without Kappy Mintie, I would be too.

My work couldn't have a finer editor than Lindsay Sagnette, whose editorial vision never ceases to inspire. Nor could it have a greater advocate than Rachel Rokicki. My thanks to the geniuses at Hogarth and Crown Books, particularly Molly Stern, Maya Mavjee, David Drake, Kayleigh George, Jay Sones, Rose Fox, and Chris Brand. Janet Silver's faith and guidance mean the world.

Finally, to my family, thank you.

In 1917 Virginia and Leonard Woolf started The Hogarth Press from their Richmond home, Hogarth House, armed only with a hand-press and a determination to publish the newest, most inspiring writing. They went on to publish some of the twentieth century's most significant writers, joining forces with Chatto & Windus in 1946.

Inspired by their example, Hogarth is a new home for a new generation of literary talent; an adventurous fiction imprint with an accent on the pleasures of storytelling and a keen awareness of the world. Hogarth is a partnership between Chatto & Windus in the UK and Crown in the US, and our novels are published from London and New York.